# THE STAIRS ON BILLY BUCK HILL

## STEVEN L. OREBAUGH

MILFORD
HOUSE

an imprint of Sunbury Press, Inc.
Mechanicsburg, PA USA

## MILFORD HOUSE

an imprint of Sunbury Press, Inc.
Mechanicsburg, PA USA

For information about special discounts for bulk purchases, please contact Sunbury Press Orders Dept. at (855) 338-8359 or orders@sunburypress.com.

To request one of our authors for speaking engagements or book signings, please contact Sunbury Press Publicity Dept. at publicity@sunburypress.com.

FIRST MILFORD HOUSE PRESS EDITION: January 2022

Set in Adobe Garamond Pro | Interior design by Crystal Devine | Cover by Victoria Mitchell | Edited by Lawrence Knorr.

Publisher's Cataloging-in-Publication Data
Names: Orebaugh, Steven L., author.
Title: The stairs on Billy Buck Hill / Steven L. Orebaugh.
Description: First trade paperback edition. | Mechanicsburg, PA : Milford House Press, 2022.
Summary: Kurt McCain, a gifted young anesthesiologist, falls passionately for a successful financial analyst who manipulates him to obtain pain medications for their mutual pleasure. When the scheme turns to diverting fentanyl from his patients, his entire career unravels, and he finds himself disconsolate, unemployed, and alone. Summoning all of his energies, Kurt must find the strength to redeem himself, regain the love of his family, and remake his career.
Identifiers: ISBN : 978-1-62006-866-3 (softcover).
Subjects: FICTION / Medical | FICTION / Romance / Medical | FICTION / Literary.

Product of the United States of America
0 1 1 2 3 5 8 13 21 34 55

*Continue the Enlightenment!*

# CHAPTER 1

"Hey. Open your eyes! Wake the hell up!"

Kurt McCain, walking home after shooting basketball in the warm twilight at a local playground, nearly tripped over the outstretched legs of a man lying, twisted, on the sidewalk. Surprised and unnerved, he bent forward and called to the motionless figure, shaking a bony shoulder.

"Come on, man, take a breath!"

Unaffected by Kurt's vigorous attempts to awaken him, the young man who was the subject of his concern lay stock-still. A waxy moon shined through an opening in the heavy cloud cover that lay over the city, illuminating the thin youth, who had fine features, sandy hair, and an unhealthy complexion. Kurt was tall but slight, and he struggled to move the man's body on the sidewalk. The boy had apparently slumped over against the side of the brick school building, sliding down onto the walkway. He was flaccid, perhaps dead.

"Jesus Christ, of all the things . . . why do I keep finding these kids?" the anesthesiologist whispered as he placed the young man onto his back, where he could at least try to resuscitate him.

A late evening stroll down to the Southside for a half-hour of relaxation had yielded this unexpected finding. The boy had stopped breathing, the victim of a substance that he'd injected moments before. The syringe lay on the sidewalk beside his limp body, boldly proclaiming its purpose and the young man's intent.

"You'd risk this to get high?" Kurt thought, grasping the slack jaw tightly with both hands and pulling it forward in an attempt to open the airway.

Nothing happened.

This wasn't merely a somnolent junkie who'd gone a bit too far and who simply needed his airway opened. Deep within this limp body was a brain that had been essentially turned off, the spirit ushered off to an uncertain place, while the body was precious close to cashing it all in. At least he still had a pulse.

"Well, son, you're in luck tonight," he said, mindful that no one could hear.

He pulled a packet from his back pocket, ripped it open, and pried out a nasal insufflator that seemed to be too tightly ensconced within its plastic confines. A moment later, he had shoved the nozzle well into the boy's right nostril and squeezed. Impatiently, the physician watched and waited, his kneecaps painful from kneeling on a cement sidewalk.

Within a few seconds, as if a miracle were in the offing, or as if Lazarus were responding to the commands of Jesus himself, the lifeless form began to move, struggling back to consciousness, sputtering and gasping. Unpleasant snorting sounds emanated from the airway.

In the deepening twilight, Kurt could see the bright blue eyes, two sky blue disks, wide open with anger and surprise.

"What the fuck? Who the hell are you?"

"You're welcome. Don't shoot heroin without a friend to watch over you, OK?"

The attitude was classic wake-up-from-opioid-land, nothing but unpleasant and ungrateful. In the past, it had made Kurt feel surly and unappreciated, but now he just went with it. He tossed another naloxone packet onto the lap of the unhappy junkie and stood up.

"There's an ER right over there or at least an urgent-care. You know—the old Southside Hospital. It'll take you about two minutes to walk yourself over to them—they should still be open."

Kurt stood up and turned to walk away.

"If you want to cut this shit out, they'll set you up with a program to help you stop the abuse. Like tomorrow. But you have to want it. I'm not gonna stand here and pretend that you'll listen to me."

Kurt had no illusions about the boy's future. He'd had more than a few interactions with addicts, going back to his days working in the ER as a medical student and again as an intern. Sometimes, tough talk worked, sometimes it didn't. He began to pick his way back along the darkened street, toward the high bluffs that reared up over the Southside. The young physician had had to intervene in similar circumstances twice before, in just the past two weeks, after he'd made his way down the cascade of stairs below his townhouse. He'd struggled to resuscitate one of the victims, with little effect until the medics arrived with an ampule of naloxone to counteract the opioid overdose. Now, as September waned, it was getting dark much earlier, and he had started to notice how seedy the back streets were becoming once the light failed. Opioids were coursing through the neighborhoods, like sewage-ridden floodwaters, bringing carnage and destruction.

Each day, Kurt injected potent opioids into people's veins. The drugs were an essential aspect of anesthesia. Without the pain relief that opioid drugs offered, patients would awaken to agony after surgery. Even so, his entire thrust at the university hospital was to minimize opioids, with nerve blocks to numb the surgical area, and with drugs that attacked pain by routes different than those of the opioids. Fentanyl, morphine, and their brethren, the families of natural and synthetic opioids, were indisputably valuable pharmaceuticals in the right setting, with the appropriate indication and monitoring. But this? The streets were awash in narcotics, a virtual floodtide of pills and elixirs for crushing and snorting and shooting and . . . death.

None of this made sense to him. Why did so many young people indulge in a habit that they knew could kill them? Why did they yearn so much to get outside of themselves? Didn't they understand the consequences?

At this point, the young man had staggered to his feet, shuffling in the other direction, cursing Kurt for the life-saving intervention that had interrupted an experience that was both intensely pleasurable and inevitably lethal. The anesthesiologist looked back over his shoulder and saw the syringe on the ground, a drop of blood congealed next to it.

"Damned heroin," he muttered, turning to pick it up, figuring that at least he could find a safe way to dispose of it.

He watched the lanky youth gradually disappear into the gathering dusk, certain that the boy was not interested in heading over to the urgent care, at least not this evening. Things would go one of two ways:

the young man would either overdose on the drugs with no one around to help him, or he would seek help and try to break the habit. It was about a fifty-fifty proposition. And no one but the boy himself could determine which direction it would go. Kurt hoped that he would choose to get help for his problem. It was easy to dismiss them, these helpless zombies, stumbling from one fix to the next, but he'd seen more than a few ex-addicts begin life over and really make a go of it. Potential sometimes flickered in their eyes. Sometimes.

Kurt approached the long staircase that stretched from 18th Street up to Clinton Avenue. The spindly structure was curiously alight as the evening darkened, small linear fluorescents embedded in the concrete steps just beneath the treads. Glowing parallel lines led upwards into the overhanging vegetation. As he reached the top landing, he walked forward and disappeared into a tunnel of this verdant coverage. Looking back, he found that he could no longer see the streetlights on the boulevard below, though he could hear the cars racing up and down the steep hill.

He reached Clinton Street, then walked up the small hill that led to Pius, a narrow way framed by rows of townhomes on each side. Then, he turned and walked beside some large, dilapidated buildings. The diocese of Pittsburgh had long maintained a substantial campus here, spanning a century and a half, but the structures had fallen into sad disrepair.

Passing rows of townhouses, he turned up into an alley that led directly to another set of staircases, which made their way up the long hill. The stairs wound between a cluster of homes clinging to the steep gradient. Kurt found himself wondering what the occupants were up to as he passed each of them: Mr. Obramawicz, a widower, who kept to himself but was pleasant enough. Probably, he was watching the Pirates, who'd long since lost hope of making the playoffs, and were likely being thrashed by the Cubs. Mrs. Koholik, middle-aged, divorced and clinging to life in her large, vacuous house on the slopes. She had innumerable cats in her overgrown yard and welcomed conversation with anyone who ambled by on the steps. Like her home, she was ill-maintained, but her kindness showed in her friendly banter with passers-by on the stairs and in her unceasing adoption of feral cats and kittens. He saw her silhouette on the blinds, moving slowly through her kitchen. Probably filling bowls with milk, he thought, readying the evening service.

His thighs began to ache, and he'd long since lost count of the steps. There were over 300 of them, from bottom to top, and they took their toll. Finally, at the top, he took a short breather, then headed in. A quick snack, a few minutes lingering over his research project, then it would be time for bed. Sometimes, he wished he could have a dog, a companion to come home to, but his hours were too crazy, and it wouldn't be fair to the canine. His evenings had been achingly lonely for the past couple of years since Cassy had gathered her things and moved to the West Coast. For a year, he had simply been broken inside, unable to look elsewhere, unwilling to concede that she was gone. After that, he'd accepted her departure as a fact but couldn't rebuild himself emotionally and had little interest in his social life. The void was still there, the wound was still raw, the regret was too profound. Nobody else would compare to Cassy. Nobody.

Kurt flipped on the kitchen light and began to carve a cold chicken breast for his lunch the next day. A bun, some swiss, a small bag of chips, and a tangerine. Some biscotti for breakfast on the way in. He looked around at the white walls of his kitchen, so bright in the glare of the fluorescents, and became conscious once again of the starkness of his existence. Then, mindful of all that he had awaiting him, he descended into the encompassing haze of professional obligation, of preoccupation . . . of ceaselessly being "busy."

Powering up his laptop, he looked over at the cell phone and noted that someone had left a voicemail. Katy, of course. His sister contacted him frequently, worried about him incessantly.

"Hi, Kurt. When can you come to dinner? The boys would love to see you. So would I. I'll make something you really like—just give me some notice. Maybe later this week? Give me a call."

He blessed her. Why did she care so much? She was busy raising two young boys while maintaining the house and keeping her husband fed and happy. She even held a couple of different volunteer positions. Still, she never failed to consider Kurt. Their mother, long deceased, would have been proud and likely would have seen something of herself, and her own devotion to duty, in her beloved daughter.

Looking around the kitchen, he sighed. It was a perfect place, a starter home. A woman's touch would have lent the décor some life. He'd had that in mind when he bought it and hoped to bring Cassy to live with him there. But it hadn't worked out after they'd dated for a couple of years—she'd gone her own way, he'd stayed in Pittsburgh. He'd expected her to come back after a few months on her own. But she had not, and since she'd gone, the evenings were steeped in melancholy, especially in autumn, as the shadow's lengthened and the days shortened.

He sat at a small desk where he did his number crunching, data synthesis, and writing. Medical research was rewarding but also demanding. He was honored that the division chief had included him in some of the protocols, and he did his best to keep up his part in them. Most of the research that Kirk engaged in was related to regional anesthesia, a subspecialty of anesthesiology that involved placing nerve blocks to control pain and reduce the need for opioid drugs. Other protocols involved pharmaceuticals for pain management, which lay outside the opioid family, alternatives to the drugs that were destroying American society. The research work was exacting and often extracurricular. But somehow, it contributed to the quality of his existence, elevated him above the daily grind, provided a sort of beacon in the night, leading him towards truths that were not yet established.

He lay down on his bed in a room with windows facing the broad river valley—a half-empty bed with a view that he seldom beheld. The emptiness of the space never ceased to touch him.

Soon his eyelids began to sag, and he realized that he'd better get to sleep. Five o'clock would come soon enough, and showing up late would not do. The early mornings at the hospital were frantic, as he and the others struggled to get the first cases into the operating room on time. This had become a fixation, almost a mania, for the administration. The anesthesiologists, who had little choice, danced to the tune. By the end of the day, his head and his back would ache, and his spirit would sag. It had become relatively predictable.

As sleep began to overtake him, he thought again about the addicts he'd recently found on the street. Three young boys lying at death's doorstep in only two weeks—it was deeply disturbing.

# CHAPTER 2

The operating room had become eerily quiet, save for the frequent tones of the pulse oximeter, which had begun to decrease in pitch. This was a reminder that something bad could happen to the patient very soon.

"Try to angle the tip up a little more."

Kurt was startled at the difficulty they had encountered in placing the endotracheal tube. Glancing up at the monitors, he noted that the oxygen saturation had decreased from 100 percent to 85 percent and was now falling ever-faster. This was ominous. The video-laryngoscope presented a tantalizing glimpse of the patient's airway on the screen at the bedside. But for whatever reason, the anesthetist could not manipulate the tip of the tracheal tube into the airway opening.

"OK, come out and let's ventilate with the mask."

Sandy, the nurse anesthetist, was always well-prepared, and he was startled to see the earnest concern on her face. She quickly pulled the blade out and placed the mask on the man's face. Already his lips and mucus membranes had become dusky, an unpleasant purple color that reflected oxygen deprivation. Moreover, the tones emitted by the pulse oximeter had begun to sound frighteningly low.

"Am I going to lose this guy?" Kurt wondered, pulling on the man's meaty jaw as forcefully as he could to aid the anesthetist's attempts at mask ventilation.

The patient had been escorted some minutes before down into some deep and featureless plane of unconsciousness. Almost certainly, he would have no memory of this brief departure.

Sandy fumbled a bit with the clear mask, then managed to apply it tightly to the patient's face, making a firm seal.

"C'mon Christopher," Kurt murmured, imploring the unconscious patient, "let us get some oxygen into you."

The saturations continued to drop. The patient, a heavily muscled, obese stonemason, showed little evidence of chest rise. They'd been able to deliver gas readily with a mask before they started poking around in the man's throat. Had they stirred up so much swelling in the delicate tissues around the opening of the airway that ventilation by mask was no longer possible? As Kurt pondered this, a sense of dread began to settle upon him.

It was extraordinary how quickly things could change in anesthesia. Five minutes earlier, he'd been joking with this affable, corpulent blue-collar worker, who'd been injured in his line of duty. He had suffered through a frustrating run-around at the hands of the workers'-compensation system and had finally been granted the right to have surgery on his injured knee. Christopher was bright and garrulous, and after a bit of sedation, managed to humor the entire OR staff. Now, unexpectedly, the induction of anesthesia was not going well.

"There's a blip," Sandy announced as a bit of exhaled carbon dioxide registered on the monitor.

But the oxygen saturations continued to fall. The two understood that there would be a lag between any actual improvement and the monitor's display.

"He's gonna start dropping his heart rate if we don't get some decent ventilation . . . do we have a laryngeal mask airway ready?" Though he tried to disguise it, the tone of Kurt's voice betrayed his concern.

"There's a size five over there, open and lubricated. You want me to put it in?"

He looked at the anesthesia machine, on top of which had been placed an odd-looking airway device, the laryngeal mask airway, or LMA. The purpose of the instrument was to cover the opening of the larynx and deliver gas to the airway. Despite its unimpressive appearance, the device had saved many lives.

The exhalations of carbon dioxide from the man's lungs continued to register on the monitor, a confirmation that at least some volume of gas was now regularly being delivered. This was a lifeline in the mind of the anesthesiologist; he didn't want to interrupt the process. But why wouldn't the saturations come up? He had begun to assist Sandy with the ventilation, adopting a two-person, three-handed technique for this plump, plethoric man. He pulled fiercely on the jaw, edging it forward in an attempt to open the airway, felt the moisture begin to coat his hands inside his gloves.

"I'm sure he has sleep apnea. He told me he snores but had no other symptoms."

No one commented. The orthopedic surgeon, Michael Daley, stood at the foot of the bed, a mixture of impatience and expectation on his face. This was his patient, but it wasn't his fight.

"Starting to come up . . . we're at 85 percent," Sandy announced.

The pitch of the pulse oximeter tones was climbing, proclaiming a higher degree of oxygen delivery. This was lovely music to the anesthesia team—no sound could have possibly been more welcome.

With a firm grip on the mask and the man's face, Kurt began to feel a bead of sweat trickle down his neck. If that's what it took, he figured, he could hold it for an hour. They simply had to get the saturation high enough to give him time to work on placing the endotracheal tube again. At that point, he knew that it was time to amass his resources, to make sure that every contingency was available.

"Velma! Can you get me a smaller tube with a stylet in it . . . make it a 6.0? Bend it in a really tight curve . . . And have someone bring the bronchoscope in here, with the difficult airway cart."

Velma was not the world's fastest anesthesia technician, but she was in tune with the needs of the staff; when he wanted things done, she got them done.

"We're back into the 90s."

"OK take the mask off."

Sandy quickly placed the laryngoscope blade back into the throat. Then, watching the screen intently, Kirk introduced the tip of the smaller tube and guided it back into the throat, maneuvering around the bulky handle that obstructed so much of the mouth opening.

"Oh, come on," he grunted, gently twisting the tube, hoping to get its tip higher in the throat. He used his other hand to maneuver the larynx backward against the spine to improve the angle of approach.

The little group of OR nurses and techs at the side of the bed watched on, fascinated.

"There we go!"

The words came out of his mouth with a clear note of relief. It was essential to get SOMETHING into the airway to rescue the patient and proceed with the surgery. Even if the tube was smaller than they wished.

The three of them—anesthesiologist, anesthetist, and technician— sighed in unison as the tube slid home.

"Good deal. There's the CO2. Let me listen to the breath sounds, and we'll get positioned."

He looked over at Sandy and grinned. The two had coped with many difficult airways over the years when working together, and he was glad she was at his side.

Sandy, meanwhile, was a whirl of activity, taping the tube, flipping on the ventilator, adjusting the volume for each mechanical breath, put- ting values into the computer record.

He nodded to the foot of the table, where the attending surgeon reacted with his own expression of relief, perhaps less from seeing the problem solved than from wanting to get the case going. He was confi- dent in the anesthesia team and would have been surprised if they'd not been able to cope with this situation. In the eyes of an orthopedist, the crisis represented a mere bump in the road.

"Did you get the antibiotics in?" Daley asked, a trace of sarcasm evident in his voice.

"Ah, yes," Sandy affirmed."The life-saving cefazolin! We gave it right before induction."

Taping the tube, Kurt listened as the OR team move perfunctorily through the "time out."

"I'm off to preop. You stable?" He was already in motion, glancing at the vitals on the monitors as he headed for the door.

"Sure thing, Kurt," she affirmed."I'll call you when we're ready to extubate."

He knew that he could leave Sandy alone for the entire case, and that she would be fine, absent any significant complications. But staying alert, informed, and vigilant was the essence of his calling. He would be back shortly to check on the patient and the progress of the surgery once things settled down in the preop area.

He sped down the hallway against the sea of blue-clad OR and anesthesia personnel, who were guiding patients back to the ORs. Stretchers surrounded him on every side, and the chatter was distracting in the confines of the hallway. Kurt knew all of them, nodded, and smiled as he went.

"Dr. McCain! I have the abstract all ready to go for the meeting. I've been roughing in some parts of the manuscript. Can I send you the introduction and the methods?"

Elena, one of the senior anesthesiology residents, was perpetually involved in research and administrative activities, along with her expected clinical workload. She had worked with Kurt on a study to evaluate the impact of spinal and epidural anesthetic techniques on outcomes after knee and hip joint replacements.

That's great, Elena. Just send me an email," he called over his shoulder, moving quickly down the hallway.

After his residency training at the university, he'd taken a staff position. Now, he had almost a decade under his belt as an attending physician. The OR staff praised him for his enthusiasm and willingness to help out in any eventuality. His co-workers in anesthesia regarded him as bright and assiduous in his application of anesthesia principles. And trainees lavished him with praise for his teaching and mentorship when they filled out their evaluations. Over the years, Kurt had gained the trust of prominent surgeons in the University system, which came only with time, experience and, baptism by fire. A few hints had been dropped that he would be in line for leadership positions in the division when they came open. It was a source of great pride for him, but he did not dwell on the idea.

Sometimes, though, he marveled that he worked with so many people, trained so many residents, attended so many meetings . . . and still felt estranged. He lived in two different realms, one brimming with intelligent, enthusiastic people, the other lonely and forlorn in his home perched high over the city. His sister insisted that he was "socially awkward" and needed to get out more, a pronouncement that occasionally rang true to him. He would laugh when she chided him—given the option, Kurt liked to sit alone, look out over the city, and think.

But right now, even with the unexpected airway issue resolved, he remained considerably stressed. Two other patients needed his attention in the preoperative area. One was a young girl waiting for a nerve block before the surgery could start. The second, an elderly man, was confused and didn't really seem to know why he was there at all. It was impossible to get consent for the anesthesia for someone that was not grounded in reality. Kurt had briefly spoken with the man earlier but was called away to attend to the airway issue.

He grappled with the frustration that was coursing through him. Too many things had to happen in a short time, with unerring precision, for him to launch all the cases on time. Just one hiccup and he'd be back on his heels. He pulled his OR cap off, ran his fingers through his short-cropped brown hair, and assured himself that he would be calm and gentle with the old man. His voice took on a soothing tone as he approached the bedside.

"Sir, it's me again, Dr. McCain, the anesthesiologist. I need to talk to you about your anesthetic."

The patient, slow in his response to any stimulus around him, turned his head slowly towards Kurt. There was a vacancy in the watery eyes, which had been dulled by age, and perhaps by disease as well. He reluctantly brought those eyes to bear on the anesthesiologist, meeting his gaze, but offering no hint of recognition.

"My what?"

"Your anesthesia—you're here for surgery; you understand that, don't you? You also need to have an anesthetic—you know, to sleep through the surgery—so it doesn't hurt."

The man appeared doubtful, gazing deliberately around the bed at the assembly of nurses and techs who had collected there.

Aware of time slipping away, Kurt felt his stomach churning.

"Doc, we're ready when you are."

Dorothy, one of the nurses, was peering expectantly from behind a curtain, which she'd pulled around the patient in slot 6, to afford a measure of privacy. Doubtless, she had made preparations for him to carry out the block, and now she awaited him.

Kurt thought anxiously about having the old man sign the consent once he understood what was happening, and the need to perform the nerve block in the girl. And then, he had to get them both into the OR and take care of his charting for the first few cases—all in the next seven minutes.

"Do you know why you're here, Mr. Jenkins?" he spoke loudly in case the old man's hearing was an issue.

The uncertainty in the man's eyes grew more apparent.

"Do you know where you are?"

With each question, the man appeared more uneasy. Kurt began to feel sorry for him. He was confused and disoriented, with just enough insight to sense that his mentation was impaired. What must it be like, he thought, to constantly feel as though your mental faculties were dulled and out of your control?

Shaking his head gently, Kurt looked up at the group of expectant observers.

"Can we get Dr. Rosenblatt in here? To the bedside? Maybe that will help him remember. If he recognizes someone, then he can start to figure things out. Even if the man signed consent for surgery in the office, we can't take him back like this. Is there any family or a caregiver here with him?"

Where the hell is the surgical team? Kurt thought.

Then, he had a realization. This temporary halt, this disruption, was precisely what he needed at the moment. While the little crowd dispersed to find a surgical team member, he figured he could move over to the other bedside with Dorothy and place the femoral nerve block. Ducking quickly behind the curtain, he announced himself.

"Hi, Dena. It's me, Doctor McCain. Remember—I spoke with you about a half-hour ago? Unfortunately, I got tied up in the OR. But now, if you're ready, I'm ready!"

He patted the young girl's shoulder, engaging her. She was pretty, with just a bit of acne on her chin. Her long blond hair had been gathered up and placed inside a bouffant cap as she lay, impassive, on the stretcher. Some teens were terrified, others remarkably composed for these preoperative nerve blocks. It was simply an injection, but it unnerved a lot of patients. Dena's parents looked more startled and concerned than she did.

"Now, this 'nerve block' is something you do for anterior cruciate ligament surgery all the time?"

The mother's eyes flashed with concern, the look of a woman protecting her young.

"Sure. We find that patients need less anesthetic, less pain medication, and wake up more readily with less pain. They usually spend less time in recovery and get out of the hospital quicker if they have the nerve block. As we discussed, there are some risks, but we work very hard to keep these nerve blocks safe. We see a lot less nausea and dizziness after the general anesthetic when people have nerve blocks for the more painful procedures, and that often translates into going home earlier."

"And you've discussed this with her orthopedist?"

"Well, actually, he expects it. If there were any unusual concerns, I would discuss them with him. He came by earlier to mark her leg, I believe?"

She looked at her husband and nodded.

Kurt was leaning toward shutting the questions down and ushering them out, at least until he had completed the procedure.

"And, did you get a chance to address your questions with him?"

"We did." He sensed the woman relaxing a bit. "And thanks for being so patient, she's our baby."

He smiled, aware of the impact that children's surgery had on parents, who sometimes felt the pain and anxiety more keenly than their kids did. The father was tall, bearded, bespectacled, and as calm as the surface of a glassy pond. He nodded and helped to usher his inquisitive wife out.

Kurt looked knowingly at Dorothy, raising his eyebrows in an expression of relief, then turned back to Dena.

"OK, young lady, let's get going."

They performed the "time out," asking her all the relevant questions, and he picked up the ultrasound transducer, having sterilized the skin of the groin with a prep stick.

After numbing the skin, he picked up the block needle, driving it through the skin in the same spot. It was immediately apparent as a white line on the screen, passing obliquely through the layers of tissue toward the nerve.

"Wow. This is so cool," the teen pronounced.

"Dena told me that she wants to be a doctor," the nurse said, as proud as if this had been her own daughter.

As he directed the needle just above the nerve, she flinched.

They'd given her a small dose of midazolam and fentanyl, a sedative and an analgesic. She appeared glassy-eyed and content.

"You OK?"

"Yeah. I feel great!"

He laughed softly. The girl had probably never had a drink in her life. Now she was in the grips of sedatives that rivaled the world's finest champagne, or cognac, or Scotch. The drugs produced a feeling that was delicious, fulfilling, and impossibly pleasurable. That was one of the most feared consequences of such medications: Once experienced, the sensation invited those who indulged back again, sometimes ceaselessly.

"OK, I'm where I need to be. See the tip? Watch the fluid come out."

The girl was mesmerized.

"Give me three milliliters right there," he directed the nurse, who complied. She repeatedly drew back on the syringe to ensure that there was no blood vessel in the path of the needle.

After he advanced the needle a bit, Dorothy emptied the syringe. He watched with satisfaction as the fluid appeared to coat the superficial surface of the nerve, spreading beneath the fascial plane that lay just above it.

"That should do it."

The adolescent giggled as Dorothy wiped the gel from her thigh.

"Dr. McCain."

He heard his name spoken outside the curtain. He pulled it aside quickly, coming eye to eye with the general surgeon who was waiting to operate on the confused, elderly man. A tall and lanky figure, he dwarfed the tiny man in the bed, who looked from face to face of those gathered around him. Unfortunately, Rosenblatt had a bit of a short fuse, and when he was stressed, he took to folding his hands in front of his chest while tilting his head back and forth from side to side. The surgical residents had a ball with this unorthodox dance when it came time for year-end satirical skits. Kurt found it endlessly amusing, except when he was the object of the man's ire.

The surgeon's jaw muscles became in turn taut and relaxed as though he were a guard dog preparing to tear into an intruder.

"Why haven't we gotten this patient back to the room?"

The physician assistant, similarly attired in blue scrubs, cowered behind her supervisor. Rosenblatt was tilting his head briskly from side to side.

"Have you spoken with him, Bruce? He's disoriented and confused. There's no way I can consent him for anesthesia like this. Doesn't he have some family with him to help him understand all this? Maybe a talk with them at the bedside, without all of us watching on, could convince him that this is for his own good."

Rosenblatt's head-tilting slowed noticeably as he began to think through the problem.

"He was fine in the office. I reviewed the physical exam and the consent with him. He understood perfectly well what I intended to do and why it was necessary. His daughter was with him and witnessed the whole thing."

Adopting the manner of a wizened and kind counselor, the surgeon turned to his elderly patient.

"Claude, it's me, Dr. Rosenblatt. Remember me from the office? I told you all about the surgery we had planned for today. We've got to fix that hernia, or you may end up with an emergency, which could make you very sick—it could even be life-threatening."

The old man looked bemused and perhaps even sensed that he knew the surgeon, but he did not embrace the concept of surgery. Instead, he turned his gaze from the surgeon to the anesthesiologist to the PA.

"Flora, you were there! You saw him sign it! Where in the world is his daughter? Can you go find her, please, so we can get this procedure started?"

The slight, affable PA skittered away.

"Jesus, Kurt. I've got a full schedule, and I have the office at noon!"

Kurt felt a twinge of sympathy. General surgeons worked incredibly hard and weren't always the most polite or politically correct. But they routinely saved lives and were faithfully dedicated to their profession at all hours of the day. He often wondered how they did it.

"Bruce, go sit down in the lounge. Have a coffee. We'll find the family and get this straightened out if we can. If not, we'll move on to the next."

The notion that some sort of progress was being made had a beneficial effect on the frayed nerves of the big man, who nodded and mumbled gratefully. He then ambled off in the direction of the doctor's lounge.

Kurt grabbed the portable "pickle" phone from his hip and called the front desk.

"Arlene, can you send for Rosenblatt's next case? We may need to delay this one."

He quickly moved up the hall after the procession escorting Dena to the OR on her cart. The young woman was giddy from the drugs, perhaps a little disinhibited.

"Oh, there you are—I thought you'd left me!" she cooed.

While her eyes were still misty after the emotional embrace she'd received from each of her parents, the girl smiled as soon as she saw him.

"All right, young lady," a deep voice boomed, "we'll get you some warm blankets. It's always cold in the OR."

The anesthetist, Robert, was professional and calming as he offered this bit of solace. At this point, she was uninterested, uninhibited, and unfazed. Her eyes closed, and a contented smile spread over her face.

Kurt looked around as the anesthetist placed the mask over the patient's face. He quickly scanned the monitors, the anesthesia machine, the patient and, the breathing circuit, satisfied that all was well. Then, he began to inject propofol, the standard drug for anesthesia induction. The comparison of anesthesiology to aviation had been aptly made many times. Kurt sensed that he was indeed in a cockpit, readying the airship for takeoff. The glowing numbers, the dials, the indicators . . . anesthesia people lived their lives beholden to them. Like pilots, they ensured the health and safety of others based upon what these devices displayed. But instead of altimeters, fuel gauges, and velocity displays, the anesthetist devoted his attention to the electrocardiogram, the blood pressure readings, and the blood oxygenation. When he had first begun his anesthesia training, all of this had seemed so glorious and romantic. Each breath was closely recorded—flow and pressure and volume—each heartbeat was displayed electrically from two different vantage points. The blood pressure the heart created as it pumped fluid throughout the vascular system was carefully sampled every few minutes. Even the intensity of electrical brain wave activity was monitored, filtered, run through an algorithm, and clearly quantitated by the bispectral index apparatus for the anesthesia team. Indeed, the very substrate of life, oxygen, was measured as it flowed through the bloodstream to waiting tissues, along with the complementary exhalation of the carbon dioxide. Both were registered as colorful waveforms on the glowing screen that provided extraordinary reassurance as to the patient's well-being.

"OK, you can count backwards from a hundred, and we'll be calling your name to wake up when surgery is over."

Kurt watched with satisfaction as her face became pacific, with the eternal calmness of non-existence. The serenity that seemed to overtake people as they slid off into anesthesia was a precious thing in an endlessly stressful world. The temporary descent into a nether-world fascinated him, sometimes frightened him.

Strikingly, once the patient was at an appropriate plane of drug-induced unconsciousness, the mask of serenity typically remained upon the face, the gift of anesthesia. This despite incisions, openings in body cavities, or trocars pushed forcefully through the skin and into the joints.

"She's ready, I think," he noted, eyeing the vital signs, which reflected the drop in blood pressure so frequently seen with propofol.

Robert used a wooden blade to compress the fleshy tongue, slippery and unruly and threatening to disrupt the entire airway management process. Then, deftly, he slipped the laryngeal mask airway into the back of the throat.

"Great. Let me take a listen to the lungs . . . Equal, clear. Did we get the antibiotics in?"

The anesthetist nodded and turned to begin charting as Kurt taped the tube in place.

"Nerve block?" Robert asked.

"Yeah, femoral block. It was setting up nicely as we came in. Should give us pretty good pain control."

"Great. I have some Dilaudid in the drawer if we need it."

He arrived back in the preoperative holding area to find that several family members were now at the bedside of the elderly man.

The daughter, her eyes alight with both concern and frustration, was frowning.

"He's this way a lot—he comes in and out. He has early Alzheimer's—isn't that in the chart? I mean, in the office, he was composed enough to give his permission for surgery."

Kurt stepped back slightly, giving her room to vent, folded his hands, tried to look contrite.

"Here's our dilemma: we know he needs surgery, and I trust that Dr. Rosenblatt spoke to him and got his permission, with family support, in the office. But I don't know him or the situation well enough to simply whisk him off to the OR and put him under anesthesia against his will. Even if he has dementia, it wouldn't be appropriate. I need to get his consent."

She looked tearfully at her father, who had set his jaw and was scowling.

"I was hoping," the anesthesiologist continued, "that when you came and talked to him, he'd remember the conversation and consent to anesthesia with you beside him. I'm comfortable proceeding under those circumstances if you are."

He turned to the patient, whose eyes had registered some flicker of recognition of his daughter and the situation at hand. Clearly, her presence had made a great deal of difference in his tolerance of these strange surroundings. His white, wispy hair stood up on the top of his head like the fibers of a cotton applicator as he turned his head from side to side.

"Dad? The doctor showed you a picture of how he was going to fix the hernia—remember? And you joked with him about how he was going to 'zip you up' after he put the mesh in?"

"Oh . . . Wait. He showed me a picture. A drawing he made."

Hesitantly, the old man appeared to begin making connections in his mind. He turned from his daughter to Kurt and then looked at his swollen legs lying before him in the hospital bed.

"Oh."

He paused again, looking at his daughter's face with a recognition that had not been there moments ago.

"Right. The picture."

"Well? That picture was you. This hernia isn't going to get better unless he fixes it. And it could become an emergency in the middle of the night—it's a lot more dangerous to fix it when it's an emergency."

This seemed to satisfy the man, and in moments he'd scrawled his signature on the consent form. He was briskly escorted to the OR by the waiting team.

Kurt injected the propofol and the muscle relaxant, succinylcholine. Within 30 seconds, he could see the fine fibrillations of the eye muscles. The jaw relaxed, the breathing stopped, and then the chest rose and fell rhythmically with the efforts of the anesthetist as she squeezed the bag.

Where have you gone, Mr. Jenkins? Kurt wondered. Are you better able to speak and think and remember, wherever you are?

Despite the difficulties in the holding area, the induction proceeded uneventfully.

"I'm gonna go see the next patient, Constance," he called, above the din of the surgical team and the strains of "Saint Elmo's Fire," blaring from a digital player in the corner.

He ushered himself out, pleased that the blood pressure was stable and that the patient was actually tolerating a reasonable level of anesthesia. The rest of the morning was a whirlwind. He provided two more nerve blocks for knee surgeries, then supervised anesthesia in another abdominal surgery case, followed by a foot procedure. When noon rolled around, he found a bit of time to slip back to the anesthesia office, hoping to gobble down his sandwich without interruption. And the busy afternoon seemed to pass just as quickly. A few hours and five cases later, he delivered the last of his patients to the recovery area and walked down the long hall to his office, prepared to clean up the charting and head home.

"You late this evening?" asked one of his partners, hurrying off in the other direction.

"No, not till tomorrow. Tonight—I'm a free man!"

# CHAPTER 3

Kurt changed quickly out of his scrubs, and walking to his car, reveled in the waning, late autumn sunshine. He thought with delight of his sister, who was coming over in the evening for a visit.

The shadows were long, and the leaves almost all down, though a few gnarled ones still clung to branches of spindly trees that poked up through the sidewalk on Fifth Avenue. Waiting for the walk signal, he turned back to look at the Medical center. An amalgam of eclectic architectural styles, some over a century old, others modern, gleaming glass edifices, the structures towered above the Oakland neighborhood, a beacon to suffering patients from across the region, the nation, and the world. The evening fell hard and fast, and in the failing light, the cluster of hospitals was suddenly illuminated, a radiant bastion of health and healing.

His commute spanned just a couple of miles, something that his friends in other, larger cities envied. The Southside Slopes neighborhood, where he'd purchased his hundred-year-old frame townhouse, was a mish-mash of different construction materials. Some of the homes were of wood, some brick, others stone. The houses had been carefully constructed along the sloping, twisting roads that led up the long embankment from the level floodplain along the river that people called "the flats."

The flats had undergone a boom-bust-boom cycle, the site of sprawling steel mills for a hundred years, later beset by economic devastation when steel left the "steel city," followed by three decades of gentrification with higher property values and the appearance of innumerable stores and restaurants. But in the last few years, much of it had become seedy, the neighborhood tainted by weekend drunkenness, trash on the streets, and rumors of widespread drug activity. Stores had begun to fail, and the ethnic halls and Churches, once the backbones of the social milieu of the Southside, had tumbled into disrepair, many closing outright.

The hillside neighborhood that Kurt called home, upon the "slopes," was altogether different. The area was a testament to a bygone era when the Diocese of Pittsburgh had played an essential role in the lives of so many of the immigrants who came for work in the mills. In successive tiers on the steep gradient were an ornate Catholic church—recently purchased and converted to condominiums—a convent, a rectory, and a retirement center for aged priests, the latter of which was an enormous, red-brick dormitory. At the top of the steep ascent, and surrounded by a well-manicured garden filled with statues of Saints and the Mother Mary, was a monastery. Another towering Catholic Church stood right next to it.

Kurt's own religious devotion was somewhat fragile, but, as he'd told Katy while moving in, the environment could only serve to strengthen his commitment. He considered the religious buildings to be relics of a time when men's thoughts and moral fiber were heavily influenced by Catholicism and its clergy. The dilapidation of the once-proud structures reflected the deterioration of religious influence in the lives of most people. Freed of the innumerable rules and ethical constraints, men were now permitted to devote themselves to whatever self-indulgent causes and notions should please them. And down below, in the teeming streets of the Southside, he could see the consequences of this newfound freedom.

Set against the hillside were the many staircases, clinging precariously to the steep terrain, leading from one street to the next as they worked their way to the top. Once of wood, these pedestrian ways had eventually been replaced with concrete. Pittsburgh's Millworkers had used them faithfully for almost a century. In ages past, the steps had been paralleled by several inclined railways, which served a similar purpose, ferrying men and freight up and down the bluffs at a time when roads were ill-maintained. Automobiles were seldom seen in front of the humble homes of mill workers.

Kurt was fascinated as he walked the staircases, knowing that great crowds of men had once gone up and down these same stairways in the morning, afternoon, and late evening of each day. A veritable tide of workers had tromped up and down the steep hills to and from their modest dwellings above the foul vapors of the great steel foundries, the rhythm of their lives dictated by the time clocks that marked the rotating shifts in the rolling mills, coke ovens and furnaces in the valley below.

From his street, high up on a protuberance that had been named "Billy Buck Hill," the stairway appeared to topple pell-mell down the steep hillside. It paralleled the harrowing roadways, stopping for rest at a landing or two until finally alighting on the sidewalk of Pius street. After a jog to the left, Kurt could then access another set of steps, perched out over the edge of a steep, rocky incline, making its way down to Eighteenth street, right beside the railroad trestle. Several sets of these ramshackle steps descended in parallel, like ladders from a children's board game, testimony to how important they had once been as a mode of access to the flats below for the populace.

In summer and fall, the stairways were embraced by a riot of vegetation that rose up from the black soil of the hillside, entwining the cement piers, reaching up over the rails and treads, as if attempting to pull the structures downward into the very substance of the earth. It was a display of power and persistence that elicited the occasional nod of respect from those who strode up and down the narrow ways, dodging the intrusive boughs and vines. Between these prolific patches of green, homes both diminutive and expansive were perched along the stairs, their stone patios and wooden decks letting directly onto the landings.

Kurth thought that life in anesthesiology was rather like the city's raucous, pitching, undulating landscape. One moment, he was carefully balancing three or four cases at once, all situated on some invisible plane of stability, the patients free of complications, the operations proceeding without incident as the surgeons plied their trade. And seconds later, he could find himself cast, unwittingly, down a slippery slope of terror as a patient became unstable, as some dreaded complication quickly gathered energy as he struggled to understand and control it, using whatever means he could summon.

Katy would come to visit him once or twice a month from her modest home in Polish Hill, another hillside neighborhood across the river and north of downtown. His sister had short, dark hair, twinkling blue eyes, and a gentle demeanor. A loving mother, she nonetheless evinced a stern disciplinary streak that showed in her interactions with her boys, a trait she'd inherited from their father. He'd resented her big-sister sternness when he was young but now sought her advice and counsel in many aspects of his life. He looked forward to the moments when he could chat with her about the joys and stresses that they experienced in their lives.

When she came to see him, they would often sit on his balcony with a glass of beer or wine, looking out over the Southside and the Monongahela River. They could see the downtown beyond, marked by a tight cluster of tall buildings that symbolized the technologic, financial, and healthcare entities that had somehow prevented post-industrial Pittsburgh from sinking into its own rust.

On this humid night, he began to think about his recent experiences in the flats down below.

"Those are mean streets down there."

He gestured toward the bustling riverside neighborhood below.

"Too many drunks on the weekends? They bother you all the way up here?"

"No, not that. I've had a few run-ins with shady characters in the dark after shooting basketball down at that elementary school." He pointed to the base of the hill, but the school wasn't visible from the vantage point. "On the back streets. You've got to be careful now there are a lot of drug deals. Heroin, mostly. Some of the addicts are pretty brash. They'll mug you in a second if there's a chance. And I've found a few guys curled up, overdosed, not breathing. I had to rescue the last one with naloxone— you know, the Narcan reversal agent that everyone talks about."

She listened in silence.

"It's not like it used to be, when we were kids. If you go down those steps at night," he indicated the steep set of stairs that snaked down the long decline, disappearing between two narrow rowhouses below, "you're in a different world. It just feels . . . threatening."

Katy's eyes opened wide, and she gave a bit of a laugh.

"You live beside a monastery, a church, a rectory and a nunnery! So of course it feels 'threatening,' when you leave your little celestial cloud!"

"Seriously, Katy. Things can get ugly in a second, with no warning."

"Well, let's stay on the beaten path, I'm sure we'll be fine."

The two walked down the many steps, and over to a trattoria on Carson Street, their favorite.

"So how are things at home?"

His sister sometimes needed to decompress from her busy days taking care of two frenetic little boys and a husband who worked long hours as a contractor.

"It's all right. Stressful, sometimes. The boys drive me nuts . . . basketball, baseball, cub scouts. I need to shuttle them all over the place. Things are pretty fat for Scott right now, but it'll slow down soon. You know how tough the winters can be."

The diminutive family made ends meet, but not by much. She'd trained as a social worker but left the job when her second boy was born and planned to go back when she got him into middle school. Though he had not shared it with her, Kurt had begun to contribute monthly to a college fund for both of the boys, a secret he would covet until the first of them graduated from high school.

"Well, whatever you're doing, I think you're doing it right. Your boys are polite and respectful. I see how they treat other people. Look, they're doing well in school, and on the court. They're even friends with each other—what brothers get along like that?"

She smiled, allowed herself a bit of pride at his description."And how are things going for you—any girls on your radar screen?"

He let the wine swirl a bit in the glass and shook his head.

"No. Not right now."

"That's what you always say, Kurt. I think you should be dating."

He became very earnest as he drained the last of the Merlot into their glasses.

"I'm not looking for anything grandiose. I want to have what you and Scott have."

"And you will, Kurt. But you know you can't force it. Get to know some women outside of work, go out a few times. Sometimes it seems like you actually avoid it."

"Not intentionally."

"I know, but you could be a little more willing to get out there and meet girls—Friday evening burgers at Fatheads and cycle club with a bunch of your friends on Sunday morning aren't gonna get it done. What about joining some volunteer groups down at the church?"

"It just seems like dating is so much work, and so disappointing, mostly."

"Look, you're a really great guy. Someone who is wonderful in your eyes will see that. And then your life can be full of the endless joys of marriage!"

This last phrase was spoken with an emphasis that Kurt knew held volumes of meaning.

"It's a lot of work, Kurt. Scott and I have our moments."

He nodded, recollecting the occasional argument that had broken out while he was visiting them. He'd even brokered a few cease-fires. But in the end, they always came back together for the sake of the boys. And for the sacredness of their union.

She nodded, looking at her wine glass.

"Yeah, I'm pretty lucky, I guess. God's given me a full plate, a lot of good things. I make it work the best I can."

"Well, I'm proud of you. Keep it up."

He touched his glass to hers, sipped the bitter red wine.

"What's new in doctor-world?"

"It's all OK. My own kind of stress, you know. As if the job isn't hard enough, there's always pressure to do more, in less time."

"I know you. You always meet the expectation."

"That doesn't mean I don't worry about it."

"Worry is what moves you—it always has been. Worrying for you is stoking the fire. I'm sure they love you over there in that hospital."

There was a silence. He knew what was coming.

"But Kurt, you're alone all the time. You need to meet a nice girl, someone who'll be a real friend and confidante. I don't think it was like that with Cassy. It always seemed like you were trying to measure up to something, or someone, that she wanted you to be. You never seemed really happy when she was here."

He couldn't reply; they'd discussed it all too many times. Katy didn't understand, and he couldn't capture how special the woman had been to him in words. Just before she announced that she was leaving for San Diego, he'd been thinking of ways to propose to her. But then, when she'd simply walked out of his life, he had raised the bar, probably too high. Could he really expect the next woman to be even more perfect?

His sister touched his hand warmly.

"Guess what? I met a really nice girl in church, who just moved here from . . ."

He laughed suddenly, breaking out of his sad reverie.

"We've been through this, Katy. You can't shop for me. I'll meet someone soon enough. But, right now, I just don't have that yearning."

"How can you not have 'that yearning?' You're a single guy in his early thirties. Please."

"I don't mean THAT yearning. I just mean I'm not ready for some kind of commitment. It just doesn't feel right."

"Your heart still belongs to that girl. It's too bad—she never really deserved it."

"Well, believe it or not, I'm enjoying my evenings alone, out on the deck in the sunshine."

She didn't need to know the truth.

"I like to look out over the city, do my work and just think . . ."

After dinner, the two surmounted the first of the many sets of steps that led back up, tipsy from the wine.

"It's like a stairway that leads up to heaven," Katy laughed, hanging onto the banister. She pointed up toward the clock in the steeple of the church next to the monastery, high above.

"This is what it's going to be like . . . After all the trials of your life, you close your eyes for the last time, and the next minute, you're on this eternal staircase, walking up into the clouds to meet God."

# CHAPTER 4

"There's a call for you," Barb, the secretary for the anesthesia office, called out as he sailed by, finally able to head back to his desk to grab a snack after a busy morning.

"Who is it?" Kurt mumbled, hoping for a few minutes to himself.

"A lady from a couple of days ago . . . she needs to ask you a question."

Shit, he thought. People never called the anesthesia office unless there was a problem.

"Can I transfer it to your desk?" she asked, anxious to get the call to him so she could get back to her work.

He sat down and looked at his workspace, littered with papers, scattered about with little semblance of order, most awaiting some sort of action on his part. He hated the administrative aspects of medicine.

Looking over at the secretary, he arched his eyebrows expectantly. Barb was a terrific assistant. She knew when to bluff, absorbing administrative reach, and when to get real customer issues into the hands of the doctors.

With the shrill note of an institutional handset, the phone sprang to life, designed to irritate and ensure a prompt response. He glared at it and reached for the receiver.

"Hello, this is Dr. McCain." His most officious tone.

There was a pause, and he strained to listen. When the response finally came, it was embodied in a voice so melodic, so seductive that he felt a chill run down his spine. He knew the voice immediately, had been captivated by it just two days before.

"Doctor?" she began, earnestly inquisitive.

He made a garbled sound of affirmation, briefly unable to formulate speech.

"I was in the operating room on Monday—you took care of me for my anesthesia. I was hoping you might be able to help me."

There was a note of sweet expectation, as though she understood that she exerted some sort of control over him, no matter how remote their connection.

He took a deep breath and waited for her to continue.

She'd been a surgical patient—vulnerable and anxious but also remarkably affable. And, to his way of thinking, beautiful. No wedding ring. She'd been just a bit flirtatious after the initial sedation went in, and he was certain that she was immediately cognizant of how she affected him. When he was interviewing her, it had been difficult to remember the standard preoperative questions. He remembered stammering a bit when he went through his routine, a speech he made eight or ten times a day.

She had engaged him so effectively that he was briefly grateful that he could leave her and tend to other patients when he induced the anesthesia. When she awoke, he found himself coming to her bedside repeatedly, inquiring after her well-being far more often than was necessary.

"Well," she began, as he cradled the phone on his shoulder, "I'm honestly having more pain than I thought I would. The nerve block was great—but when it wore off the pain got really intense. And my surgeon, just my luck, is out of town. So I just spoke to the people in his office. The Vicodin he prescribed doesn't do much for the pain and it makes me itch; I was hoping you could switch me over to Percocet, or oxycodone, or whatever form of that drug you use. I know this isn't usually your responsibility, but I was hoping you could write me a prescription for just a few days of pills—he'll be back by Friday, and his office nurse said he can attend to this, first thing when he gets back."

He was buoyed by her voice: it was velvet to his ears, soothing and warm and provocative all at once. Her face was indelibly imprinted on whatever part of the brain was responsible for remembering the countenance of a lovely woman.

Her request was irregular, to be sure. Surgeons controlled the home-going opioids by their preference. It was much easier to keep track of things with just one prescriber. There was too much room for manipulation and confusion if multiple docs were writing scripts.

And by Kurt's reckoning, he'd just as soon not be prescribing opioids outside of the tightly controlled and monitored setting of the OR, anyway. The drugs had so much potential for adversity: respiratory depression, nausea, itching, constipation, dizziness, personality change, sleep disturbances. Pain control was something that doctors had to provide, but outpatient opioid scripts were becoming more and more frustrating to provide. The oversight was driving doctors crazy; everyone knew of someone who had been sanctioned by the FDA. There were whispers of loss of licensure and even imprisonment. Still, she was in a tight spot, and he'd provided her anesthesia. No one would question his actions if he helped her out.

"Uh, sure. I think I can do that. I'll write a script for oxycodone; I'll leave it with our secretary, Barb, here in the office. Just come to the second floor and call this number. She can run it out to you."

"That's so kind. I'm really sorry to bother you. I can come down around one."

He hung up the phone and looked over at the secretary.

"Would you . . ."

"I heard, sure. Do you need to see her?"

He wanted to see her, felt a tingle of desire to see her.

"No," he countered hastily. "Not if you can just give her the script; then she'll get in to see Jenkins in the office when he gets back to his office. That should be fine."

He leafed through some of the papers on his desk, trying to suppress the effects of that phone conversation, signing some of them, discarding others.

"Am I behind on my PPD?"

"Yes. You were off the day they did them—you were on call the night before. So you'll have to go down to employee health."

Great, he thought, one more stupid thing to do.

He flashed through the emails, responding as needed, deleting whenever he could.

"Hmmm. Study of a new non-opioid pain drug. Sounds promising. Few side effects, no potential for addiction. Maybe we could get some clinical trials funding with this one."

The phone on his hip buzzed.

"We're finishing up in 3."

He walked out into the OR corridor, nodding to various blue-clad people as he went. One medical student seemed particularly out-of-sorts, wandering about, trying to find his attending physician, probably. A tall, lanky, young man with radiant black skin. Kurt smiled beneath his mask, remembering how foreign and intimidating the OR had been for him at first. It was the very last place he thought he'd spend his career.

The memory of his initial, grievous encounter with a surgeon had stuck with him, ceaselessly, for over a decade, even the question the angry, overwrought man had asked him.

"What's the blood supply to the gallbladder?" the huddled figure across the table had raised his voice menacingly, directing his vitriol at Kurt. As a freshman medical student, he'd struggled to provide the answer; gross anatomy was six months behind him, and only the major points remained.

The man had repeatedly sworn and thrown instruments, a petulant tyrant in his realm. The staff had simply cowered, as did Kurt. He'd taken his shame to the call room that night and knew that surgery would not be his calling.

As the memory faded, he grabbed a stretcher from the hallway and pushed it inside the OR.

"Mr. Marcuzzi, wake up," he called, gently tapping the man's shoulder.

He looked up at the vital signs, all stable, with a respiratory rate of fifteen, a good place to be. It suggested the patient was going to emerge with some degree of comfort.

"Shouldn't be long—BIS is almost 80," he noted out loud.

The patient began to stir. The psyche was beginning to return from whatever quarter in which it had been sequestered during the chemically-induced coma that was anesthesia. It was now reuniting with the corpus. At first, the lines of expression so evident in the face of older adults began to make themselves apparent in the eyelids, cheeks, forehead, corners of the mouth. It was subtle, like a sunrise. You had to remind yourself that something was actually happening. The mask of human expression returned, superimposing itself upon the bland features that accompanied deep anesthesia, as though the man were now once again inhabiting his own body.

Invariably, over time, the reflexes and awareness returned, followed by the frontal lobe functions. Sometimes, patients struggled, coughing and reaching for the tracheal tube, with what seemed superhuman strength, as the anesthesia team held the patient's limbs. Finally, when control of the airway muscles had clearly returned, the tube could be safely pulled. With startling immediacy, the struggle ceased, the quiescence returned, the expression became far less pained.

Providing anesthesia to make surgery tolerable was a precious pharmacologic gift, derived from the brilliant innovations and tireless work of long-departed anesthesiologists. But restoring the patient to himself, observing the reunion of the persona with the body after the surgery had been completed, was extraordinarily satisfying to Kurt.

Unfortunately, for a few patients, things could rapidly deteriorate at the moment of extubation. Deprived of the noxious, almost intolerable stimulus in the airway, the agitated patient might fall back into a stupor. That was when things could get exciting and frightening, with the patient snorting, snoring, obstructing, occasionally even turning blue.

Mr. Marucuzzi exhibited none of this.

"Well, that was a sweet wake-up. Let's get to the PACU."

The anesthetist nodded and began pushing the cart. As for the patient, he appeared content, at least for the moment. Having descended to a plane of near non-existence, he had now climbed back into the land of the living. Exuberantly, he overcame the chemical forces that had aggressively shut down the metabolic processes in his brain.

Kurt arrived in the PACU alongside the stretcher, just as Ellie, the chief CRNA, was coming out.

"I think Dr. Cutler is tied up. Can you take a look at this guy? He's really been dropping his pressure. He seemed fine when we got out here."

Ellie seldom got excited, had a sort of "take it as it comes" attitude, which had served her well over two decades in the OR. She had a knack for sniffing out trouble early, although she spent most of her time in the office these days, making schedules, dealing with complaints, ensuring adjudication of squabbles, and creating or updating policies. Kurt didn't envy her; sometimes, he wondered how the woman avoided being consumed by her administrative duties. A few years prior, she'd hurt her back while moving a patient and walked with a pronounced limp, the result of a failed back surgery for disk herniation. Long clinical days were tough on her, he could tell, but she never seemed to complain, and in fact, seemed grateful to get out of the office and get to the bedside once or twice a week.

He looked at his own patient, who was sleeping peacefully. The airway was open, the vitals stable, the mucous membranes pink and viable.

Moving from the cart to a slot a few yards away, he looked at Ellie's patient, motionless on the gurney. The man looked ashen, was breathing rapidly. Kurt listened to the breath sounds, which were unremarkable.

"Mr. Johnson, can you hear me?" he asked, looking at the bedside chart."Do you have any pain?"

The blood pressure cuff registered 75/40, low by any standard. The fluids were running wide open. The man gave no answer, turned his head briefly toward Kurt, then turned away again.

The anesthesiologist palpated the man's abdomen gently. It appeared to be distended, almost protuberant.

"Can you call his surgeon—isn't it Rosenblatt? I think he's bleeding into his abdomen."

Some vessel still pumping inside. Kurt realized he needed to get things moving and fast.

" And get some blood up here—do we have a type and crossmatch on him? If not, we'll take O-negative. Have someone get another IV started in his arm. Does he have a Foley? If not, let's get one in. And some albumin, please. We need some real volume till the blood gets here."

The nurses scattered, attentive to his orders.

The medical student he'd seen earlier was at the bedside, concerned but unaware of what he should be doing.

Kurt addressed him directly, putting a hand on his shoulder, turning his nametag around so that he could read it.

"Namobi," he pronounced the name carefully."Are you with this patient? Let me have your hand. Do you feel this distension? His abdomen is full of blood. And, would you please draw a blood gas?"

He figured the student knew how to do that, and if not, he'd help him. The gas could give them some critical parameters: the blood count, the oxygen levels, the carbon dioxide, and, most importantly, the bicarbonate and base deficit. How severe was the oxygen deficit? How hungry were the cells? To what degree had they been deprived of their substrate, to what degree were acid metabolites from anaerobic respiration by the tissues building up that could poison the patient?

The young man began gently feeling the wrist, searching for a pulse, a needle and syringe clutched tightly in his hand. His timidity was apparent, the actions of a medical student who had never performed a procedure in a critically ill patient before.

"Here. You'll never feel the radial pulse with that kind of blood pressure—the peripheral perfusion is just lousy." He guided the young man's hand and used his own digits to push the long, black fingers into the patient's groin fold. He looked steadfastly into the startled student's eyes.

"Can you feel the femoral artery? It's right here."

The young man's face lit up with recognition. He handed the syringe to the student, who began to carefully cleanse the groin.

"Namobi . . . this is not an arterial line. It's just a blood gas. We may need an art line eventually, but just do the stick and get the blood. We don't have to prep the skin for five minutes to do a single needle stick."

The man was too delirious from his falling blood pressure to care about the minor pain of the needle thrust into his groin. Namobi fumbled a bit and stuck the needle in, moving it in and out tenuously to where he thought he could feel the pulse. On the third insertion, moving the needle laterally, he appeared to hit the artery. The syringe quickly filled with bright red blood, forcing the plunger back. The student suddenly adopted an air of confidence and sobriety. His posture changed from slumped to upright, even as he reached forward with his long arm.

The albumin was hung, an amber, life-saving blood replacement, allowing them to temporize until the actual blood could arrive and the surgeon could rush the man back to the OR.

"What's going on?" The general surgeon moved brusquely to the bedside, already formulating a plan for what appeared to be awry. His paper hat was stained by the sweat from his brow.

"Do I have an OR? I need to get him back in there now!"

He then muttered in a lower tone."Probably the cystic artery. I'm sure I clipped the damned thing off."

The OR supervisor was coordinating the response. A whirlwind of activity, she was slightly overweight but an attractive woman, with boundless energy and a gift for administration. Moving from room to room, she coordinated times, personnel, equipment—a very demanding position on busy days. Yet, even in the thick of things, she somehow remained calm and deliberative, despite many demands placed on her.

"They're opening five for you. We put Dr. Hiram on hold—he just has a couple of hernias."

"Great—thanks. Where's anesthesia?" Rosenblatt was already in motion, his head tilting furiously from side to side.

"We're all here," Kurt countered. "I can go back with you, and the anesthetist has already set up the room for him. We're ready to go back. Waiting for blood, but his pressure's coming up with albumin. And we've got a big line in the antecubital vein on the left; we can go."

Kurt noted with relief that the systolic blood pressure was already up over 90, with the brisk infusion of the fluids. So they were winning the volume battle, at least for the moment.

"Kurt, what's up? I was hung up in Ob, trying to get an epidural to work."

His partner, Jimmy Cutler, approached the bed, eyes quickly surveying the scene.

"I was just going to call you. This is your cholecystectomy patient from this morning—looks like he's bleeding into the belly. We've got him going back to OR 5. Can you stay with him, or do you want me to take care of him?"

"No, I'm OK. I put in some spinal fentanyl along with the epidural catheter. The lady is completely effaced and almost ready to push. She'll probably deliver within the hour. I have Brad up there—he'll do fine. He's pretty new but a really good anesthetist, very comfortable in OB. There's only a couple of epidurals running. I doubt they'll need me unless they get some bad news from the fetal monitor or something."

"OK, I'm going back to preop so I can keep things moving."

"Hey, thanks for the coverage," Jimmy nodded as Kurt walked away.

"'Course. Glad I was here. Just gave him some fluids and got some better IV access. The rest fell into place. Keep your eye on Namobi, there. He did a great job getting a femoral blood gas."

The student looked up, startled that he'd been singled out. A reluctant smile spread across his face.

Jimmy put a hand on the boy's shoulder."Did the blood gas come back? Here, let's take a look at it."

Jimmy was an excellent teacher, a natural. He understood what other people couldn't, and knew how to present it so that they could. Kurt admired that about the man; Jimmy also had an air of instant accessibility. You knew that if you needed him, he'd offer his time, whatever else he had on his plate.

Theirs was a fine anesthesia group, Kurt thought, as he moved back towards the preop area. A few old-timers to anchor the younger practitioners, to give them perspective and bore them with stories of how things used to be. And there were several people in mid-career, just ascending to the heavier administrative roles, and able to pull from both ends. Most importantly, there was now a cadre of young anesthesiologists, right out of residency, keeping the older ones honest with their endless facts and citations from the recent literature. But they also quietly asked the probing questions that suggested that they yet needed a real understanding of the practical aspects of clinical anesthesia. Add to that a slate of older and very experienced nurse anesthetists, along with a few young ones right out of training. They were very fortunate to have the inveterate practitioners, both the doctors and the nurse anesthetists. Doubtless, several retirements would come in the next few years, and he dreaded that development.

Kurt went on a quick sweep through the PACU; things seemed to be stable for his postops.

Then, ambling through the short, dingy hallway, he found himself in the preop holding area. The hospital was aging, and none too gracefully. Passageways seemed dim; floors, even after cleaning, appeared to hold onto the grime from decades of heavy use. The last major upgrade with paint and new tiles was too distant for most of the practitioners to even remember. The restrooms were dark and dank. Such were the finances of a University Hospital system.

He moved as quickly as he could through the preoperative evaluation. The man with the bowel resection was quiet, introspective, compliant. The lady waiting for back surgery was filled with consternation, suspicious and risk-averse. Probably, he thought, she was terrified.

The tiny, bespectacled woman was intensely scrutinizing her operating room permit. She barely noticed him, as she scribbled notes on a pad of paper, digesting the form one sentence at a time. He decided to be bold.

"Mrs. Appria, life has risks. Walking down the street has risks. Rendering you unconscious with multiple powerful drugs, managing your airway so you get enough oxygen, balancing your fluids in with your fluids out, titrating the line between too much anesthesia and too little . . . yes, things can go wrong. But there are something like 50 million surgeries a year in the United States, and the vast majority of them are unremarkable, and patients emerge safely, aside from pain, swelling, and a fuzzy head. We're gonna do our best to take good care of you—I promise!"

She deflected his initiative.

"It talks about vision loss here—why would that happen?"

He did his best to explain the rare risk of optic nerve injury with long procedures in the prone position.

The lady proceeded to pepper him with a litany of questions about rare outcomes, and he did his best to field them all, conscious of the time.

She set her jaw and picked up the pen.

"I guess I don't really have a choice."

"People don't like to lose control—we get that. It's our job to get you through safely, and that's what we're dedicated to."

His phone rang at just that moment.

"Done in OR two."

He looked up."OK, if you have any other questions, let us know. You'll meet Julie, who's a nurse anesthetist, shortly, and then we'll go back to the OR. We'll start some sedation on the way back."

He was silently thankful for her capitulation and ushered himself away with a conspicuous flourish so she could see how busy he was. Please, he thought, don't think up any more questions.

A hernia case was just finishing, and the elderly patient was just beginning to regain consciousness.

"Mr. . . . Elliott, your surgery is over. Wake up!" the anesthetist, Lori, coaxed. The man looked to be a long way from being cognizant of his surroundings, squeezing his eyes tightly together and attempting to reach for his breathing tube. Two of the OR nurses held his arms tightly, lest he should remove it too early and put himself at risk of inadequate ventilation.

Kurt eyeballed the vital signs. The man was hypertensive and on the borderline of tachycardia, with ineffectual attempts at respiration. He coughed repeatedly, his saturations dipping down and his carbon dioxide building up. It was a typical wake-up for an elderly patient with an endotracheal tube. The device was noxious, its presence registering in the deep, ancient centers of the brain long before there was any return of consciousness. A little pharmacologic restraint with dexmedetomidine would help settle things down.

Finally, under the watchful eyes of the OR and anesthesia staff, the man began to furrow his brow, then opened his eyes. Once again, he appeared to inhabit his own body. He continued to cough, but not so severely, and was able to take deep breaths when asked, though this often precipitated more coughing. Moments later, he was following commands with his hands, and, to the relief of everyone in the room, the tube was pulled.

"Mr. Elliott, we're all done; we're going to the recovery room!" Kurt announced this triumphantly.

It was always enjoyable to let patients know that they had come successfully through the procedure. Most of them were able to process the information, at least for the moment, smiling or expressing relief. The brain and spinal cord had not yet begun to register the pain from the surgery. He was amazed at how often patients denied pain on awakening in the OR, only to characterize it as severe a few minutes later in the recovery room.

Lori reported to the PACU nurse. Both of the nurses were busy connecting monitors, jostling the patient purposefully to keep him stimulated, and breathing.

"This is David Elliott, patient of Dr. Johnson. History of hypertension; general anesthesia for inguinal hernia repair, with an endotracheal tube. Propofol, sux for induction; maintenance with sevoflurane and 100 mics of fentanyl. No versed or ketamine, given his mental status. Minimal blood loss, 1200 of crystalloid, no foley catheter. Family is in the waiting room—he may need some help at the bedside for getting oriented."

Kurt settled briefly at a desk to update his charting. Two preop notes remained unfinished, and he now had four cases to finalize. The computer, carefully tracking every aspect of his practice, was at once an ally and a horrid adversary. They were always in the way—a demanding, ubiquitous overseer of the medical practice. He remembered the days fondly when he could scratch a note, barely legible but at that time both legitimate and acceptable. It took 30 seconds for a reasonably healthy patient. Now, the most trivial procedure in the healthiest patient required far more time—all the questions had to be asked, all the boxes checked off, all the studies documented just so. It was no longer acceptable to note that the patient was simply 'stable.' Each element was appropriate and had a purpose, he reminded himself. But in the aggregate, the requirements had made his life much more frustrating.

He felt the familiar vibration of the phone on his hip, even before it buzzed aloud.

"Can't ever get anything quite finished," he seethed to himself.

"Hello, it's McCain."

It was Barb.

"So, she's here."

# CHAPTER 5

Kurt cocked his head, tried to concentrate—what had he forgotten? Did he have an appointment with a product rep or a resident?

"Who's here?"

"Lauren. You know, from Monday—she called you this morning. The patient who needed the script for pain meds." Barb sounded a bit constrained, as though the woman was right before her and intently listening.

"Uh, OK. Did I give you the script?" He felt a bit of panic, afraid he'd have to go see her.

"Yes. But she wants to thank you," Barb gushed, "in person."

He paused for a moment, running through his cases in his mind. There was really nothing happening at the moment that he could claim would prevent him from dropping back to the office for a short time to accept her gratitude.

She was overtly kind, almost affectionate, from the moment he opened the door.

"Doctor McCain, I can't thank you enough. I've been having an incredibly difficult time with this Vicodin . . . it makes me nauseated, and I just feel awful. The shoulder is killing me—I really don't want to take those pills." Holding up the script for oxycodone, she regarded it as though it were a prize. Her eyes sought his and somehow locked them into her gaze.

"I know you went out of your way to help me with this—I won't forget it, honestly. So many doctors aren't able to help you out when you're in a scrape, and this was really kind of you."

He felt like he was melting and found himself concentrating on the clarity of his speech, as though it was an effort to enunciate."Now make sure that you follow up on Friday—that's only going to last you a couple of days."

Barb had her chin on her hands, watching the interaction intently, not even pretending to do other work.

"I will, oh, I will. Have a great day, now."

She cast one more look behind her as she exited.

His eyes, suddenly freed up, strayed to the secretary.

"What?"

"Oh, nothing. I just haven't seen you look like that before."

"Like what?" Kurt asked as he stared at the closed door. Then, returning his attention to Barb, "Like what?"

She smirked and went back to her computer, signaling an end to the interaction.

"I don't understand," he mumbled, heading back out to the ORs.

The woman had done it again. Though he was steadfastly trying to avoid any emotional interaction with her, Lauren had knocked him over as though he had no substance whatsoever. He felt the trace of her within him, felt her eyes piercing his. Her lovely expression was now etched before his eyes, like the lasting, brilliant glow from staring at the sun.

These impressions resonated within him as he hurried to the preop area and interviewed the two patients awaiting him there. But his interviews were cursory; he floated through the rest of his day like an automaton.

Later in the afternoon, he was at his desk, finishing charts.

Phil Dugan, one of the other anesthesiologists, walked by on his way out.

"Kept us busy today, huh?"

"I'll say. It pays the freight though . . . and it beats the alternative."

"Yup. You want to grab a bite and a beer?"

Phil was a short, thick, muscular man who had been a wrestler at Penn State during his college years. He liked to cruise the eateries and sample micro-brews after the day ended. But Kurt avoided drinking on weeknights. It was way too much fun, one beer always led to the next, and by 10 P.M., he was wishing he was home in bed, even as he considered ordering another round. Kurt had learned to respect this vice of his and avoid it. Weekends were a different matter, and when he occasionally went out, he could hold his own with drinking buddies.

"I'm gonna pass. Maybe next Friday?"

"OK, but I'll be at Fathead's if you change your mind. Cheeseburger in paradise."

"Now you have me salivating. But I have too many things to do when I get home—have a good night."

He watched the stocky, muscular man walk out, and listened with satisfaction as the door closed.

# CHAPTER 6

The office became very quiet, and Kurt's was the only desk light that was on. He could not help but think of the woman and the impression she'd left upon him. Lauren. Her name reverberated in his consciousness. Romance had been frustrating and unfulfilling for him to this point in his life. After college, two different women had captured his heart in succession. But once things had become comfortable, each of them had begun to pull away from him, seemed to have second thoughts. Was there something wrong with him? Or had he chosen unwisely? Had he chosen at all? The women had shown up in his life, and he'd fallen for them. Still, perhaps it had been no more than the fulfillment of a biological imperative.

Cassy had decided to go off on her own two years prior. He'd been confident that she was the one, that she'd be a great friend and lover for the rest of his life, that she was the mate he'd been searching for. They'd kept in touch for a while after she left, then the letters stopped. She was off doing locums work as a nurse, loved the travel, always yearned to be somewhere else. Finally settled in San Diego. He'd never had the heart to ask if she had found someone else. They had sometimes argued about children—he wanted some, she only wanted to wait. Their lifestyles were different, too different. What he thought had been love had begun to seem more and more like infatuation. After she left, he had become stony hard inside, had no interest in the women he met, and no real yearning to date or find a romantic partner. Until now.

Something was melting inside him, and it was disturbing. He was not in control.

Kurt looked up and shrugged. The best cure for this unsettling occurrence would be to simply avoid Lauren—which would be easy. It was unlikely he'd have to see her again. In two days, he'd be able to forget her, and life would be back to the usual, his emotions once again settled. He sighed contentedly at the thought and then began to wonder what he could dig out of his freezer for his supper. His sister had sent over some stuffed-pepper soup a week before, a favorite, which he could defrost and devour in short order.

One more pass through the PACU, he figured, and if all was stable, it was probably time to cut out.

"Good night, Kurt," a gravelly voice called from behind a partially closed door.

It emanated from the chief's office.

"Night, sir; I'll see you tomorrow."

"Right, I've got you in the thoracic room, along with some cataracts and general surgery cases. Should allow you to focus on the lung surgeries."

He popped his head around the door. Kurt adored the man. The chief always had the right answers, always kept his cool, dealt judiciously with upset patients and upset surgeons. He wished he had the man's grace, but he thanked God almost daily for having him as a supervisor. The anesthesiology private practice world was filled with malignant, mercenary players who served as chiefs in smaller practices around the city, slick opportunists grabbing up contracts and hiring young docs at low wages. At the same time, they skimmed the large share of the revenue that came from billings. They made nice with the administration and left the clinical subtleties and risks to those down in the pit. Such arrangements infuriated him. He knew good anesthesiologists who'd walked into such nightmares, then had to live out a contract that made their lives a living hell until it was up. After that, they faced non-compete clauses in the contracts they'd unwisely signed and had to move away to another city to practice.

The woolly-headed chief anesthesiologist was hunched over his computer, looking at a spreadsheet. Graying, small in stature, he was just beginning to develop the forward spinal curvature so common in older

THE STAIRS ON BILLYBUCK HILL

men. His face was creased with the lines of worry that radiated outward from the soul of one who had spent decades caring for others. His concerns and stresses had imprinted themselves upon his leathery skin like arroyos in a parched landscape. But from his time-worn countenance, he regarded the world with brilliant, deep-set blue eyes that seemed to illuminate everything they came to rest upon. With all of his administrative tasks, clinical duties, and the frustrations of leading a group of all-too-autonomous physicians, he still had time to perform meaningful clinical research. His name was well known in various academic circles, and he seemed to turn out a paper every couple of months. Kurt admired him for all of these things, had no idea how the man could be so active and so successful. He was simply the optimal role model. John Mennerberg could be biting, caustic and terse when the need arose. Still, his lieutenants were so genuinely intent upon pleasing him that it seldom did.

"You seem a little out of sorts, Kurt. What's up?"

Best to just let the question slide by and change the subject in a few moments.

Patiently, the chief asked again.

"You look like something's upset your apple cart. You sure you're OK?"

The man was very insightful, knew his people.

"Just had a busy day. Patients calling back with issues, trying to stay on time for the starts, and we had a lady with a really tough intubation— we got it. Still, I really felt like we were risking traumatizing her pharynx. Hard to coach someone when you can't quite see where the tube is on the Glidescope, you know?"

"Sure, I know exactly what you mean."

The chief waited expectantly, then broke the slightly awkward silence.

"Well, I remember a time . . ."

Like any good supervisor, the chief always had a relevant story. Kurt settled in, leaning against the door, and as he listened, he could not help but wonder if his brief conversation with Lauren had echoed through the suite.

"I've talked to you about my time in Viet Nam. A year in an Army field hospital, courtesy of the draft. There was a nurse. Let's call her

Yvonne. Eyes of vivid green, a smile that completely took me apart, startling intelligence, a searching disposition. And she was utterly devoted to patient care. I was stunned the moment I met her; topsy-turvy nuts. She did not feel the same. I used my sense of humor, my enormous cache of witty remarks, my drop-dead good looks, my professional competence . . . I put my best foot forward in every way I could. But It was all to no avail. I spent my last four months over there in a trance, a fog, an emotional fugue. I felt as if I'd been lifted from my life and placed somewhere completely alien, an unspeakably depressing valley of shadows. The place was hellish enough, the work even more so. I suppose I yearned for deliverance from the constant stress and unhappiness, placed all my expectations upon her. And she would have none of it. She was friendly enough, but it ended there. She showed me curtness, frankness, tokens of respect. I never had the courage to really talk to her about it—I knew that she was aware of how I felt. When my orders came, I ran out of my tent with my duffle bag and then to the landing pad as quick as I could go. I knew I had to get away . . . that she was, without intent, strangling me. I cried when the chopper lifted me up and out of that Godforsaken camp. It took me a long time to get her out of my soul. Then, two years later, I met the missus. Thank Heavens. It was like climbing a mountain when I was over there, one that I could never reach the summit of. You look a little like I felt back then. Just be careful—a beautiful woman can be like a drug, can deprive of your very self; perhaps even steal your soul."

Kurt couldn't help but grin at the insight the man possessed. Still, he would not go as far as acknowledging that his situation was similar, not even to himself. His soul was simply not available. Finally, he said goodnight, nodded respectfully and walked out of the office.

# CHAPTER 7

"Oh, come on!"

"Yeah . . . I don't see the connection here."

"Well, the general surgery service did. The surgeons are pretty convinced that this is a result of the anesthetic."

Morbidity and mortality conferences were always on the spirited side. The anesthesiologists and anesthetists gathered once a month to review complications, throw stones at each other, and circle the wagons. It was important to deflect criticism from other specialties whenever blame seemed to be misdirected.

"Look," Kurt explained, "it was a pretty standard case. No prolonged hypotension, no dysrhythmias, no airway issues, or hypoxia. The lady had a normal induction, a few episodes of systolic blood pressure below 90 while we were waiting for the prep and positioning, and we propped her up with phenylephrine. She responded nicely with pressures around 110 systolic, then she'd sag again. Of course, we opened up the fluids for a bit, but she had a history of diastolic heart failure, so we couldn't really just blast the crystalloids in—it made more sense to give her some squeeze to get the pressure up."

One of the younger anesthesiologists, Natalie, chimed in energetically."We do cases just like this one every single day. You can't induce anesthesia and then wait 20 or 30 minutes for the surgeons to make an incision without the blood pressure starting to sag. We take away the vascular tone with the induction agents, and give it back with vasoconstrictors—it's unavoidable!"

The chief walked in at that moment, looking sleepy and sipping a steaming cup of black coffee. He seemed to fuel his morning—and much of his afternoon—with the robust, dark draught. He ate little and was as thin as a stick, with a face that bordered on gaunt. But there was an evident vitality about him, manifest in frenetic movements and his cease-less activity. Heads turned and nodded in acknowledgment.

"This that the case from last Friday?" he asked, peering at a CT scan of a very compromised brain projected on the screen in front of the room.

"Yep, this is the one. The lady had a dense stroke, with complete right hemiplegia and aphasia. It's devastating," Kurt announced for the second time that morning, biting his lip.

"I heard about it at the med exec meeting," the chief continued."Tom Sotherby is pretty vocal about the situation. The lady is a good friend of his mother-in-law. I'm not sure he has much cause to point fingers. I looked at the record, I don't see anything concerning, seems like a well-conducted general anesthetic. When did she start to show signs of the stroke?"

"They finished the bowel resection around five o'clock. The lady emerged looking pretty much as expected, went to PACU, and woke up slowly, but she appeared to be neurologically intact. They sent her up to the floor at a little after six. She had some pain, was medicated a couple of times, and seems to have gone to sleep at around ten o'clock. Complained in the evening to her nurse about the NG tube. The nurse on nights woke her a little after 11 just to assess her and noticed nothing odd. But at 6 A.M., when they went by to deliver her meds, her speech was unintelligible, and the weakness was obvious. She seems to have had the event in the middle of the night."

"I expect they called Sotherby? And neurology?"

"Yeah, the neurologist was there within 15 minutes; he was already rounding. They got her down to CT within a half-hour, confirmed there was no bleed, and sent her over to IR. They tried to open the middle cerebral artery, but it was occluded, and they weren't able to remove all of the clot. Doubtless, some of it broke up and showered downstream. It's a big stroke, and she's not likely to get much of her function back."

"Did we miss anything in terms of her risk for this? Did she have any prior neurologic history?" one of the anesthetists asked.

Kurt went back a couple of slides to review.

"No. No neuro history. I asked her specifically about strokes and mini-strokes. She had a history of hypertension, and she quit smoking four years ago. Those were her risk factors. But no known vascular disease."

"How was her blood pressure control at baseline, outside the OR?" another called out."Maybe we needed to keep her at a higher perfusion pressure."

"She seems to have been well managed, on a calcium-blocker and an ARB. Her baseline systolic pressures ran from 120s to 140s on the floor. Supporting her around 110 with means in the mid-seventies to ninety seemed reasonable."

"Why didn't you put in an arterial line?"

"Well, we had plenty of IV access, and she was pretty stable throughout; I didn't consider her to be at much risk with her background, and this is not a particularly high-risk procedure. There were no prolonged periods with low blood pressure. Sotherby lost next to nothing in terms of blood. How would an art line have changed anything?"

"Well," came the response, "you'd have known about those hypotensive episodes earlier. Maybe you'd have treated her blood pressure earlier, and that would have affected her outcome."

"Really?" Kurt began to sense his patience growing thin."You think this is a hemodynamic stroke from poor blood flow? It was almost certainly embolic. Her 'hypotension' was minor and really short-lived. She woke up and had normal neurologic function for hours before going to sleep that night. I just can't think that low blood flow was the issue here."

A large man who'd been sleeping in the back row, emitting gentle snores, started awake. His protuberant abdomen hung out well over his scrub pants, and his face was partially obscured by a scrubby beard.

"OF COURSE it was embolic," he thundered. Heads turned, and faces reflected their amusement.

"Oh, it's alive," a colleague observed.

"I had a rough night," came the retort."That aside, this was not a hemo-dynamic stroke. Kurt's right. It's embolic. She probably has got cranial arteries full of plaque. And she woke up from the surgery a walkie-talkie. This happened during the night, and all her recorded pressures up on the floor were fine. Two minutes of hypotension do not cause profound hypo-perfusion to a brain that manifests 12 hours later with an MCA occlusion. That makes no sense to me. Here's what makes sense, okay?"

He looked around the room, almost threateningly, with bulging, bloodshot eyes.

"Surgery is major trauma, and mediators go coursing through the bloodstream the minute the bloodletting and tissue destruction are begun. It's no slap in the face to our surgical colleagues—they know this better than we do. Coagulation factors and vascular chemicals and fibrinolytic molecules and inflammatory cascades and God knows what else are let loose, for hours on end. Anesthesia doesn't protect you from all this, even with multi-modal analgesia or nerve blocks or opiates or anything else. Sleeping patients are black-boxes of ongoing pathology. We can't figure out what the hell is going on inside of them most of the time until they wake up and let us know unless it's a big MI or a cardiac arrest. Imagine this lady with a head full of partially obstructed vessels, all of which are happy enough to do their jobs until the inevitable inflam-matory changes start to affect the diseased intima of her arteries during the procedure. Then, slowly, platelets accumulate, thrombin is generated, new shear forces are created as the intima expands into the lumen and POW, it breaks off. Headed downstream until it can no longer pass. It lodges in her MCA or a major branch thereof, many hours after surgery, right when the cellular changes come to a head. THEN you have a stroke. Calling this an anesthesia complication is pure bullshit."

The chief, who had seated himself beside the perturbed anesthesiolo-gist just before the diatribe erupted, gently folded his hands and looked over at the man.

"Thanks for that, William. Eloquently stated. I happen to agree with you. What did the angiogram show?"

"There is minor occlusion of both carotids, left worse than right, on the order of 25 to 30 percent. In the smaller, intracranial vessels, the angiogram showed diffuse, mild atherosclerosis, along with the new MCA occlusion."

"Well," Willam bellowed."What else do we need to know? She either embolized to the MCA or thrombosed the vessel in the wake of surgical trauma and the post-surgical inflammatory state. What the hell are they blaming us for?"

"The literature is unsettled," the chief offered, providing the perspective of his many years of experience."Intraoperative hypotension can lead to stroke, but typically only when it is severe and not corrected for extended periods. Some studies show no association at all. The suggestion that intraoperative mismanagement of the blood pressure led to this complication is not supported by the OR record nor by the literature; that line of logic is faulty. I'll speak to Sotherby—I think he was overly emotional about this because of the close relationship he has with this patient and her family."

"Right. Well, he should've ordered a workup of the damn intracranial vasculature if he wanted to avoid this outcome." The big man shook his head and glared around at the others in the room, who had fallen silent. The two residents on-service looked as though they would have liked to find a rock to hide under. Namobi, the medical student, appeared terror-stricken."This is what pisses me off about surgeons—they try to pin everything on the anesthesia service."

"William," the chief scolded, "That is not even close to true. We work well with the overwhelming majority of our surgeons, and out-of-place suggestions like this one are actually unusual. I need you not to trumpet such sentiments about; I'd like to stay on good terms with our surgical colleagues. Further, we need to have broad shoulders and vet this kind of complication, even if it's obvious to us that it's not a direct complication of our care. We all learn from these forays through the literature. Two of the papers you cited, Kurt, are completely unknown to me and probably to most of us. The surgeons come down on each other very hard at their M and M conferences when there is a complication. It's only appropriate that we subject ourselves to scrutiny as well."

Kurt nodded. The chief never failed to impress him with his measured approach and his judiciousness.

The doctors and anesthetists got up, chatting amiably among themselves about domestic issues, politics, and the cases of the day.

"Man, they tried to jack you. What a crock," William had fallen into line beside Kurt, pulling up his sagging scrub pants and quickly enveloping the smaller man with his meaty arm.

"For what it's worth, I think you and Connie did a fine job caring for the patient. Talk about deflecting the blame."

Kurt shrugged, trying to appear indifferent, but he was actually pleased to have the backing and reassurance of his colleagues. M and M, while necessary, could be utterly humiliating. He'd had his share of ducking the mudslinging. At the same time, other practitioners scrutinized him for circumstances that often represented gray areas, the "more research is needed" specificities of clinical care. What remained iffy or uncertain in acute medicine seemed to outweigh that which was incontrovertibly established and by a wide margin. That didn't stop doctors from becoming contentious and accusatory when it came to adverse outcomes.

The group left the conference room and meandered down the hallway, a sleepy platoon in pale blue uniforms, yawning and stretching. Six o'clock conferences were trying because everyone was tired. On most days, the manic rush to get rooms and patients ready ensured that a robust level of glucose and neurotransmitters were coursing through the brain. This made it easy to stay focused on the necessary morning tasks. But sitting in a dark room at that early hour while someone droned on about a case, or a paper, was deadly.

"What do you have today?" Sheila, one of the nurse anesthetists, asked him, sipping on a drink that smelled much more like French Vanilla than coffee.

"Two thoracic cases with Sanders, and then some eye cases and a few hernia repairs. Should be a good day unless we get tagged with add-ons. But before I get started, I have to get up to the floor and see a patient from yesterday."

He ran up the stairs, two at a time, mindful of the hour but intent on seeing a lady who'd sustained an injury to her soft palate. The occurrence was utterly unexpected and, in a sense, humiliating. It simply shouldn't have happened.

He prepared himself for the visit, running a series of statements through his head, judging their effectiveness. It had not been difficult to place the airway. Still, neither he nor the anesthetist had been able to see the tube when it was initially thrust down into the mouth and throat. As she tried to advance it into the view of their camera, it had met the tender tissues of the tonsillar pillar on the right and pierced the mucous membrane. He had been shocked when the bloody tip of the tube appeared on the video screen. However, she was able to easily guide it into the airway. Blood had quickly begun to pool in the back of the mouth, and as they suctioned, he'd been able to see the rent in the pink tissues.

The patient was asleep at this early hour, snoring softly, her mouth wide open. He assessed the scene, felt a twinge of guilt and regret for what had happened, acknowledged that he needed to take responsibility and offer an apology.

"Mrs. Shapiro?"

She started, looked dumbly at the anesthesiologist, and quickly became oriented.

"Hello, doctor."

"I came to check on you. I know your knee is hurting, and, worse yet, we caused you a lot of pain in your throat. I apologize. I wasn't aware, until after we placed the breathing tube, that we'd created this injury to your palate."

She was controlled in her response, rubbing her eyes and focusing on Kurt. Her voice was raspy and hoarse, doubtless an effect of the trauma they'd caused in her throat.

"I just don't understand how this could happen."

"Well, our video-laryngoscope gives us a great view of the vocal cords, but we didn't see the tube impacting on your palate. When we appreciated it, coming into view, it had already done its damage."

"It's really hurting. I can barely swallow."

She waved towards the breakfast tray that had been placed at her bedside. The food and juice were untouched.

"I'm terribly sorry. The only bright spot is that injuries inside the mouth usually heal very rapidly—I think you'll be able to eat and drink pretty normally in a couple of days."

An infection from such a tear could spread rapidly through the neck into the mediastinum and actually become a lethal process, though such an outcome was rare. The ENT consultant had responded promptly, irrigating and sewing the laceration right after the knee surgery. With a few days of antibiotics and oral rinses, Kurt was confident that she would heal rapidly and get on to rehab her new knee.

"Her throat hurts her worse than her knee does!" Her husband, a large, lumbering man, had just walked in. He carried a vendetta with him as though it were a loaded firearm.

"I understand. I'll do anything I can to help her feel better. We could use a mouthwash that we use for cancer patients with stomatitis-sores in the mouth. I think it could soothe the soreness."

The husband scowled and said nothing, but at this suggestion, Mrs. Shapiro brightened somewhat.

"I would appreciate that, doctor."

He seized on this brief, favorable moment.

"I'll order it, and you can ask for it whenever you need it—it's a 'swish and swallow.' I doubt if it tastes good, but I think it can make all this more bearable."

"Will I have to stay here in the hospital longer because of this?"

"Well, the ENT surgeons will want to observe you for a couple of days and make sure the antibiotics are effective, that no infection develops. So, yes, I think you'll have to stay a bit longer."

The silence that permeated the room was deafening. Kurt had nothing else to add. Nodding respectfully, he exited, making a mental note to put a follow-up note in the chart. While he had little in the way of meaningful therapy to offer, at least physicians on the other services would see that he was taking responsibility.

He almost bowled over the ENT consultant as he sped out of the room.

"Kurt, that laceration in the tonsillar pillar was pretty impressive."

As if, Kurt thought, he needed that news.

"Looks good today, though," the surgeon continued." I think it will heal without incident."

"I appreciate that. The sooner, the better," Kurt confided."Many thanks to you guys for coming to the OR so quickly to address this."

"Of course. It's our pleasure. This is the second major lac in the oral cavity in the past couple of weeks. What's going on—do you have new people on the service, or what?"

The anesthesiologist winced. The other occurrence had been an urgent intubation, a real struggle with an injury to the posterior pharyngeal wall. The patient later developed a severe infection in the deep spaces of the neck and had nearly died of sepsis. Not his patient, but the appearance of two significant throat injuries caused by intubation attempts in such a short time was an ugly one.

The oral injuries would be the topic for another M and M conference, probably in the next month or so. They would likely include the surgeons who'd been present to add their own particular brand of critique. He could hardly wait. In the meantime, he said a prayer for Mrs. Shapiro's recovery and headed back to the OR. As in life, evil occurrences in the OR seemed to come in little bursts. Kurt hoped for an uptick in outcomes soon, with a long, complication-free interval.

# CHAPTER 8

The holding area was buzzing with activity. The nurses from the OR were already out and greeting the patients, while the preop nurses scurried to obtain and dispense the necessary medications before the surgeries started. The arrival of the anesthesia teams crowded the preop ward that much more, with jostling bodies and intense interrogations.

A lean, asthenic man, with a gaunt face and sparse white hair on his head, lay before Kurt, gravely speaking with the circulating nurse from OR 2, in which he would undergo lung surgery. The ravages of 35 years of cigarette smoking had caught up with him. In addition to early obstructive lung disease, the patient had developed a nodule in his right lung, suggestive on CT scan of a malignancy. A few days before, a biopsy performed during bronchoscopy had confirmed the diagnosis, and he was now booked for a thoracoscopic removal of the right upper lobe. Fortunately for him, the determination had been made that the tumor was removable and hadn't yet begun to spread.

"Mr. James—I'm Dr. McCain, a pleasure to meet you. I'll be taking care of your anesthesia today along with Dora, a nurse anesthetist who'll be working with me. You'll meet her shortly. What will your surgeon be doing for you today?"

The man became still and quiet. He turned to Kurt and greeted him, offering a limp handshake and a weak, watery gaze from green eyes that had lost all luster. The glance embodied complete and utter despair—mind, body, and soul in unison. It was as though he had fallen into a deep rent in the earth, inside of which hope could no longer even be imagined.

"Doctor says I have lung cancer. Says he's gonna cut it out."

Kurt let a respectful moment of silence pass.

"I see. I'm sorry to hear that, but if they've offered you surgery, then there is at least hope of a cure. Even if you have to get radiation or chemotherapy afterward, we can be hopeful about your outcome."

The man nodded, looking down at his feet. He looked very small in the oversized patient gown, lying prostrate on the stretcher. Kurt could see his masseter muscles dancing as he gritted his teeth together rhythmically.

"Let me ask you some questions about your medical history. I have a lot of this from the computer chart—and then I'll talk to you about the anesthetic."

After the interview, the patient was taken to the OR. Once the case was in progress, Kurt made his routine rounds on the patients in the other ORs he was covering, then found his way back to the preop area. After interviewing another patient for the cataract room, and a patient with a hernia who would undergo repair with a nerve block as the anesthetic, he sat at the computer and began charting. The burden of computer record-keeping had become ever more demanding. In addition, care of patients had become increasingly frustrating as more and more requirements were laid upon the providers by out-of-touch mid-level managers. Certainly, the administrators needed to ensure hospital compliance with endlessly proliferating rules emanating from state and federal governments. But that didn't make it any more satisfying to spend a greater amount of time seated at the computer than at the bedside.

He shook his head with exasperation as he typed aggressively at the keyboard.

His phone rang, distracting him.

"Hey, it's Kurt," he chirped, trying to sound enthusiastic.

He recognized the officious voice on the other end. Barb.

"Doctor McCain, Lauren is here. Again"

He froze. The name alone elicited an intense visceral response within him. Then, briefly, his world stopped spinning.

"Ummm . . . did we request her to come back? Did she lose the script?"

"No, no. But she has developed a lot of pain at the incision site, and she wants you to take a look at it. She thinks she might have an infection. But, remember, her surgeon's out of town."

He was startled but felt a delightful sensation course through his body. Despite his reluctance, and only a day after her first visit, he really did want to see her.

When he got back to the office, Barb inclined her head towards a small consultation room located at one end of the suite, suppressing a knowing smile. He found the lady sitting patiently within, already in a gown, the shoulder conveniently exposed for him, the arm dangling limply in her sling. He reached out, instinctively, to examine and perhaps to soothe. Her wound was developing a severe inflammation, rings of red radiating angrily around the tidy white bandage that had been placed over the set of small arthroscopy incisions.

As his fingertips touched her warm skin, she pulled away and gasped reflexively.

"Sorry. That's really tender—you're getting quite a cellulitis around this. We've got to get you on antibiotics. Hopefully, this is simply a superficial infection, in the skin, not down into the joint."

"Doesn't that figure? I guess everyone who gets an infection says 'why me'? They tell you this is like, one in a thousand cases. Probably doesn't do any good to wonder why I was chosen."

He nodded as he inspected the inflamed area.

"Anyway, you took such good care of me the first time! Since I had to come back, I'm glad I get to see you. It's like you're my personal anesthesiologist!"

He looked up, startled, and blushed. When he met Lauren's piercing, dark eyes with his own, he felt a jolt of excitement. He'd not yet removed his hand from her shoulder, was still gently compressing the supple skin beneath his fingers. He retreated, with his digits, to a less tender area but couldn't entirely withdraw from touching her.

He then became aware of the setting, admonishing himself, as a voice from somewhere within sounded in his mind: This woman is a patient. You cannot develop an attachment to her.

He offered an embarrassed smile, mumbled a thanks for her compliment, and tried to move on to medical matters.

"Well, you should get an IV dose of cefazolin to cover the likely skin bacteria. I'll contact the surgeon's office and ask them to see you right away. That dressing should come off to examine the wound directly, to make sure it's not oozing."

"Well, that's just it . . . he's not due back till tomorrow morning. Could you take a look at it and just start me on that first dose of antibiotics—I could go to the office to see him tomorrow. And this is much more painful than I expected . . ."

He shifted a bit uneasily. It didn't seem appropriate to take on the antibiotics before the surgeon had a chance to lay hands on her. Was she really infected, or just inflamed? The pain issue, on the other hand, he was comfortable with. She certainly had a reason to need more aggressive pain management. And she'd probably already gone through the few oxycodone tablets he'd prescribed the day before.

"Well, actually, I can. But I need to call the surgeon's office to let them know what treatment we apply and make sure he'll see you tomorrow. I don't want this to go much longer without a surgeon seeing it."

She offered the bare shoulder to him, letting her gown slip down off her shoulders. Her bra, partially obscured by the sling, was lacy, low cut, a bit more revealing than he thought proper for a visit to a physician. He carefully pulled the tape off the incision, attempting to be as gentle as possible, wincing himself when he saw how her expression reflected the soreness. Then, removing the gauze dressing, he noted the wound itself looked relatively clean, with no exudate.

"This is gonna hurt—I need to push on it a bit to make sure it doesn't have any fluid collection."

She moved the shoulder closer to him.

"It's okay. I know what to expect. Thanks for being so gentle."

He realized that the interview had to be completed, and soon, before he began to ask her personal questions and, just maybe, to ask her out. It seemed achingly clear that this was what she wanted. All of this was starting to edge towards the borderline of ethical behavior; he felt himself traversing that line, despite his awareness.

"Right, I'll get that together. For now just sit back and we'll get an IV into you for that first dose of antibiotics, and something for the pain."

Lauren settled back against the back of the cart. She looked awkward with her shirt removed, her red shoulder painfully obvious, the clunky sling almost enveloping her trunk. He looked around for someone who might be able to come and start the IV, hoping to get away from her for a few minutes. This would at least allow him time to consider what had just transpired. Unfortunately, no one appeared to be unoccupied.

"Let me get some supplies, and I'll put the IV in."

"I've got nowhere else to go," she reassured him, smiling, holding up her right arm, presenting the dorsum of her hand.

He sailed briskly out of the room, began collecting the supplies.

"Hey, don't you have to start a case in OR five?" his partner, Rodney, asked him as they passed each other."I could put in an IV if you need me to."

He looked over at the bed space where one of his patients had been a moment before. The anesthetist had already taken the man back to the operating theatre, so they'd be calling him in a minute or two to come and begin the induction.

Kurt paused, nodding to the other man. He was tall, dark, and regarded as impossibly handsome by the OR nurses, who gossiped ceaselessly about some of the younger doctors. He suddenly did not want to give up the time he would have at her side.

"I'm okay. I'll just put this in to get the antibiotics going and head back to the OR. I think I've got a couple of minutes."

Having gathered the equipment, he hastily went back into her room, self-conscious of the attention that others might be paying to his personal ministrations. Certainly, he could have asked one of the preop nurses to start the IV and handle the antibiotics since other patients were already waiting for him. But he'd identified the problem and wanted to take care of her rather than add one more burden for the busy nurses on the floor. Glancing around as he entered her room, he wondered how many of his colleagues were aware of his focus on this attractive woman.

"Wow, Gorgeous veins," he assured her, gently caressing the dorsum of her right hand.

She beamed.

"Well, I do try to take good care of them. I played piano for 20 years, and that really brought them out."

"So I see. A pinch, and we'll just tape it in place."

"You're terrific at that. Hardly felt a thing," she chirped.

"Well, I haven't actually put it in yet. That was just some lidocaine to numb the skin."

She laughed effortlessly; his spirit was buoyed.

"Okay, now hopefully, you'll just feel some pressure."

She looked away, stole a glance, and he was already taping the catheter in.

"Ah, my confidence in you was not misplaced. It was really painless."

He stood up, feeling a bit heady.

"All in a day's work," he confided proudly."These antibiotics will drip in over about a half-hour, and then we can get you going."

"I'm in your capable hands," she answered, playfully engaging him.

"I'll be back in a bit, and we'll just take this out."

There were three more patients to see in the meantime, and he had to duck back into the thoracic surgery room.

"Hey, how's he doing?" he asked the anesthetist as his eyes roamed over the monitoring screens.

"Pretty well. I'd like to see the oxygen saturations a bit higher. I called you twice, but you didn't pick up. His saturations were dropping, so I put some CPAP on the operative lung—I think it helped. He's up to 92 percent."

Kurt gritted his teeth. This was a decision he should have been involved in. However, he acknowledged to himself that she did exactly what he would have recommended. Had she really tried twice to reach him? He glared down at the pickle phone hanging off of his hip. Was he so caught up in treating Lauren that he hadn't even heard the phone?

Tall and lanky, with coarse facial features, Dora was a bold presence on the anesthesia side of the ether screen. She proudly related the experiences of decades in several different ORs around the city, from small hospitals that had since fallen by the wayside, to trauma centers. Her facial expression alternated between disinterested and incredulous, while her hands were of legendary proportions. She could make a better face mask seal on a bearded, large-jowled, obese patient than any of the anesthesiologists could.

The anesthetized man's oxygen saturations were marginal, barely in the low 90's. This was perhaps the best they could expect in the face of his lung disease, the surgical position, and one deflated lung. Kurt was content for the moment to keep things as they were.

"Give me a call if they fall any further. Sometimes these damned phones get turned off and you don't even know it. I'll check it. Looks like the hemodynamics are stable, the patient is making adequate urine, and you're keeping him warm. The blood loss is modest. It all looks pretty good for the moment."

"I'll call you if any changes," she intoned. "I think they'll be done in about a half-hour if they stop letting the resident piss around in there."

Kurt grimaced, then ducked out of the room. Of course, the surgeons had to teach their trainees, too, and wouldn't appreciate her grousing, but that was Dora. He quickly checked into his other two rooms, where the surgeries were proceeding satisfactorily, then doubled back to the PACU.

"I'm back."

He rushed in, noted the empty infusion bag, and started to take down the IV. She was silent for a moment as he removed the catheter from her hand and placed a small dressing, again kneeling by her side.

"How long do you have to go to school to be an anesthesiologist?"

"Well, college, then four years of medical school, then an internship and three years of residency, then maybe another year of fellowship. So it's a long haul."

"I'd love to hear more about it. I'm having a party with a few friends at my apartment next Friday. Some fascinating people. It would be great to have you come and meet them."

She looked at him, expectantly."And, technically, after I leave today, you're not my doctor anymore."

He began to feel unsteady as he stood up and quickly leaned back against the arm rail of a nearby chair. Her words were everything he wanted to hear, but he was startled to listen as she actually pronounced them. And he could not, for the moment, respond.

She quickly began to recant.

"I'm sorry—too forward?"

She was everything he could envision in a woman: attractive, intelligent, fit, sensitive, articulate, forward when it suited but deferential when necessary. So why not accept the invitation? There would be no long-term professional relationships between Lauren and himself, so what harm could there be in meeting her outside the department for a drink and a chat?

He pressed her hand a bit more firmly and regarded her with a hint of a smile that he hoped would pass for self-assuredness.

"Ah . . . that would be great. Sure."

He tried to avoid sounding too enthused; it never made sense to wear the heart on the sleeve, at least not too early on.

"Oh, that's terrific! Now I know it's not likely, but if this thing gets worse, and I have to come back for surgery again, I want you to be the one to take care of me—okay? And, well, I guess we'd have to do a raincheck."

He was happy to turn the conversation back to the business at hand.

"Naturally . . . I understand—I'd be happy to do it. Let's hope it doesn't progress; I think we're gonna be okay here. These superficial skin infections usually get better quickly with the antibiotics; I don't believe it's in the joint, but I will defer to the orthopedist. You have to make sure you get in to see him tomorrow. And here's a script for the oral antibiotics—it's cephalexin, one every six hours."

She eyed the script and noted the second slip of paper. He followed her glance.

"And, I wrote for more of the oxycodone—I'm sure this is more painful than usual. If the infection is not in the joint, he'll probably have you start some range-of-motion right after seeing him and setting up the physical therapy. Joint motion is pretty painful after these surgeries, at least for a week or so."

Her enthusiasm was nearly palpable.

"You are so considerate! Thanks for the counseling and starting the antibiotics—this will probably make all the difference. Here's my address for Friday. I'll give you a call early next week to let you know my progress . . . if that's all right."

"Right. I'd really like to know. Here's my cell number."

His mood shifted. He was involved now. No turning back. The cellulitis on Lauren's shoulder would probably clear up with the antibiotics in a couple of days. But there were echoes of doubt and hesitation within him. At no time had he ever dated a patient, not even a former patient. Still, it had been such a very long time since he'd held hands, or shared a kiss, or indulged in a passionate embrace. Maybe the walls had been too high, too unyielding, for too long.

# CHAPTER 9

On a Friday morning, more than a week after he'd treated Lauren for her infection, Kurt rose with excitement that he was especially conscious of and which he tried to subdue. Giddy as a schoolboy, he thought, and how silly—it's just a date. But a titillating warmth suffused through him as he imagined spending the evening with this woman. The idea of embracing her made him breathe just a little deeper, emotional and physical arousal that Kurt had seldom felt, of late.

"Hello, Mr. Wayne!"

His ebullience spilled over as he anticipated the evening that lay before him.

The man was curled on his side, he'd disdained the idea of covering himself with a blanket. His spindly legs looked curiously bird-like as he lay on the stretcher, glaring at the anesthesiologist. It was a pretty odd presentation.

"I see you're here for a . . ."

"Right. A knee scope. Look, I've been to six doctors, had eight imaging studies, two shots of cortisone, been fed a line of crap by everyone. Can you get this knee fixed?" he rolled onto his back, fixed his eyes carefully on the ceiling, and went on, "It's been 68 days since I've been injured, and no one has been able to help me."

Kurt stepped back. This was going to be difficult. He already felt an intolerance growing for the anger this man displayed—he knew that he would have to consciously tamp it down. He prided himself on getting on the good side of frustrated patients.

"I'm sorry to hear that. Hopefully, today, Dr. Taylor is going to change all that for you."

"You'd think so," he scowled. "And he'd better. I've got six weeks until the Boston Marathon. I qualified this year, had a PR at New York. Missing this race is not an option."

The guy was 69 years old. Kurt was impressed. "So, you're a marathoner."

"An ultra-marathoner. I run fifty—and hundred-mile races, too. But Boston is pretty special, and I've got to be there. I was first in my age group two years ago. I expect to do that again."

"Wow. Fantastic. You're like, a world-class distance runner."

"Well, I was. Now I'm old. I can win my age group by five or ten minutes sometimes, but no one else is any good. People get old, and they can't run distance anymore. I'm the last man standing. But I aim to keep it up."

"I bet they would have called you a 'hard-charger' in the Navy." Kurt's father had spent four years in the Navy and often used the expression.

"I don't know about the Navy. I was a light colonel in the 82nd Airborne. You know, 'Death from the sky.' We just got it done and asked questions later."

An amazing man, Kurt conceded. Intolerant, demanding, and even rude, but that probably explained his success as an endurance runner and senior officer in the army.

"Well, let me ask you the basic questions about your health."

"I'm fine. Tip-top shape. No problems, no drugs, no conditions. What else do you need to know?"

"Well, that kind of sums it up. Let me mention the organ systems; you tell me if you have problems, okay?"

He wanted to get his questions in without irritating the man, who obviously was ready to dismiss any inquiry into his health.

"Heart-chest pain? Palpitations?"

"No"

"Lungs—I know you're a runner. No wheezing or shortness of breath?"

"Hell yes, I get short of breath. Do you get short of breath if you run six-flat miles for an entire marathon?"

"Uh, not something I can do. But I get your point," Kurt continued, "GI: ulcers, heartburn, diverticulitis?"

"No, no, and no,"

"Nerve-related issues? Numbness, weakness, seizures?"

"No." Initially bored, the man appeared to be growing impatient.

"Bleeding or clotting problems? High blood pressure? Diabetes?"

"All no. Are you trying to insult me?"

Kurt swallowed.

"Of course not. Just need to ask. I take it you don't smoke. Alcohol?"

"Sure. Two drinks a night. Keeps the pipes clean. If I'm with a lady, might be a couple more. And I don't need Viagra. Got it?"

Kurt suppressed a smile."Sure, got it. Let me listen to your heart and lungs."

The man sat up reluctantly as if grudgingly giving ground in a tug-of-war.

"Nice, very clear. Now open wide."

The airway examination was fine.

"Now, let me just get your signature as permission for anesthesia. We'll put you under, then place an airway and pull it out just as you awaken. While you're under, we'll monitor all your vital signs, watch for adverse reactions, which are rare, administer pain medications, and . . ."

"I'm not afraid of pain. I run a hundred miles a day sometimes—remember?"

It was a humiliating sort of interview. But Kurt really did admire the man, despite his curmudgeonly nature.

"Right. I always like to get consent for a postoperative nerve block, just in case the pain is greater than we expect. A nerve block is . . ."

"I won't need that. Trust me."

Kurt had heard this many times before, only to find that a knee scope patient had postoperative pain far beyond what the patient had envisioned, so severe that it was refractory to opioids in the PACU. The femoral nerve block could be a true deliverance, a nearly immediate form of relief. He'd learned to seek the signature ahead of time. It was difficult to get consent from people who were howling in pain and who'd been compromised in their decision-making by three or four doses of intravenous opioids. But somehow, he believed Mr. Wayne.

"I get it. We'll deal with any pain that you have with medications."

"I probably won't need those either. I don't intend to take any drugs after this. And if you didn't forbid it, I'd get in my car and drive home today."

"Well, our drugs will be circulating in your body and brain for many hours, so we always recommend no driving until the following day."

The man raised his eyebrows as if this was incomprehensible. His dark eyes darted about, but he seldom actually made eye contact. Once he'd signed his anesthesia consent, Kurt moved to the next patient. A wry grin was etched on his face as he thought about this retired Lieutenant Colonel and his over-the-top attitude. The man would probably do just fine and be running in less than a week. In fact, he'd probably be running in two days, whether he was fine or not, regardless of anything he was told.

"'Morning doctor, we're in 14 together." Tina, a friendly, middle-aged nurse anesthetist, greeted him with her peculiar sing-song voice. "We have the cutest little lady for a lap chole."

"Right. She came in two days ago with pain and nausea; bilirubin was up, and she had an ERCP to get the common bile duct stone out. I saw the preop note. Sounds like it all went fine."

Tina produced the written note. She always had a stack of printed notes on her patients. Unlike some of the younger providers, who simply brought the chart up on the electronic record in the room, she liked a hard copy."Keeps me mindful."

"The lady has hypertension and mild aortic stenosis. Sounds like she's well-compensated. Pretty spry for her 80 years," her melodic voice boomed through the preop area. Everyone knew when Tina was nearby.

"Good. I'll get over to interview her."

She led the way to the bedside.

"Hi, Honey, this is Dr. McCain. He and I are going to take care of you during anesthesia."

She was so effusive, patients could not help but feel comfortable in her care, he decided. Calling all the elderly ladies "honey" or "dear" without exception, she raised no one's ire in the process.

"Hi, Mrs. Martinez, I understand they just put you to sleep two days ago to get that stone out of your bile duct."

She was still icteric, her eyes a sinister yellow hue. But her bilirubin levels were dropping rapidly towards normal. She was a tiny lady, spry and youthful, with a soft and engaging voice. Intensely respectful and polite, he learned that she was a retired teacher of grammar and English.

"We used to put more emphasis on proper diction and polite speech in those days," she assured him.

The exam was unremarkable except for a substantial murmur over the upper chest. The stenotic aortic valve was reluctant to let blood exit the heart, producing turbulence and loud protest by the rushing liquid.

"I've had that forever. When it's quiet, I hear it in my ears. I've learned to tolerate it—like the ticking of a clock. It kind of comforts me at night."

"After we go to sleep, I'll also put a small IV catheter down here by your wrist," he indicated, palpating her radial pulse.

"Whatever you say, sweetie," she acceded, nodding to her husband, who sat silently in a chair beside the bed.

Old people often developed an extraordinary sense of acceptance, he thought. A forty-year-old would have been chewing her fingernails, anxious as can be, or maybe clutching her side, overwhelmed by the pain of a spastic gallbladder. But this silver-haired octogenarian simply sat placidly, awaiting her fate. It was alien to him, but he could see how a gradual evolution towards inner tranquility would be valuable and appropriate. Kurt had many years before him to consider this new philosophy. Still, he hoped to be as accepting as she was when his health began to deteriorate in his eighth or ninth decade. That was one thing that physicians had a leg-up on, compared to many in the lay population: you knew what was coming and that you could neither ignore it nor evade it. The best you could do was preserve the health that God gave you as well as you might and accept the inevitable downgrades with grace. It would be inspiring, someday as he lay helpless in a hospital bed, to think of people like her.

He went through the particulars and prepared to go on to the next.

"Call me, Tina, and I'll be back for the induction. I'm going over to see another patient."

"I'll see you back there," the patient called as he walked away.

Kurt gave a friendly wave and walked into an adjoining preoperative slot.

"Hello, Mr. Obramawicz," he said cheerfully.

"What is your surgeon doing for you today?" Kurt asked, shaking the man's hand.

The patient looked dour.

"This shoulder. Fourth operation. No one can seem to get it right. It just won't heal up."

"I see. How did you hurt it?

"Coal mines. I'm from up Scottdale way. Worked in the mines for twenty-two years. Then, one day, I was picking up a framing timber, and something snapped. That was two years ago. I've had no peace since that day. It always hurts, especially at night. I can't get any sleep! Mostly, I sleep in a recliner, but I just doze and wake up a lot. I went to my first surgeon twice, but it didn't help. I don't wanna stay on Comp—that's no life. And the Comp doctors all treat you like you're fakin' everything, like you're trying to cheat your way into easy money. Twenty-two years workin' my butt off down below, and that's what I get."

Kurt quickly went through the particulars of the nerve block and the general anesthetic that would follow. Obtaining consent, he promptly moved to place the nerve block. Despite his large frame and thick, muscular neck, the nerves were readily located with ultrasound.

Just as he completed the procedure, a gruff voice was audible, close behind him.

"Perfect timing."

The surgeon had been watching the block quietly so as not to disturb the proceedings.

"Let me just mark your shoulder, and I'll go change my clothes. I'll see you in the OR in a few minutes. Any change in your symptoms since I saw you in the office?"

The man shook his head.

"Can we go back now, doctor?" Karen was among the older crowd of CRNAs, finely tuned for the types of cases she usually found herself managing. She'd been a nurse in a coronary care unit for decades, and decided, somewhat later in life, to go to nurse anesthesia school. She had a good eye for trouble and would call quickly if things started to slide in the wrong direction. It was the essence of the anesthesia care team, anesthesiologist and anesthetist, to manage complications together. Some of the anesthetists were reluctant to call for help before they figured out the problem or before it was severe for fear they'd be admonished or berated. When they joined the practice, he assured new anesthetists that they need not stand on pride or ceremony on his account. An early call was appreciated.

It was going on 0730, so the din and the bustle in the preop area were intense. It was almost impossible to hear someone a few feet away. Carts and teams were speeding off in multiple directions, intent on entering the OR before the scheduled time to avoid a write-up and the need for an explanation.

"I have to see one more patient. I'll be back shortly."

Karen nodded and pushed out of the PACU.

Kurt made his way to another bedside and met a patient who was slated for laparoscopic hernia repair and quickly entered the note in the computer.

He liked to be in the room when the shoulder cases started to make sure his block was effective when the scalpel hit the skin. As he opened up the door to the OR, donning his surgical mask, he saw Karen lowering the head of the bed frantically, from the beach chair position, with help from the circulating nurse.

"Call Dr. McCain—now!" she called out, just before she looked up to see him."I've got no blood pressure!"

The propofol infusion had been started, and the patient had just been going off to sleep when the pressure began to slip. Karen had given a dose of vasoconstrictor to push it back up. He hustled to the bedside, asked her to cycle the pressure, and began palpating the groin for a pulse. When there was no apparent response, she cycled the cuff again, noting the systolic pressure in the low 60s. Not deadly yet, but almost into CPR territory.

"I don't really feel anything—check the carotids."

The cuff failed to register any pressure at all. He reached up to make sure the IV infusion was working and then grabbed a large syringe, attaching it to the stopcock of the IV line and using it to blast fluid into the vein as quickly as he could.

"The propofol's off, right? And did you give epinephrine?"

"Not yet—just ephedrine."

"Doesn't look like it helped. Let's get a hundred micrograms of epinephrine in. Or we'll be giving a lot more if he arrests."

The team coalesced around the patient. The anesthetist called for help, and the chief nurse anesthetist suddenly showed up at the bedside.

"I brought the glideslope just in case. Can you ventilate?"

Karen was raising the chest readily with her face mask ventilations.

"It's easy. Can you give the epi?"

"Get ready to intubate, please," Kurt advised, palpating the neck and eyeing the monitors. The pulse oximeter wasn't reading, and the blood pressure was still not registering. The EKG looked comparatively normal, suggesting the heart was getting both blood and oxygen, but that could change within seconds.

"I see no rash." He spoke loudly to no one in particular."I don't think this is anaphylaxis. The heart rate is low—was he this low when you hooked up? I don't recall him being in the 40s out there during our block."

By this time, three more nurses had hurriedly pushed the code cart through the door. They were preparing to put defibrillator pads on the patient, whose pallor was just beginning to give way to a healthier pinkness.

"He's got no heart disease, he has no reason for a pulmonary embolus; he could have a pneumothorax, I guess. But we were nowhere near his lung with the needle," he was now thinking aloud, letting the team know what possibilities he was considering.

As he spoke, he listened to the lung sounds. The endotracheal tube had just been placed, and vigorous ventilation gave him apparent chest rise on both sides accompanied by breath sounds.

"Sounds fine. No pneumothorax, at least not a big one."

"I've got a carotid pulse now," he noted with some relief and satisfaction.

"What drugs did he get before this started?"

"Just the antibiotics, the propofol, and a small dose of ketamine. I guess it could have been an allergic response," Karen countered, looking back and forth from the anesthetized man to the monitors.

"Doubt it, Karen. No rash, no wheezing. And he wasn't tachycardic—if he developed a sudden loss of vascular tone, an intact sympathetic nervous system should've met it with an increase in the heart rate. He's not on any drugs that would prevent that. I can't rule out anaphylaxis, but it isn't a typical picture. Probably a reflex response to sitting up in the beach chair during anesthesia."

"We able to operate?" the surgeon had poked his head into the circle.

"Yeah, I think so, as soon as we have a stable blood pressure. We're gonna have to sit him up slowly and watch that pressure. He may drop again as soon as we have him upright."

The cuff now read 140/79, and the heart rate had rapidly accelerated into the 90s, just what Kurt wanted to see, at least for the moment.

"This always scares the shit outta me," he confided to the anesthetist.

"You? I'm the one standing in here watching it all go downhill. I guess it only took you a few seconds to get here, but it felt like three hours."

Kurt nodded."I'd go faster if I could. Never in the right place at the right time. I think that's the way they like it. Keep us moving, supervising lots of rooms, hanging on the edge."

"Yup, the way of our world. Now, this guy's hypertensive. Where do you want me to keep the pressure?"

He looked at the surgeon, who was biding his time while they discussed the particulars. The ortho resident had already begun to prep the shoulder, maneuvering a mechanical extension of the table that held the arm and could easily be adjusted with a foot pedal.

"You know I like it low. How low are you comfortable?"

"Well," Kurt eyeballed the man and thought back to the blood pressures he'd registered during the nerve block. It was really all he had."He was just fine between 120 and 140. I think we could let him go down to about 110 systolic."

It was a judgment call. Drops in blood pressure were virtually inevitable with most general anesthetics. It was expected that the blood vessels would lose their tone when the sympathetic nervous system succumbed to the central nervous system effects of the drugs. This was almost always exaggerated in the sitting position, when blood tended to pool in the dilated veins, especially in the lower half of the body, in response to gravity.

"That should be fine. Let me see what kind of visibility I have with the scope in there, with those pressures."

He was an easy man to work with, who really lent an ear to the anesthesia team's concerns. For that, Kurt was very grateful. Not all of the surgeons cared so much about what happened at the head end of the table, as long as they saw no adverse surgical outcomes on their end.

The day wore on with a series of shoulder cases. Fortunately, the remainder of the patients were relatively stable during the anesthetic. The pain control for the patients in the PACU was excellent. This, of course, pleased both the anesthesiologist and the PACU nurses. No extra pain meds were required, a significant benefit of the nerve blocks.

At last, he had the final case in recovery. He looked around at the other patients, watching some of the anesthetists and anesthesiologists drift through. Most looked haggard and worn. Theirs was an excellent specialty, and on most days, an arduous one. Standing in the OR, watching the monitors, and responding to the little things that tended to go awry was stressful. So was running from one place to another, seeing patients for multiple rooms and stamping out fires. Today, there had been mercifully few complications to tend to, and he felt a sigh of relief escape him. The more time he spent in the OR, the more he yearned for a quiet Friday evening, with the demands of the workweek behind him. But this night promised to be so much more enjoyable than usual—he felt a touch embarrassed as a boyish thrill rose within him. A provocative lady had invited him to a party, nothing more. He simply had to show up. And, now that she was officially out of his care, perhaps he could relax enough to actually ask her out on a date.

# CHAPTER 10

"This is nuts. I shouldn't be here," Kurt thought. He felt the familiar screws tightening inside of him. Seated beside Lauren on a comfortably worn leather couch, he accepted the glass of wine she'd poured.

"I figured you'd like this crowd—a bunch of young professionals. You'll fit right in." Her voice was kind and reassuring.

"Hey Lauren, how are you? It's been a long time," a man in a navy sport coat with tight jeans nodded to her and cast a sidelong glance at the physician.

Her face lit up. "Kurt, Marc is a financial advisor with our firm. Kurt is an anesthesiologist at the University Hospital."

The man's expression suggested that he was suitably impressed but had no reason to like him.

"Good to meet you," Kurt called above the din of the party, grasping the man's hand as firmly as he could.

The crowd was young, fashionable, attractive. Nobody was actually dancing, but there was a very festive air about the place.

Lauren caught his attention with a playful squeeze of his hand. She was a lovely and pleasant woman, to be sure. Still, he could not fight the sense that he was violating everything he'd ever learned about relations with patients by being there with her. She'd been so casual and demure with her invitation, had worked her way into his consciousness so thoroughly that he hadn't even contemplated turning her down. And he knew the wine would temper his guilt and anxiety.

He suddenly realized that it had been over a week since she started the antibiotics he'd prescribed.

"How's the shoulder?" he asked, trying to maintain some professional bearing. But his thoughts turned to embracing her and kissing her, as the wine suffused through him, warming him, loosening the tight rein that he maintained around his psyche.

"So much better. Dr. Jenkins saw me last Friday and again yesterday. He says I'm really improving."

Her eyes were sparkling as she pronounced this, as though he had saved her very life.

"That's great—is the pain easing off, too?"

"Oh, it's much better," she reached up and patted the shoulder, as if to demonstrate how the tenderness had resolved."And I thank you again for helping me with those prescriptions."

He thought of her lying on the stretcher, in her bra, ample breasts outlined against the delicate, lacey material. There had been just a hint of a desirable scent when he'd examined her, perhaps that of a body lotion. He smelled it again now, to his great satisfaction. Sipping the bitter red wine, he began to relax; a gauzy aura of perfume and intoxication swirled around him, dimming his sensibilities and whetting his desire for her. She had launched into an amusing story about getting her car stuck in a snowbank as some friends gathered around. He couldn't follow the story in detail, but everyone began to laugh. He found himself laughing loudly as well, a fondness growing inside of him for these people that he did not know. They were friends of hers, and that already pleased him.

She turned, leaning towards him amiably, yearning to introduce him to her crowd.

"So, how'd you decide to become an anesthesiologist?"

He nodded. Many thought of anesthesiology as a curious profession —"passing gas," as the old saying went.

"Well," Kurt answered, noting that he had a small, devoted audience, "I really love animals."

The crowd erupted at this odd retort, and he began to feel comfortable among them.

"No, honestly. When I was little, I couldn't stand to see animals suffering. I thought I'd be a vet. Then I learned you have to train to take care of horses. Horses terrify me. And you can't talk to dogs and cats. So, I decided to go the people route, you know, and take care of them when they're suffering. It's pretty gratifying, really. People tend to be very thankful. They come in, filled with fear, you gain their confidence, reassure them, maybe put in a spinal or a nerve block, escort them to 'La La land' with some drugs, and put them out. Then, when it's over, you turn it all off and wake them up. They always seem shocked when you tell them the procedure is over as you take them to recovery."

She smiled broadly, her lips parting to reveal perfect teeth, her dark eyes flashing. She briefly put her uninjured arm around him.

"Well, he certainly made me feel fantastic for my procedure," she announced triumphantly. "You really have a way with people. I think you landed in the right place."

Her comments suggested a familiarity that made him blush. Or maybe it was the wine. Whatever, he felt extraordinarily complemented and was developing an earnest affection for this lovely woman, feelings that welled up within him despite his efforts to suppress them. Some part of him wished she'd not told all these people that he'd been her physician; it seemed so awkward. But now, he didn't really care. This party, these people, her attention—it was all so enjoyable.

Lauren's embrace made him feel secure and desired, something he had desperately wanted the moment he sat with her. When she moved her arm while chatting to a friend Kurt followed the lithe movement of that slender extremity with inebriated fascination. He could not help but imagine intertwining the thin fingers with his own and caressing them.

She turned to him to see his reaction to what she'd been saying, looking for affirmation, but he was unable to hear, with the music and all the chattering voices. So he just stared back in a sort of contented reverie. Kurt wanted to sit beside her all night, to watch her talking and laughing with her friends, to be the companion she kept turning to. Little cliques of guests kept forming around them, then reforming into new groups . . .and then, for a moment, it was just the two of them.

"So—you never asked me about me," she began as if trying to judge whether the anesthesiologist was quietly contemplative or simply in a satisfied state of intoxication.

"What about you?" Kurt countered, realizing she was right, and he was suddenly intensely interested.

Her aura, her beauty, her magnetic persona had been all the mattered. He hadn't, until now, really needed to know much more.

"Well, I'm from Kentucky, around Louisville . . ."

"Nice town—I was there for a conference, once, and a brilliant fireworks display over the Ohio River. But you sure don't sound like they do."

She tossed her dark hair and sipped again at her wine."We moved when I was six. I still go back sometimes and visit my relatives. Doesn't take me too long to get that drawl back."

"And do you say 'y'all' when you've been down there for a few days?"

"I suppose I do; it sounds a lot better than 'yunz' doesn't it?"

They both laughed at the reference to the blue-collar dialect of Pittsburgh.

"And what brought you here?" he continued.

"My father was transferred here, and he brought us up here after a year when it looked like he was going to stay. I went to Catholic grade school, then to Oakland Catholic. I went back to the University of Louisville and then came to graduate school here at CMU."

"Where do you work now?"

"I'm at a financial firm downtown—I do wealth management for a small group of clients."

Business and finance were an alternate universe to him, mysterious and perhaps even incomprehensible. Still, he knew that a person had to be gifted to move in those circles—no financial firm in those downtown skyscrapers was hiring mediocre performers. There was a sense of control and determination about her that he found fascinating and alluring. The woman betrayed no sense of inadequacy or self-doubt; every statement was issued with complete self-assuredness. Perhaps, he thought, that self-confidence was the very nature of her business. Even the slightest evidence of hesitation might divert a wealthy client in another direction, to a different adviser.

"That sounds fascinating," he acknowledged, inclining his head towards hers, waiting to hear more about the day-to-day life of a major-league investor.

"Oh, it is," she retorted, "I'm really fortunate to have found my way to Federated. A wonderful series of coincidences got me the position. Then, I had to run with it."

His praise charmed her. As she turned her face back to his, he found himself dangerously close to her. In a sort of magnetic attraction that required no volition, their eyes met, their heads tilted slightly, and they brought their lips together in a gentle, searching kiss. Pressing these most sensual of organs together for a moment, they parted, adopting the intense and penetrating gaze once again into each other's eyes.

For Kurt, the world ceased to exist, but for those eyes. He brought his lips to hers several more times, felt a delicious vibration course through his entire body, and wondered if she was beset by the same extraordinary feelings. Whether it was the alcohol or the woman's beauty, he was unsure. But he felt himself sliding, losing the tight control of his emotions.

"Oops—sorry! Can't find my purse!"

The lights flickered on suddenly, as one of her friends returned to find her handbag. Whatever magic had arisen between them quickly dissipated.

Kurt was suddenly conscious that everyone had gone. The room was quiet and empty, though the candles still burned. She would have been his if he'd simply wished it—she was so desirable to him that it was not possible to turn away. But as he paused to think, in the stark white light that filled the room, the desire that had arisen between them was extinguished. It was late, and he suddenly felt too sober to try to reclaim it. She, too, seemed to have escaped whatever feelings had developed in those quiet moments.

"Well, I better go. Everyone just kind of snuck out. I didn't really see them leave." Kurt laughed uneasily, trying to add a bit of levity to the empty and expressionless feeling that had come over him.

She was terse. "I understand. Let me get your coat."

Ashamed of how awkward he was in romantic situations, Kurt was painfully aware of his limitations. He knew that he needed to proposition her, and quickly, or all would be lost. "Can we get together sometime—for coffee or a bite?"

She seemed surprised and suddenly was enthused once again. "That would be great! Maybe next week? I have late meetings with clients on Tuesday and Thursday, but I'm free on the other nights."

He nodded, relieved, and became conscious of how his heart had been palpitating within him. "I'll call you. I may have to play it by ear if that's okay. Sometimes my days don't end when I think they're going to—it all depends on emergencies and add-on cases. So let's try for Friday, say about seven? I'll call you by five if it looks like I'll be late."

"That sounds fine, just fine," she confirmed, a note of pleasure in her voice.

Kurt sat in silence for a few moments, lost in the warmth of her approbation, simply watching her as she walked to the closet to get his coat. It unsettled him as he thought about the passionate moment that had been building between them—how rapidly she'd become cool and dismissive. He realized that if his life and hers were to become intertwined, this aloofness would likely be used effectively against him when she felt the need. That was the power of a woman.

Moments later, sitting in his car, he shook his head to clear his thoughts. The wine was wearing off, and he began to wonder if this was the right direction for him—his tightly constrained life might become a bit disordered. Perhaps that was the cost of bringing a lover in, depending on someone else for emotional satisfaction. A smile crossed his face. He tended to overthink things. A lot. Spending some time with Lauren might be just what he needed to loosen the strings a bit.

# CHAPTER 11

"I think things are going pretty well, overall," the chief announced to the anesthesiologists, who sat sleepily sipping coffee out of "Proud to serve Starbucks" paper cups from the little gift shop in the lobby. Most were distracted, thinking about the cases they'd soon be starting.

The once-a-month, early morning business meeting. Kurt dreaded them; it seemed the news was never good.

"We're going to add one person to the group come July. Name is Jennifer Saxton, comes to us from Wake Forest, did her medical school at Vanderbilt. Sharp lady, interested in regional, now in acute pain fellowship, also at Wake. Very solid CV, great letters, interviews well. You're all going to like her, I think."

That was met with some relief around the table.

"It's been a long year, I know," he said sympathetically."Losing John was painful, and we were already short-staffed. But he heard his calling and couldn't wait to get back up to New England. His whole family is from up there—I don't think he ever really believed he would stay here in the long run. But the position here presented itself when he needed one. He's a good guy, and we'll miss him. Till Jennifer comes on board, it'll be tight. In order to get people vacation time, I'm gonna have some of you work on your post-call days. I know that can be miserable. If you're up all night, we'll do everything we can to get you out early. I just don't have any alternatives right now."

"What about borrowing someone from one of the other sites? Isn't that supposed to be an advantage of this vast, multi-center system?" Phil called out, a sardonic grin on his face.

"It is," the chief explained calmly."But every single division chief is poor-mouthing right now. There's no fat at all in the system; they keep it too close to the bone. An illness or a family leave, and we're all sunk. Not to mention when someone leaves for another position, as we are currently experiencing." I

Angry comments began to ricochet around the cramped conference room. The dark, knotted paneling seemed to lean in on them, constricting the tense crowd gathered around the faux-wooden table.

"No foresight, no forethought."

"That could be the mantra of these administrators. Didn't we see this same bullshit just ten years ago—they shriveled the place up, got rid of anybody they could, then panicked when the caseload went back up? Do they not teach any sort of planning for the future in MBA school?"

"Not, I'm afraid, if plans cost money," the chief continued. "Hospital margins are thin. My perception is that they will do anything to save money today, with little thought of care delivery tomorrow—consequences be damned. Isolated adverse occurrences are easily obscured or settled. They seem to have a great deal of confidence in your ability to stretch yourselves very thin, indeed."

"Great," Phil muttered."Fewer docs, more rooms, less time."

"This just adds up to more pressure and stress on us and less safety for the patients. So why don't they get that?" another frustrated anesthesiologist called out.

"Oh, they get it. I don't think they care," came a cynical retort.

Kurt looked around at the expressions of frustration on the faces of his colleagues, wondering if their respected leader could see that things were getting out of control.

"Folks, this isn't helping."

The chief adopted one of his "shut up and listen to me" expressions, and the room quieted.

"We're doctors, in a setting where change never stops. We all have to adapt, and we will. There's help on the horizon, but I need everyone to give a little more till we get back up to speed with our numbers. We've been through worse than this. I don't mind if you get your inspiration from the adversarial relationship we all have with the administration. But doctors gave away administration a long time ago, at least in our system. If you feel things are unsafe, you let me know. I frankly don't foresee that, but life will be more stressful. We make very good money, and the people in charge expect us to earn it. That means stress is inherent in what we do. But stress and lack of safety are different things—if you are pushed so hard it's unsafe, I expect you to speak up and delay cases. I'll take the heat. Send an angry surgeon to me. But let me know what's going on before he arrives, so I can at least act informed. I'll defend you and take your side, but I've got to have communication."

The words had a soothing effect, and the emotions of the small group began to calm. Kurt did not believe that the chief's gentle admonition equated to an acquiescence towards the powers that be. There was a feeling among those in the room that their leader would be willing to sacrifice himself to make his points to the administrators, to stress to the clipboard carriers that their edicts carried real-life consequences at the bedside and in the OR. But there was also concern about how far he could go, without something terrible happening. He was probably expendable in the eyes of those that made decisions, and they could hire another chief for the site in a snap. Someone who was more intent on carrying out the orders from on high, cracking the whip, ensuring efficiency, and at the same time showing less sympathy to the worker-bees.

There was no certainty of anything, it seemed, except change and an increase in the work burden.

The door popped open, and someone's head appeared, replete with a blue cap and a mask.

"Sorry to disturb you all, but Kurt, they need you up in Ob—it's a stat C-section, I think."

Grabbing his coffee cup, he bolted out of the room, the words of the chief ringing in his ears, concern for the future hollowing him out from the inside.

# CHAPTER 12

"They're in four," the Ob charge nurse called, relieved to see him as he came out of the stairwell.

Jeannie, a senior anesthesiology resident on service, had already transported the patient, 37 weeks into her pregnancy, into the tight operating room. She was crying out in pain with each contraction, as she'd arrived late in labor, and there was little time for an epidural to be inserted. The fetal monitoring tracing began to show a troubling pattern almost immediately, which progressed quickly to "late decelerations," a sign that the fetus was receiving insufficient oxygenation. It was now essential to get the baby out, with little time to spare.

"Do you have everything pulled up?" he asked hastily, looking at the spinal kit the resident had opened.

"I've got bupivacaine 0.75 percent hyperbaric, some lido for the skin. Here are size 8 gloves for you. I'm ready to prep."

The labor and delivery nurses had already helped the patient over to the stark, black operating table, its stirrups projecting officiously skyward. A sheet had been placed carefully over the none-too-comfortable black cushions that lay atop the cold metal frame. Suffering from frequent contractions, the lady had great difficulty moving onto the table. There had simply been no time to place an epidural, and she'd been rushed to the OR.

"What's her name," Kurt asked of the resident, as quietly as he could.

"Shasha."

"Shasha, we need to get your baby out as fast as possible. I'd like to do a spinal anesthetic; it's best for the baby and best for you. I'm going to have to put a needle in the low part of your back and then inject a small dose of local anesthetic . . ."

She began to cry out in pain, no longer able to pay attention to him.

"We gotta go, now. Can you please put the spinal in?" The obstetrician was flustered, the ability to monitor the fetus now compromised by the need to scrub her abdomen.

"There's a small risk of . . ."

"I went through all that—spinal headache, infection, nerve damage, bleeding. She signed her consent in the room."

Good resident, he thought gratefully. Always prepared. Kurt turned his attention back to the patient.

"Okay, you're gonna feel a pinch back here."

She was desperately uncomfortable, moving about on the table almost continuously, and she was terrified for the outcome of her baby. Kurt tried to ignore his concerns for her as he went about placing the spinal. However, he could not help but briefly have a flash of sympathy for this woman, who was consumed by pain, and whose mind was filled with thoughts of brain damage for the baby, or worse. Her pitiable husband was silent and white as a sheet, sheathed in a white paper 'bunny suit' that matched the pallor of his skin. The man was molded into a seat behind the proceedings where he could scarcely bear to watch what was unfolding.

The woman did not react to injection of the lidocaine to numb her skin in preparation for the much deeper insertion to follow. This moving target, he knew, would be a challenge for the resident. Still, she was not a junior, she'd done dozens of the procedures, and she deserved a shot at delivering the spinal anesthetic. But he'd only give her one, and if she didn't get CSF with the first stick, Kurt knew he'd have to take over. The obstetric team was almost ready to incise and would be expecting a numb abdomen very soon. He could tell from the clamor below the stirrups that they were about to get very demanding. The instruction to his resident would be surreptitious as possible; he didn't want the others to hear him coaching.

He grabbed the gloved fingers of the resident, with whom he'd worked a few times before, and pressed them against the protuberant backbones. He guided her to palpate an inviting sulcus between two spinous processes at the L3 or L4 vertebrae. She nodded confidently, had probably already done a practice run or two in her mind while tending the patient and waiting for him to arrive. As she picked up the spinal needle, the patient shuddered and moved forwards, uncontrollably responding to the contraction.

From the moment Jeannie had begun her residency, she'd professed an interest in obstetric anesthesia. A small, energetic lady, it was her expressed intent to spend a year in an obstetric anesthesia fellowship after she completed the residency, hoping to run a service eventually.

"Okay, now come back to us, honey . . ." He suddenly couldn't remember the patient's name and hoped she wouldn't mind the paternalism.

He grasped her side through the drape to help stabilize her and inclined his head toward the low back.

"What's going on up there?" The obstetricians were ready to incise, and needed an anesthetized field.

"Almost there, hang on." This was an assurance he wasn't quite ready to give, but he gave it anyway.

Jeannie pushed the introducer needle against the skin, and Kurt impatiently watched it tent the elastic membrane inward. She quickly followed with the flimsy spinal needle, passing it through the introducer. Once again, the lady began writhing as she felt the agonizing waves of pressure coursing through her uterus.

Over what seemed an eternity, he watched the long needle progress inward, meeting no boney impediment to its progress. Finally, at what appeared to be a bit of a shallow insertion, the resident gave a nod and pulled the stylet from the needle. At first, he could see no evidence that they were in the right place, and he pressed his teeth together, letting a curse of exasperation quietly pass his lips. A scant second later, the clear fluid began to slowly seep into the hub.

"Excellent," he pronounced, proud of her performance under duress.

She hooked up the local anesthetic syringe to the hub of the long needle and gently withdrew the plunger. The fluid from the spine began to mix with the drug, creating a curious swirl within the barrel of the syringe. Jeannie promptly drained the syringe into the patient's back, pulling back once again as she finished to ensure that the needle tip was still in the correct space. It all came off flawlessly.

"You should start to feel numb in just a few seconds," Kurt announced, as much to the OBs as to the patient herself.

"Can we go?" came the demand from the Ob doctors below.

"You should be getting numb now. Give her a test, please."

The obstetrician grabbed a toothed forceps and forcefully grabbed the taut skin overlying the uterus.

"Shasha!" the name suddenly reappeared in his consciousness, "can you feel that?"

She was just coming down off of the extraordinary surge of pain that accompanied each contraction.

"Feel what?" came her weak retort.

"OK—you're good!" announced the resident anesthesiologist, with a confidence borne of the pride in her performance.

She need not have bothered—the obstetric team was already slashing through the abdominal wall, blood briefly spurting from the transected arterioles. Bleeding would have to wait unless extreme. All else was secondary to getting the infant out as quickly as possible. Obviously, the utero-placental lifeline was failing and within minutes irreversible damage to susceptible tissues would occur. Neurologic injury would be devastating, possibly all-encompassing. The future well-being of a tiny human was starkly suspended in the bustling room; the outcome was now tied inexorably to the actions of the obstetricians.

In a few seconds, it was over. The purple fetus was hauled out, covered with blood and wet membranes, and delivered to the neonatologist, who busily went to work. The husband, seated at the head end of the table beside his wife, appeared ready to go down; he was quickly supported and moved away from the table by a sympathetic nurse. There was murmuring from the surgeons and a course sucking sound from the bassinet. A loud cry then erupted from that quarter, accompanied by a collective sigh of relief from the pediatric and OB team.

"I have APGAR scores of two and eight!"

"Two. Wow—that was close," Kurt said, turning to the resident.

She was beaming, having played a vital role in what appeared to be a life-saving or at least brain-saving drama. Now, the focus would change back to the mother.

"Is he okay?" the young woman asked weakly.

"The baby is out and appears to be breathing on his own," Kurt reassured her.

At this point, the pediatricians had sufficiently cleaned and suctioned the little bundle; there was confidence that he did not need any further invasive maneuvers. The team had swaddled him in a soft cotton blanket and placed a light blue stocking cap on his head to preserve his body heat. This sputtering, wailing, rosy infant, his features distorted by several hours of labor, was placed ceremoniously in his mother's arms, and the most profound of human bonds was initiated.

Initially, the young mother peered into her baby's eyes with an intensity that moved anyone who was in a position to observe it. Then she held him in her arms with a gentle caress the belied the strength she had displayed as she accommodated the tumultuous period of her labor.

# CHAPTER 13

"I can't breathe," the young mother pronounced suddenly.

Kurt looked at Jeannie, who peered intently back at him. He'd seen the dose she injected, which was pretty much the standard. The patient shouldn't have developed a high spinal level, but sometimes it just happened.

"Can you move your arms?" asked the resident, which seemed a senseless question since she was holding the baby.

"They feel . . . weak," she responded, her voice tenuous as she began to show the strain of ventilation. Her chest muscles were becoming profoundly weak.

"Listen, Shasha," Kurt whispered in her ear.

"Sometimes the spinal level goes higher than we want, even when we are careful. We have to make you numb, or bad things happen during the C-section. This is your spinal making you feel the way you do. We're gonna help you breathe for the next few minutes, but we have to take the baby back until you feel stronger."

He grabbed the oxygen mask and applied it tightly to her face, gently assisting her ventilations by squeezing the bag as she attempted to inspire. Then, finally, the consternation in her features began to ease, her sense of panic to relent.

He turned to Jeannie, who was now reinforcing his hold on the mask, so he could let go.

"What else are you worried about?"

Her eyes darted from the mother's face to the field. The surgeons were industriously controlling bleeding while sewing the layers of tissue that they'd incised on the way in. Then, after a pause, she presented a list of concerns, the manifestations of a high spinal anesthetic level.

"Breathing, oxygenation, blood loss, hemodynamic instability . . ."

As if on cue, the monitor began to alarm, and the new blood pressure value flashed up on the screen: 75/44. And despite the blood loss, the heart rate had ratcheted down from the 90s to the 60s.

She nodded and turned to grab a vial of drug that would increase the pressure and accelerate the heart rate, in essence, a weak form of adrenalin.

"Ephedrine—right. What's the genesis of the hypotension and bradycardia?"

Now that things were manageable and the infant appeared safe, it was time for some actual teaching.

He liked teaching the residents, especially in the aftermath of critical physiologic perturbations caused by delivery, or by surgery, or by their anesthetics. This was a shining example of pharmacology in action, the profound effects of the drugs on display across the illuminated screens of the monitors.

The young woman at this point was quiescent, apparently comfortable, though still showing some increased work of breathing. Kurt turned the ventilation back over to Jeannie, focusing for the moment on documentation of their interventions.

The obstetricians began to encounter difficulty with bleeding from the uterus.

"Can you tighten her up with some Pitocin, please?"

"What's your EBL down there? The pit's running."

"It's getting better; the uterus is clamping down. I'd say we've lost about 800."

That was a relief. The lady was breathing on her own, requiring less support, seemed more at ease. It was clear from the movement of her arms that she was getting her strength back, and her breathing pattern showed that the capacity of her chest cage had returned. With the slowing of blood loss, they caught up with fluids, and her blood pressure was once again stable. He felt he could leave things in the hands of this competent resident and get back down to the ORs.

# CHAPTER 14

"They keeping you busy?" asked one of his partners, Ross, a chubby but vigorous man, who was moving quickly from one preop bay to the next to keep up with his patient assessments and a slate of preoperative nerve blocks. On this afternoon, his red face was a testament to his efforts.

"Not bad. Ob is under control, finally, and I've got a couple of rooms of minor cases down here. So what are you dealing with today?"

"Foot room. You know, Dr. Johanssen. He wants a nerve block catheter in everybody. Eight patients, seven catheters. Takin' me forever. He's got no patience. Doles out the demands, can't give you the time to fulfill them. Gets pretty damn stressful."

"Well, it's Friday—cheer up. This will all be a memory when you have a drink tonight."

"I think I'm gonna have a few drinks tonight!"

Kurt looked around to see if any patients were privy to their discussion, but no one seemed interested.

"I'm ready when you are!" Dorothy called impatiently.

She stood at a bedside expectantly, awaiting Ross for the next catheter insertion. She had a terrific knack for keeping the doctors on-task in the preoperative area. She'd track them down in the ORs, the office, even the locker room when necessary. The patient was already lying prone in preparation for the time-out.

"Ready for the next." Ross waved his arm, indicating his newest recipient."If you get bored, Kurt, I'll let you put in a couple of my catheters. But you gotta be nice to me."

"Sure. I'll be real nice. But I have to be ready to go upstairs at a moment's notice, so I think I'll let you continue with this one."

Ross greeted this news with an expression of sincere disappointment, then hurried off behind the curtain.

Kurt nearly floated to the locker room when the call team took over the Ob suite. All of his surgical cases had finished. He could think of nothing but a date with the girl that had taken over his dreams. He'd not been able to sleep the entire week, lying in bed and thinking about Lauren—his efforts to steer his thoughts to other matters, to avoid over-analyzing their budding affection for each other, had come to naught. Each night Kurt eyed his quiet cell phone, which he placed on the kitchen table, thinking how much he'd like to call her, hoping she might call him—but the date for their rendezvous had been set, and he wasn't yet confident enough to start calling her to discuss the cares of the day. So instead, he looked in the mirror several times each evening, clipped a few nose hairs, examined his teeth, tried on a couple of different pairs of glasses—tortoise shell or gold rims? He even rehearsed a few conversations, introducing what he hoped were interesting topics that he could bring up if the two of them should fall into an embarrassing silence.

Filled with a delightful sort of anxiety, Kurt made sure he was precisely on time. As he walked up to the café she'd recommended, he saw her in the window, her back to him, brown hair cascading down upon her shoulders. She was leaning forward, seated in a darkened corner, silhouetted by the dancing candle flame on the table, intent on something in front of her, perhaps the menu. It made for a tranquil picture, to see her there, waiting for him, and he let his imagination drift, wondering if the two of them would have a future together.

He entered, smiled at the hostess, and pointed toward the corner table. The young lady nodded demurely in recognition, seemingly aware of what he was feeling for the attractive lady sitting by herself.

"There you are! I was afraid I had the wrong night."

"I'm sorry—I had a bit of a problem finding a parking space," he said and sat across from her, briefly taking her hand in his.

He simply had to touch her. Whatever doubts he may have had about her regard for him instantly vanished. Her eyes were radiant, her smile genuine.

"I'm delighted to see you," she proclaimed. There was not a modicum of pretense about her.

"Me too—I've been thinking about tonight all week."

She looked down with just a hint of embarrassment or perhaps reluctance to accept the compliment.

"No, really, I have."

Her cheeks flushed."Well, how was your work week?"

He shifted in his seat, not really wanting to talk about anesthesiology but recognizing that, perhaps, it was something that held an interest for her.

"I'd like to say it was different than every other week. But, the things I do happen over and over again. I guess when I'm there, I'm really engaged in it; when I come home, I try to forget it."

She nodded sympathetically and looked at him with something akin to admiration.

"Is it really stressful, dealing with surgeries every day?"

He laughed."Sometimes it's the surgeons more than the surgeries!"

"Tough breed, huh?"

"Well, I'm kind of exaggerating. Most of them are terrific, amazing people. But we focus on different things. They bring patients to the OR to get a surgical intervention accomplished. Sometimes, my priorities for patient safety stand in the way of that—and then things can get hot."

"Are there are a lot of arguments?"

"A few, but mostly people are pretty professional. It never serves me to get mad, even though I let it happen. The older I get, the more I realize that."

He nodded intently as he pronounced this as if to affirm this conviction in his own mind.

"I think what you do is really noble. And exciting. You keep people safe in dangerous situations and help them with their pain. What job could be more fulfilling than that?"

He tilted his head, thought about it.

"I guess because the challenges never stop coming, you don't stand around thinking of yourself in that way. But, then, in quiet moments, somebody really nice, like you, reminds you that you have one of the best professions on earth. So, thanks."

"I bet you're a good teacher, too."

"I do enjoy teaching," he returned, careful to avoid too much self-satisfaction in his answer.

"The residents and students make it all worth it. They get real satisfaction out of learning to run things and doing it right. I had a student the other day who just kept botching the IVs. That can be really stressful for both the patient and the student. I remember when I was learning to put them in—I had a tough time. I kept going through the vein, then it would bleed under the skin, and the patient would get a big hematoma, a blood blister. Even during the first year of residency, when it was always my job to put the IV in, I was much worse than the other residents in my class. Then one day, it clicked."

She appeared to be interested, so he continued.

"And now, I get these things. I know how to do the technical stuff, and most of it isn't some sort of unattainable art. When I can teach a frustrated resident, or a medical student filled with self-doubt, how to do something right, something that contributes to medical care, it's a fantastic feeling. Nothing else makes me feel quite so good. Maybe it's because, in caring for patients, good patient outcomes are expected, and mostly, that's what happens. It becomes kind of humdrum. But when you look for what makes you feel important and validated, something you do out of the ordinary that changes a life, teaching is right up there. I don't even know HOW to teach. Most of us have never been trained in educating other people. But when you see the light go off in someone else's eyes, you know you did something right, something meaningful. You don't need a teaching degree to get that."

He was suddenly conscious of how long he'd been speaking; perhaps he'd had said too much.

"I'm sorry—I keep rambling on. I hope I'm not boring you."

If anything, though, she seemed intent upon his words, her head inclined, gazing warmly at him as he spoke.

Kurt didn't want to share too much of himself, to risk the disasters he'd had in the past when he mistook a mild interest or a passing fancy with actual affection. But she had invited him to share his thoughts and seemed to embrace his sincerity.

"What can I get you two?" asked the waitress, a squat woman with a round face and affable manner.

"Umm—you in the mood for wine?" he asked, glancing at the list.

"Sure—I like a Savignon Blanc."

"OK. We'll take a bottle of this New Zealand 2010."

Kurt turned his attention back to his date.

"How about you—what makes you tick?"

"Me? I really love my job. Love meeting new clients, examining the ups and downs of investments in different products, bringing the deal home. That makes me feel very satisfied."

She was staring into the wine glass as she pronounced this; her eyes glittered with the ripples in the golden liquid, and she appeared to him as something supernatural, a goddess or a siren, with abilities he could only guess at.

"You get to do that a lot?"

"Well, there's always room for more clients, but things have gone very well; I've had my victories. Shall we toast?"

"Uhh . . . here's to new adventures and new experiences."

It was lame. He'd wanted to say something about new relationships or affection, but something inside gave way.

"And exciting new people?"

"Yes," he acknowledged."Exciting new people."

The wine was superb, the steak succulent, the vegetables roasted to perfection. Some kind of reduction sauce on the meat gave it remarkable flavor. His intoxication with Lauren enhanced every aspect of the meal.

"Dessert?" asked the waitress, handing them the short menu.

"I have some homemade apple crisp . . . and really great vanilla ice cream," Lauren offered.

It was an invitation to her place. And ice cream.

"Real ice cream?"

"Oh yeah. Hagen Daaz. Vanilla."

"French vanilla?"

"Yup."

"I'm there." Simple enough. Apple crisp and ice cream as a pretext for visiting her apartment. And maybe a bit more. He ached for a bit more.

Kurt looked gleefully at the waitress.

"Check, please."

Recognizing her defeat, the lady pulled the dessert menus off the table and reluctantly surrendered the bill.

# CHAPTER 15

Kurt helped her with her coat, put his hand on her slender waist as she exited, and held the door. Together, they walked gaily down the brick sidewalk. The charm of the little shopping district on Walnut Street buoyed both their spirits—the streetlights glowed like warm candles in the chill air, and each shop window was filled with glittering items, colorful distractions that beckoned in a mirthful way. The shoppers were happy and distracted, as though there were no serious pursuits in the world. Pear trees shimmered seductively in the warm breeze, still clinging to a few leaves that were tinted along their edges in orange and yellow.

"The key sticks," she said apologetically after a quiet elevator ride to her floor in a towering downtown high-rise.

"Want me to get it?"

Important to take charge with mechanical issues, he thought, a virile display if ever there was one.

"There it goes," she purred as he rattled the key forcefully.

It was a beautiful apartment in an old-world, luxurious building. Her home was a throwback to a time of genteel affluence that had concentrated in the center of the city and the closest suburbs. When he was at her party, the lights had been low, and he hadn't appreciated how inviting the décor was. She preferred the charm of antiquities, had impeccable taste in decoration. The couch was plush, velvet perhaps, inviting, and laden with soft pillows that had a motif carefully chosen to accent the material they were placed upon. The furnishings, the carpets, and the draperies were in perfect harmony. He sat as she rounded up the dessert, fussing with the portions and the china.

"Can you dish the ice cream?" she asked, handing him a spoon.

Surely, he thought, she doesn't do this often. She was svelte, thin even, with roundness in all the right places. Maybe an exercise hound, perhaps a walker.

"How do you stay so fit?"

"Spinning. I go to class every day at 6 A.M."

"Then you go to work?"

"Well, after a shower, yes. Don't look so surprised. There are 20 people in there with me, and they all do the same thing."

"I'm usually at work by 6, or just a bit after. But, I'll tell you this. If I didn't have to be at work until 8, I'd be sleeping till seven. I can't imagine exercising my brains out at that hour. You must have incredible energy."

They combined the apple pastry and the ice cream and headed for the couch. Sitting close together, they sighed their way through the desert.

"My mom made apple crisp when I was growing up. Haven't had it since. Delicious."

She nodded in agreement."This is my mother's recipe—she was a really good cook."

Lauren had poured two glasses of port, a delectable follow-up to the dessert. As he sipped, she moved closer, and he felt the contact of her body against his. When she turned and looked as though she'd posit another question, he faced her and pressed his lips to hers, suddenly and as firmly as he could. There was no hesitation on her part; her lips willingly embraced his own, and her arms intertwined with his as both of them struggled to catch their breath. Then, she turned and flipped the lamp off as he waited, yearning for what he was sure was to come.

In a few minutes, they were lying beside one another, embracing, as he slowly began to remove her clothes. She yielded, breathing heavily as he placed his lips upon each newly exposed site, playfully kissing her body, licking her smooth skin, trying to imbibe the scent of the perfume that hovered just above her warm flesh. Finally, he pulled off his own shirt and felt her press her face to his chest. Too fast? He briefly wondered, but the pull they had upon one another had developed its own energy, and neither could deny it. He felt at once both helpless and enthused. Their lovemaking was slow, soft, sweet, and gentle, a defiance of the frantic pawing that he had experienced too often with other women. She erupted in moans of release and satisfaction, he followed in seconds, and they collapsed in a tight embrace.

They remained quiet, dozing on and off for hours, occasionally awakening, one or the other applying a gentle kiss, then settling back again to rest.

"Did you have a good time tonight?" she whispered.

"I have no words. Just happiness. Can't really describe it. You?"

"Sublime."

He loved the experience, reveled in the moment. And couldn't begin to think of leaving. Did she expect him to stay? Again he dozed, content and still a bit inebriated.

"You know, the wine was excellent," she said, hesitantly.

"Agreed. I don't know a lot about it, but I liked it."

"Kurt."

"Uh-huh."

"I probably shouldn't tell you this."

"Tell me what?"

"I took an oxycodone tablet with the wine. It really sent me."

He considered her statement. There was a real fear of patients mixing opioid medications and other depressants for physicians since it could lead to an overwhelming CNS depression, respiratory insufficiency, perhaps even death. But two glasses of wine and oxycodone? What, he thought, could be the big deal? When he was a teenager, it wasn't uncommon to smoke some marijuana or even eat a brownie laced with hashish while drinking cheap beer. Nothing bad ever happened.

"All right. I can't get excited about it. Sent you where?"

"Somewhere wonderful. With you. I felt like I was in another orbit, you know?"

He was drowsy and not inclined to talk about it.

"No, I don't know."

"It was awesome. I've got some more. Will you try one with me?"

He was awake now, trying to ground himself in the situation.

Her lovely face was next to his, eyes wide open and peering intensely into him.

"I think I'm good with the wine. I'm a doctor. I don't mix things like that."

Why hadn't he seen this coming? The request for oxycodone, running short on tablets after only one day, the request for another script. Had he been played?

She giggled. "I can't begin to tell you how enjoyable it was. You just have to try."

He was more alarmed.

"No, really, I can't. I prescribe these for pain. I can't use them for . . . recreation."

"I see." She was immediately withdrawn, perhaps even pouting in the darkened room.

Shifting away from him on the couch, she began to put her clothes on. He regretted what perhaps had been too forceful a repudiation, hated that he'd interrupted their affectionate interlude.

"Look—I do understand the attraction. I once had an endoscopy. You know, where they look down into your stomach. They put both fentanyl and midazolam into my IV for sedation. And I remember, both before and after, the effect that I felt from those drugs. It was terrific, indescribably terrific. But that scares me—I have access to those drugs every day. If I start having fun with them, I might not be able to control my own impulses. These are powerful things."

He remembered the feeling as the drugs enveloped him, the inescapable sense of being pulled downward as blackness closed in, of a strange euphoria, then the briefest snatch of wonder at the helplessness he felt, even as he was adrift in sensations of pure pleasure.

She suddenly was bright and cheerful once again.

"Ah, so you do know what I mean! But you know what you're dealing with. Someone like you is not going to fall into a dark pit of opiate abuse any more than your joy from wine is a dangerous thing. You're clearly not an alcoholic—you can control your cravings for alcohol, right? Didn't you tell me you don't drink on 'school nights?' How can anyone as disciplined as you lose their ability to discriminate what they want? I just don't see you becoming a druggie."

There was a degree of logic in what she said. He enjoyed beer, wine, scotch but kept them in their place.

"And pills aren't the same as injections. That's heavy stuff—these are for a little fun now and then, that's all."

He desperately wanted to please her. Yet, somehow he sensed that she was challenging him, seeing how far he'd go for her and whether or not she was worth it to him.

"OK, maybe I can try it. But tonight, I'm tired. So I've gotta get going."

"No, you don't," she said playfully, wrapping a comforter around her near-naked body.

She sprang up and disappeared into the kitchen, then came back with a small glass of wine and one of the opioid pills.

"The night is young, and so are we. Here, take this. Just once. It's not going to hurt you, you know that. Let's see if you feel as good as you did when you had that procedure."

He set his jaw, wondering how things had come to this. A woman he strongly desired, an insistence that he indulge in a drug he had no interest in. But he ached for her companionship, for her affection—he'd never felt so much warmth with Cassy. A quick demonstration that he was willing to try it for her sake, to satisfy her this one time. He recalled a few episodes of low back pain from an old basketball injury, and twice he'd received a few opioid pills from the ER just to get through the spasms. The drugs gave him no real pleasure, just some pain relief. Surely, there was no reason to fear a single dose.

Closing his eyes, Kurt took the pill and chased it with the wine. He patted the couch and invited her back down beside him. He desired her again, hoped she could be convinced to feel the same.

# CHAPTER 18

They embraced for a few minutes, and he began to feel something . . .unusual. Each sensation, each kiss, each caress, even each of his own breaths, began to take on the quality of intense pleasure. Euphoria was not sufficient to describe the sensation.

She pulled back from him, looked intensely at his eyes.

"Now you know what I'm talking about, don't you?"

Her perfect eyebrows arched up inquisitively.

He nodded, as a broad smile crept across his face, and then began to laugh indulgently.

"Yeah, I know. Maybe I'm a little uptight about things like this."

She folded her body into him, and somehow they were making love again on the floor, then the couch, then a chair. The deliciousness of her flesh was overwhelming to him, and his body felt electric. In a few minutes, they were spent, clinging to each other, barely able to keep their eyes open.

He awakened a few hours later, crept about the room collecting his clothes as a thin gray light crept into the windows. The night had been without parallel. But he felt somehow compromised, guilty, and indulgent. He needed some time to collect his thoughts and process all of this. He tiptoed toward the door. Suddenly, there was a playful tapping upon his shoulder.

"We can have many more good times," she offered.

Her hair was mussed, eye makeup askew, teeth not yet brushed, marks from the seam of a pillow on her cheek—and still she was the most beautiful woman he'd ever encountered.

He turned to her with a pleading expression.

"I can't really do this, you know."

"Of course you can," she insisted, in a soft, throaty voice, watching as he dressed, admiring his broad back."You're a doctor. If you can prescribe a few more of these for my shoulder, we can have some . . . extracurricular fun."

"Yes, I get that. But I know you. Prescribing opioids for a . . . friend is, well, unethical. You aren't really my patient at this point."

"Yes, but I'm still a patient with an injury and a need." She stated this simplistically, her calculus irrefutable, tilting her shoulder in his direction.

Turning to regard her, he met those eyes with his. His heart skipped just a beat or two as the full impact of her gaze fell upon him. Thoughts went careening through his mind. If dating her had been a transgression of his moral boundaries, what of writing opioid prescriptions for obvious pleasure? But it was simply one more script for a few oxycodone tablets. What could it matter? The world was awash in opioids. How much harm could it do? He felt a churning inside of him, and thought for a moment he might throw up.

His voice seemed to respond before he had actually formulated an answer.

"OK. Just a few. One more time. Since you're still coping with the pain."

Certainly, he thought, after the tablets from this script were gone, he'd have to hold out against writing any further ones. He'd play along . . . for a bit. But it gave him a chill to realize how much influence she could exert over him.

He suddenly felt her hands rubbing his back, caressing him, then pulling him around to face her. She pressed her body against him, and he felt himself rise, the blood throbbing in his temples, heat spreading rapidly throughout his being. He had acquiesced, now came his reward. She was simply irresistible to him in her beauty and her longing. Embracing her, he felt himself drawn along some ill-defined course that promised endless pleasure and excitement, a rapturous existence that stemmed from her extraordinary femininity. The attraction was more powerful than any he'd ever felt, an inexorable force that awed him.

# CHAPTER 17

"Now what?" he wondered.

On a somber Saturday morning, Kurt contemplated what had occurred in the past 24 hours as he sat alone in his home. On only the second date, he'd become the lover of a woman who had cast a spell over him that defied his sensibilities. Sex three times in the same night. This was three more times than he'd experienced that delightful feeling in the past several years. He was a man who considered himself staid, controlled, reserved, the master of his destiny. That belief had been shattered. Now that he was alone with his thoughts, the entire sequence of events was almost inconceivable, like some crazy romantic fantasy that he'd suddenly awakened from. But this was real, and he'd compromised himself profoundly to cater to his whims, or perhaps his needs. It was hard to figure exactly what aspect of his nature was being served by her amorous attentions. Still, he felt a hard and bitter disappointment at the fact that he was incapable of maintaining his bearings when she began to stroke him. He felt at once manipulated and indulged; the dissonance left him frustrated and demoralized.

His back ached considerably, a testament to the vigorous activities of the night before. There hadn't been much sleep, perhaps a few hours, between their embraces and the soul-revealing talks they had afterward. He liked her very much as a person, and when they lay, side by side, comparing notes and perspectives, it was satisfying. But he couldn't escape the humiliation that he felt at how effectively she could change his mind for him, turn his considered objections on their ends, and move right past them, so that, in the end, he changed his way of thinking to fit hers. Popping the oxycodone tablet had been a serious violation of his personal ethics, but somehow, she had prevailed upon him. When he felt the effect of that drug and the wine together, he knew that his self-imposed barriers had been severely compromised. And if she suggested popping a pill again while they embraced and laughed and spoke in low, affectionate tones, he'd be that much more susceptible to taking it in pursuit of the delightful feelings it could produce.

He'd crept out of her bedroom while she still slumbered, gently slid a pillow against her while she cuddled it. Saying nothing, he had dressed and made for the exit, a hangover draped over him like a wet, foul towel; Lauren probably thought he was up to go to the bathroom. She would call him in a few hours, he knew, and he needed to clear his head before she did. What would he do? Make another date, anticipating the same pleasurable interlude? Exhausted and perplexed, he felt no enthusiasm for the prospect, but he knew himself, was aware of his own aching loneliness and his needs—by that evening, he'd undoubtedly be thrilled to hear from her. Dejected, he sat and considered the contradictory nature of his own personality—he knew he should not do exactly what he was going to do. And he had no effective way to maintain his current, sober mindset to guard against the self-indulgence that was to come: the woman was simply intoxicating.

# CHAPTER 18

As the growing light made its way inside the house, he lay on his couch, but the emotional turmoil continued to grow within him.

"Am, in control of my life, or not?" he demanded angrily, glaring at his face in the mirror.

He gave up any thought of rest, resigned himself to staying up the whole day. It was certainly no worse than being up most of the night, on-call at the hospital, and then trying to stay up the next day to avoid screwing up the sleep-wake cycle.

Kurt looked out over the city from his balcony. The narrow, three-story house high on the slopes looked out over an impressive panorama of the Monongahela River valley, from the forested bluffs above Hazelwood to downtown's skyscraper-studded golden triangle. But he could see little in the early dawn. The narrow, steep roads that led to his townhouse, twisting up towards Knoxville at the top of the hill, were a nightmare when it snowed, but there was an inspiration in the view, and sometimes even clarity of thought, when he needed it. He'd paid dearly for the place, even in its disrepair, and then spent much more to have it fixed up to what he considered habitable. Still, he dreamt of the major renovations that would make it an incomparable find on this hillside of brick and frame houses, most over a century old, some perhaps twice that, almost all in need of major maintenance. A hundred years before, luxury housing on these steep bluffs would have been a laughable idea—the layer of smog that hung over the mills in the river valley below would have obscured any view of the city or the river. The wealthy in those days mostly made their homes in the East end, well away from the industrialized Mononga-hela valley, even as they siphoned the profits from the factories and mills into the mansions that lined Fifth Avenue.

Pittsburgh was not beautiful in the chill, foggy, dampness of this early December morning. The city wore necklaces and epaulets of verdant foli-age, cascading down its impossibly steep hills, from April until Septem-ber, then bedecked itself in a riot of yellows, reds, and oranges briefly in October. But when the bleak, gray season arrived, it became difficult to regard her with cheer. Barren, stark tree limbs reached upwards toward the seamless layer of low clouds as if in desperation at the lifelessness that prevailed.

The decision he'd rendered in Lauren's arms the night before weighed upon him heavily. There was nothing for it but to walk a bit, he thought, at least down to the flats, maybe even across the bridge to downtown if his energies could take him there. And from there, he'd let his feet guide him to wherever might seem appropriate, as he considered the impact of his transgression. It was too wet and cool to cycle anyway.

Just outside his front door, the long, steep stairway led down Billy Buck Hill to a different world: he stood at the top, narrowing his eyes, and he could see that a few hundred steps down, the stairs disappeared into a thick, lurid fogbank that obscured everything in the river valley. He held tightly to the rail, stepped carefully down toward the gray cloud of fine drizzle, felt the steps rock just slightly with each footfall, and was beset by a sense of foreboding. He'd been down this set of deteriorating steps dozens, perhaps hundreds, of times, but somehow the way now looked, and felt, menacing, as though his surroundings had shifted in a way that he could not quite apprehend. The neighborhood was quiet; he could almost hear the fog wrapping itself around the homes, pressing its cool tendrils between them.

The steps were locally famous, a symbol of a city that had enmeshed itself within an impractical, almost forbidding topography, long before massive earth-moving machines were able to level five-hundred foot elevations with relative ease. Pittsburghers were doers, enablers, hard workers, survivors. Their hillside neighborhoods were literally laced together by long stairways, bridges, and steep, twisting streets that defied vehicles in the winter. Of late, the crumbling steps had become reminders of the fraying fabric of society. As the stairways buckled, crumbled and shifted, so the fine lines of neighborly communication and mutual support had pulled away, leaving people in ever-more isolated pockets, gazing vacantly into their televisions and their smartphones. Meaningful engagement with people was slowly being replaced by pandering for games, entertainment, thrill-seeking.

Making his way down the long, precipitous staircase, between multi-hued houses with balconies dangling precariously off each story, Kurt landed on Pius street, walking along the narrow roadway, passing the soaring church and the rectory across the street. He found the next staircase tucked between two row houses, and walked to the bottom, vaguely aware of the moisture that hung in the air. He considered how every morning in ages past, thousands of men in dungarees and shabby, stained shirts carried lunch buckets and walked these same rickety staircases down to the steel mills, foundries, and coke ovens, eking out a demanding living. The smoke and soot pouring from the tall stacks had collected in dense clouds above the flats, a foul effluent that loomed over the low parts of the city; he wondered what their feelings must have been as they descended into the brown-gray haze for another day of toil in the exhausting heat.

Carson Street, the epicenter of the small commercial district of the South Side, bore the residual of a Friday night of heavy partying, the numerous bars and restaurants emanating intoxicating effluents of their own. The humble bars served as reminders of many taverns that had lined these streets, just outside the fences of the mills and factories. For the exhausted mill-workers, these unpretentious watering holes had helped to raise their spirits with a "shot and a beer" as they made their way back home, before facing the domestic cares that awaited them as they trudged upwards once again at the end of the day.

# CHAPTER 19

"You got a buck, buddy?"

Kurt was startled as he looked up, and side-stepped the man, sweat-stained and dirty, lying limply on the sidewalk. There were supine, disheveled figures on the heating grates on every block, solemn reminders of the societal costs of too much alcohol, too many drugs, and too few opportunities. Looking back, he could not help but be reminded of the boy he'd found lying on the sidewalk, unconscious, a few blocks away. The sinister influence of opioids was everywhere, like a poisonous ether that moved silently through the communities.

He thought of Lauren, her beauty and seductiveness—could such a lovely woman somehow be touched by all of this? He shook the image out of his mind. She was of a different ilk, moved in different strata altogether.

As he continued down Carson, he was reminded of how alluring the Southside had once seemed to him at night. The main drag was alive with a kind of heady excitement, the windows of the shops and bars all alight, neon signs flashing advertisements for every type of beer imaginable, the artistic signs of the tattoo parlors almost as numerous as those of the bars and restaurants. Young lovers, groups of singles, and solitary marauders cruised the sidewalks on weekend nights, some joyful, some inebriated, some mindless, brushing and shoving each other in their quests to get somewhere. By midnight, the crowds were boisterous, restless, tumbling into the streets, arresting the progress of the traffic. And by 2 A.M., catcalls, fights, and public urination made the scene increasingly unpleasant. The detritus from this late-night debauchery continued to writhe on the sidewalks in the early morning while delivery trucks and men hauling boxes picked their way along, bringing in the substrate for the next night's revelry.

Kurt plodded through the small business district, ruminating on what had transpired the night before and what it meant to him. When he reached the Smithfield Street bridge, he turned to cross, and perched himself over the center span, looking down into the turbid waters of the Monongahela. A low blast reverberated along the channel, and he looked up to see a long line of barges being pushed by a riverboat, emerging from the fog. Transfixed, he watched it glide silently beneath the bridge, not a soul evident on the barges or decks of the towboat, a ghostly scene in the quiet morning. Towering piles of gravel pushed the flatboats low in the water, destined for some industrial plant down the mighty Ohio River.

His frustration and anger at himself were so intense that he suddenly had the urge to run alongside the barges, down to the confluence of the rivers, to parallel the riverboat as it moved mysteriously along, in a vain attempt to leave himself behind. He judged that it was probably making no more than 5 knots, and, if he could get off the bridge quickly enough, he might be able to get to the point just in time to watch it move across the invisible transition from one river into the next—and so, he ran.

Moving as fast as he could to the end of the bridge, he turned to the left. He paralleled the river on an elevated concrete roadway, watching his reflection in the windows of storefronts that were at least 150 years old, meticulously refurbished. Once the sites of purveyors, purchasers, and shippers, they had become the dwelling place of lawyers and accountants. His breath came in great gasps, and he wondered if he could continue the pace for the half-mile that lay between him and the point.

He crossed Fort Pitt Boulevard in front of an angry driver, who sounded the horn as he realized he'd run against the light.

"Jagoff!"

It was the classic Pittsburgh insult, and Kurt knew that he deserved the slander. As he crossed a small concrete bridge that arched over a water feature, entering the park that occupied the confluence of the rivers, he again picked up his pace, crossing the outlines of the long-vanished Fort Duquesne, which had been marked with cobbles in the turf.

The fountain at the point was just in front of him now, a disappointing concrete basin of water, lacking the spray that attracted tourists in the warm season. Beyond the wet sidewalk that surrounded the fountain, the Monongahela ran headlong into the cooler waters of the Allegheny, which rushed briskly down from western New York. The two rivers mixed tumultuously there to create the Ohio, one of the few places in the world where three major rivers came together.

Just as he moved past the fountain, Kurt felt his legs ready to give way and came to an abrupt stop, bent forwards, and placed his hands on his knees, wondering if he'd vomit. But, to his satisfaction, the specter of the mist-shrouded riverboat was just passing the point.

"You sure run fast!"

He turned to see a man who obviously stayed nearby, making his home in a sleeping bag on the concrete surrounding the fountain.

"Well, only once in a while. Not in the shape I once was."

"Yeah, well, who is?"

He was an African American man, lean, with a pockmarked face and a dark blue baseball cap that bore the name and silhouette of a U.S. Navy ship, but the stains made it impossible to read.

"You sleep out here?"

"Mostly."

"Isn't it cold?"

"Yeah. If it gets too cold, I go to a shelter." He paused and looked up at the fountain, "But I like it out here."

Kurt followed the man's gaze from the downtown skyscrapers to the carefully arranged landscape of the diminutive state park around him, to the briskly flowing waters of the rivers, and then over to the bluffs that overlooked them, barely visible in the shroud of gray vapor. The barges and towboat were just past the point now and disappearing under the span of the West End Bridge.

"Well, you do get to see a lot."

"Oh, yeah. Especially at night," the man said with some satisfaction.

The physician thought about that, about the boulevard lights out-lining streets carved into the hillsides, about the brightly illuminated Catholic Church high on the summit of Mt. Washington. And the glit-tering windows of the skyscrapers, along with the bridges that arched over the rivers, their girders and piers and towers outlined in the night by bright amber spotlights. The city was spectacular in the dark. Kurt was able to see it all from every window on the back of his townhouse. But his perspective, from a perch high on the slopes, was decidedly dif-ferent from the one this man witnessed as he shivered in his sleeping bag. Somehow, here, on this somber morning, the muscular hills and bluffs that surrounded the rivers towered over a man, loomed out of the fog, gave him the impression of being channeled or penned in, as though his life was determined by great, threatening forces that he could not resist.

The young physician felt an odd kinship with this destitute man as he stood beside him in the misty air, but there wasn't much to say. The two stood there in silence for a few minutes, watching the riverboat disappear from sight down the waterway.

"I'm sorry if I scared you." He realized that in his haste, he'd almost run over the man in his bag, had been startled to find him underfoot.

"What was you runnin' from? I thought you were goin' right off the edge and into that river!"

"I don't know." Kurt took a deep breath as the weight of his decisions from the previous night had returned: "I really don't know what I was running from. Sometimes you just run, maybe to find that out."

"I guess I've done some runnin' myself." The man's eyes turned away again, off toward the river.

"From what?"

"I got mixed up with drugs pretty bad some years back. Lost my wife, lost my family. I hurt a lot of people. I got clean, though."

"Crack?"

"No," he looked at Kurt, "Heroin. I was shooting heroin."

The two were silent again.

"Do you know what an aquifer is?" Kurt surprised himself when the question popped out of his mouth. He thought that perhaps as someone who lived here on the point, the man would have some insight.

"No. I don't know what that is."

The anesthesiologist continued, watching the mist envelop the trailing edge of the boat at last."When I was a boy, I used to visit my grandparents up on Mount Washington. Sometimes I'd stay with them. My parents lived south of the city—it was kind of the country back then. Anyway, they'd send my sister and me to visit, and we'd come downtown to see movies or sometimes to just walk along the river. My grandfather told me that there was some kind of underground river that ran underneath the point.

"He said that this fountain," he nodded towards the large circular basin of water, "was filled with water that bubbled up out of that river. Later I heard someone say that an underground river like that is called an aquifer. Did you ever hear about that?"

The man chuckled heartily."Yeah, I heard those rumors from my granddaddy, too. He even told me that once an airplane crashed into the Mon river, full of top-secret atomic devices, and the next day, the Air Force tried to get it, to pull it out, and they never could find it! He said they thought that airplane went down so far into the riverbed that it went into that underground river and washed away downstream.

"But," he continued, "this here fountain, I don't think it gets its water from the underground river. A couple of weeks ago, I saw some men here fixing it. I think they just use the regular city water for this."

Kurt nodded pensively.

"That old story sounded too good to be true," he said, looking over at the man, who suddenly adopted a wizened air.

"A lot of things are like that, you know—when you find out the truth, when you can really see things like they are, it makes you sad."

"It makes me sad that you live here."

The man pulled a threadbare, camouflage poncho around his wiry frame."There are worse places. The VA wanted to put me in the dom, you know, their old-folks home, with a whole bunch of old, sick men. It seemed like a place to die. I didn't want that. I got some freedom here, and if I need a shelter, I can go there."

"You get enough to eat?"

"I get by."

"What if you get sick?"

"They got these doctors that drive around and help out. From Mercy Hospital, I think. They're students, like, but they can get you medicine."

"No more drugs?"

The eyes were suddenly alight.

"No. Not ever. I was down there. All the way at the bottom. I'm never goin' down there again."

His words were spoken with determination, and Kurt understood immediately that the man would sooner die before than start taking opioids again."I'm glad to hear that. Well, thanks for the information—about the fountain, I mean. But, I'm gonna move on, I still have a long way to go."

"Where you goin' to, today?"

"Polish Hill. My sister lives there. I gotta go see her this morning."

"All right. Well, I hope you find what you're lookin' for."

"Me, too." Maybe I'll see you out here again, sometime, Kurt thought.

# CHAPTER 20

Kurt took leave of the genial vet and walked briskly through the nearly deserted streets of downtown. An icy wind was funneled cruelly between the towering buildings, the pinnacles of commerce and investment—it met him full in the face as he paced down Liberty Avenue. During his boyhood, these same streets would have been teeming with shoppers by this time, especially as the Christmas holidays approached. Much of the retail had left the city's inner core, relocating to the upscale suburban malls or simply disappearing altogether. It was sobering to see such desolation at the heart of a modern American city, but Pittsburgh had shifted with the economic forces that played across the land: entertainment, drinking, and dining, the idle past-times of the evening, had gained traction. The the city now supported a thriving cultural district, ringed by blocks of trattorias, tapas bars, and bistros. The steelworkers of the preceding generation would hardly have recognized the place.

He reached the limits of the downtown and paused to rest a moment on the corner beside the Greyhound station. He'd ridden those crowded buses many times when he was young, visiting aunts and uncles out in the country and one cousin up in New York City. A strange, sympathetic twinge rose within him as he smelled the diesel fuel from the idling vehicles and saw a group of rag-tag, backpack-toting, sleepy-eyed people disembark from a bus that had come in overnight from New York City. He looked northward along Liberty Avenue, where a long, straight length of sidewalk disappeared into the distance, paralleling commercial structures on one side and a steep hillside on the other. He seldom walked here, it was too far from his house, but he always felt cheerful when he drove along this stretch in the car. He knew that in a few moments, he'd be at his sister's house, a place where he would be welcome. She'd be up by now, fussing with the kids, getting them to their Saturday activities, and had probably already sent Scott off to work—a hardworking contractor, he almost always had jobs booked for Saturdays.

Kurt walked a bit more jauntily now, found himself at the bottom of the road that ascended to Polish Hill, and started up. Even though he made an effort to stay in shape, jogging when time permitted and riding his bike along the river once a week or so, he was startled at how difficult the climb was, how the Pittsburgh topography taxed him. His backache persisted, an intermittent, unwelcome visitor since he had taken a very hard fall at the end of a basketball game in college—he was sure that he'd left a dent in the wooden floor of the old Field House.

Halfway up the long hill, he turned to the left, walked another half block, and then carried himself up the front steps to the broad front porch. There were probably a hundred thousand of these big brick houses in the city; his brother-in-law had worked ceaselessly on his days off for the first five years they lived in the house, trying to make the old place presentable. It was now the belle of the block, a beautifully appointed, century old Colonial Revival home. Scott had painstakingly restored the leaded glass in the double-door entryway, cleaned and reconstructed several original stained glass windows from the stairway, and pulled down, stripped, and refinished all the oak trim. It was an impressive statement by an industrious and fastidious craftsman. Kurt had a lot of respect for his brother-in-law, but seldom got to actually see him, with their conflicting schedules.

He looked at the campy, old-style Christmas decorations his sister had put out. Passed down from their parents, they bore the joyful memories of four decades of holidays before his mother and father had decided to move to Florida for good, both of them succumbing not long afterward to the ravages of old age. The life-size plastic statues of Frosty and Santa were still illuminated in the dim morning light, perhaps would stay that way all day and into the night again. Katy's two little boys adored the figures, as Kurt had when he was a child. Large, colored, glowing bulbs on strings surrounded both front windows, blinking periodically to add to the charm. He didn't come here often enough, he thought, and was happy every time he did.

"Knock-knock," he called, opening the door.

"Oh! Kurt, it's you! Can't you call first? I'm in the middle of a hundred things."

Katy was pretty with large blue eyes, dark, pixie-cut hair, and a fair, flawless complexion. Even when she frowned, she radiated kindness, along with a certain approachability and affability that Kurt simply did not have. At the local parish, St. Gwendolyn's, she was renowned for her pierogis, from their mother's recipe, one that had probably come from many generations back. Once a week, Kurt's sister cooked her own version, along with a few other women in the parish, to be sold on Friday mornings to raise funds for the church's missions.

She possessed a lovely soprano voice, leading the congregation as a cantor at mass on Saturday evenings, which he would occasionally get to, though not nearly as frequently as he wished. She filled the soaring sanctuary with her fine voice. Sometimes, when he listened, felt moved to tears. Throughout the week, she volunteered at the elementary school beside the church and read to kids at the library. He was very proud of her, idolized her volunteerism and her tight infiltration into the community. Kurt liked to think that her relentless bossiness when they were children had set him on the right path, had pulled him back from some strange and feckless diversions, had perhaps even given him the self-discipline to become a physician.

"I never call—you know that. I just love to show up and fill your life with joy."

She looked up, put down some utensils she'd been holding in front of a bowl of flour.

"Christmas cookies—it's that time."

"I know. But . . . I needed to talk to you."

"I like to talk to you. But you should make an appointment," she laughed, "It would be a lot more convenient."

He almost smiled.

"What's wrong? You seem kind of put out," she continued, eyeing him.

"You know me so well."

"I do. Who is she?"

He launched into an explanation of how he'd met her, the awkward-ness of the situation, the warmth she projected, his inexplicable attrac-tion to her, the suddenness of their intimacy.

She shook her head, scoffing. He'd always been able to be frank with his sister; she'd been his prime counselor in romantic relationships.

"Maybe I don't need to know so many details . . . You did all that? On only the second date? I hope you put BOTH of your socks on the doorknob. Why do you tell me these things? And you're a Catholic."

"Part-time," he assured her.

"Is she a Catholic?"

"Hmmm. I don't know. I just know that I'm crazy for this girl, and I'm aching inside, and my judgment isn't good when I'm around her."

She whirled, smacked the hand of her ten-year-old son, Thomas, who had snuck into the kitchen and attempted to sneak a warm cookie off the tray.

"It's not even lunchtime yet. Go help Dougie get ready for basketball."

The boy waved humbly to his uncle and skipped off to play with his younger brother.

She turned her attention back to Kurt, engaging him as firmly as she could with a stare.

"You have to be careful, Kurt. You had two disasters not so long ago. That . . . affair you had with Cassy. It nearly tore you apart. I don't think your judgment is good, generally. Maybe you learned something from those other relationships, but you get rusty, you know? You're like a schoolboy now, suddenly dancing around in some kind of infatuation. What you really need with this girl is to take your time and get to know her, let the affection develop gradually and naturally, not like some tidal wave that breaks over you and destroys everything in its path. You're susceptible to that kind of thing."

He furrowed his brow, nodded slightly, and turned to look her in the eye. "It just . . ." Kurt began, frustrated by the truth of his sister's words, "it feels terrific to care about someone. And have her care about me."

"Of course it does, Kurt. That's like saying it feels good to pat a puppy. Everyone needs affection, and everyone needs to give it. It's . . .

elementary. But it was like you put up these barriers when Cassy went out to California, and you left yourself in solitary confinement. Now, the walls aren't just coming down; they're being bulldozed: you're not in control of your emotions. It sounds like you're leading with your loins—you could get hurt. Real bad."

He shifted his weight, leaned over onto the counter, put his head on his hands."I feel like I know what I'm doing and how to not get beat up. I'm a big boy; I can see when danger is coming. This feels really right for me, like nothing has in a long time."

Now she widened her eyes, incredulous at what she was hearing from her brother.

"That's exactly the point. You don't have your wits about you right now . . . like you're in a spell. I've seen you like this twice before, and it didn't turn out well. Look, I'm your sister; I'm giving it to you as straight as I can. Did you come here to tell me about this situation so that I would give it a thumbs-up? You know me better than that—I'm telling you what I really think. You're already way over-committed with this woman, and you can't control it. Until you really get to know her, you should pull back and hold on to your affection. So you have to wait—what's the big deal? 'Waiting makes the heart grow fonder.'"

"It's 'absence makes the heart grow fonder,'" he corrected.

"OK, then show a little abstinence. And let your heart grow fonder."

It annoyed him that she could so easily twist his words around and make a good point.

"I'll try. I will try. I know that you're right. It's just not easy to pull your heart out of this kind of a passionate . . . interaction."

"'Nothing that's worth it is easy.' Dad always said, and you used to say that all the time when you were under the gun in medical school when you felt like you couldn't open one more book or memorize one more fact. So what's different with this?"

He grabbed a cookie and sampled it.

"Just like mom's. Well, what's different is that I was thinking back then, philosophizing. This isn't like that. I'm just feeling something that I can't control."

"Well, maybe thinking about it will help you control it. That's the best advice I can offer. Here."

She gave him a brown bag that's she'd put a half-dozen cookies into.

"Now, I gotta get these guys to their basketball practice. Come say hi and bye."

"And don't make any wisecracks about a new aunt, please," she added. He followed, scoffing."Of course not. It's way too early."

He found his two young nephews dribbling and passing in the garage.

"Uncle Kurt! Uncle Kurt!" called Doug, a diminutive, sandy-haired, blue-eyed boy, just turned five.

He hugged the youngest and gave a fist bump to his older brother.

"Here, guard me—both of you!"

The boys menaced him with their extended arms, attempting to slap the ball out as he dribbled in tight circles, forward and back, between his legs, keeping the ball just out of reach.

"Wow!" the younger boy called."You're really good! Tommy said you played in high school."

"Course he did—he played at Mt. Lebanon. He started on Varsity when he was just in tenth grade," Thomas instructed the younger brother, who had undoubtedly heard all this before.

"He even played a year in college at Pitt!"

"Well, yeah, as a walk-on, Dougie." Kurt feigned a bit of modesty but was endlessly proud that he'd been able to make a varsity team at the college level.

"But it took way too much time," he continued, "I just needed to study more, and the coach didn't buy that. You have to give it everything at that level, and I wanted to go to medical school. Anyway, I had a lot of fun. I even got to play a few times in home games up at the Field House, in the end, if we were winning by a bunch."

The boys charged him, ignoring the basketball, and made to tackle him. He collapsed, laughing, and they climbed over him as he lay on the ground.

"OK," their mother called, "look sharp. This train's leaving."

She heaved the side door to their mini-van open so the two could crawl in.

"How's your back?"

"It's OK. You know, ups and downs."

"I'll see you again soon, right?"

"You know you will," he called cheerfully.

Kurt walked alongside the vehicle as it eased out of the garage, making faces at his nephews, who gleefully made them back. As they disappeared down the block, he kept his hand up, waving. He had carefully avoided mentioning the oxycodone tablets. That would be his little secret. Despite their closeness, Katy definitely would not understand and could not be made aware. He would make sure of that.

# CHAPTER 21

Heading for home, Kurt descended the long grade back to town on a seldom used sidewalk. This route led through the Duquesne University campus, perched high on a bluff overlooking the river, and down a spindly steel staircase to the Tenth Street Bridge. As he crossed the river, he again paused to look down into the fast-moving, green-gray waters. Though he'd been buoyed briefly by his visit to see his sister and the boys, he remained troubled. His decision haunted him, and guilt lay like a mantle around his shoulders as he hunched over the railing. He moved through his life with what he assumed was an iron-core, irrefutable set of values that determined his actions, but what had occurred was a glaring act of self-contradiction. His ill-advised decision was clearly rooted in loneliness, desire, and the need for love and acceptance. He'd been aware of all of these influences within himself and yet could not explain how they had somehow taken precedence over a principle that he had formerly believed was inviolable.

Staring down at the current, he felt a sort of awe for the power of the rivers, their turbulence, and their unpredictable nature. These broad valleys into which hundreds of thousands of people had channeled their lives had been carved by the waters over millennia. He was amazed by this irresistible force, the simple trickling of rain waters that somehow moved entire mountains. All around, there were signs of the water's undeniable power, of men's failure to contain or control the unceasing flow: the deep gorges and steep bluffs, the deterioration of walls into piles of rubble, massive blocks of stone that had tumbled into the channel, the rusted underbelly of a capsized barge. The rivers were incessantly at work, carving the terrain, pushing ever deeper into the crust of the earth, generally placid on the surface but tempestuous beneath, titanic influences that escaped the casual observer.

An hour later, he arrived with aching legs at his townhouse, fatigued and hungry. How far had he walked? Ten miles? As he slapped together a ham and cheese sandwich and stuffed a handful of pretzel sticks into his mouth, he looked at his cell phone and saw that he'd missed a call. Probably his sister with an invitation. She usually had him over once every week or two. Still, she had been so flustered getting the boys to practice and lecturing him that she hadn't mentioned it during his visit.

Instead, he heard the irrepressibly cheerful voice of Lauren.

"Hi, Kurt! Miss you already. You left so early—just like a doctor. When you have a chance, give me a call!"

He tried to bear his sister's wisdom in mind as he repeatedly listened to the message and fashioned a response. It wouldn't do to appear too eager. He'd give the whole thing some time, some space, then he'd give her a call for another date. The very idea reverberated through him, a lovely feeling. Yes, he could wait a bit. And yes, he'd call back.

# CHAPTER 22

"His pressure is going to shit."

"I can see that. I gave him propofol, succinylcholine, antibiotic, ketamine, glycopyrrolate . . . and the patient had fentanyl and midazolam on the way back to the room. This could be just hypotension from the propofol, may be an allergic reaction . . . are the fluids open? Is the anesthesia off? Can we put his legs up? Just hand ventilate him, turn off the ventilator . . ."

The anesthetist cycled the cuff again and set it to cycle every minute.

"I can feel a thready carotid pulse . . . nothing else."

"You gave ephedrine, twice, then phenylephrine ?"

"Yeah, he had just a short bump up with his pressure, then he dropped again."

"I think he's got a rash over his chest—take a look!"

The OR staff had gathered close by, craned their necks to see what Kurt was pointing to.

The surgeon stood with his hand clasped, gloved, and sterile, awaiting the outcome of this drama.

"Do we need to cancel, Kurt? Where are we?"

"I think he's having an anaphylactic reaction—probably from the muscle relaxant, maybe the antibiotic."

He surveyed the scene, winced at the blood pressure displayed before him, flashing, accompanied by an unceasing alarm bell.

"I'm giving 100 micrograms of epinephrine . . . let me have Benadryl 50 mg . . . and 20 of Pepcid, please."

The problem was a relatively rare one, but the response was often practiced; every anesthesiologist had stood in the simulation center and recited it.

"He's coming up. We're at 70/40."

"Great. No CPR. That's a lot less paperwork."

The CRNA nodded with satisfaction.

"OK, and I need 125 milligrams of Solu-Medrol. Are the fluids wide open?"

"Yes, and Terry is starting a big IV, so we should have plenty of access."

"Are you OK, Kurt?" Natalie was swept in with the tide of humanity that made its way into the room, brimming with curiosity.

"What can I do to help?"

"Can you pull some serum for tryptase levels? Let's make sure that this was really an allergic issue. We can get him to an allergist to test for all of these drugs that we gave. I don't think we can proceed. I have no idea how he's gonna respond to bleeding and fluid shifts during this surgery. Let's bring him out of this and plan for another day, a safer day."

The surgeon appeared to scowl behind his paper mask but had little reason to argue the point.

"I see," he sighed."Can we call for my next patient?"

The clamor began to die down, and Kurt called the ICU to make arrangements to take the patient there after surgery. When the intensivist answered, he sent forth a litany of questions. The gatekeepers kept very close track of ICU beds, ensuring that a patient really required admission there.

"Full-blown? Well, yeah, Khalil, it was pretty damned full-blown. I think we were on the verge of arrest. Another few seconds, and we'd have been doing chest compressions. He's still anesthetized with a tube in. Pressure is marginal, we're pouring in the fluids, and I have him on an epinephrine drip. He's had all the usual stuff, except steroids, which we're about to give now . . . I don't believe he's stable enough to extubate right now, but maybe in an hour or two, if he doesn't manifest any airway swelling, he'd be all right to get the tube out . . . I think we caught the whole thing early . . . probably the muscle relaxant is the culprit; it's the most common cause among the drugs we gave . . . yeah, we'll have him up there in about 20 minutes or so . . . I'll start an arterial line. He's got a Foley catheter; we're probably OK without a central line unless things deteriorate . . . right, see you then."

"Dr. Khalil always has a lot of questions," the anesthetist said, pulling up the components of a transducer so that an arterial catheter could be placed and used to observe the blood pressure from second-to-second.

"Yeah. He's really thorough, which I appreciate. And he'll ask them all again when I get up there, probably."

He carefully prepped the patient's right wrist after taping the hand back to keep it in place. The pulses were by this time bounding, courtesy of the epinephrine infusion. It took but one quick needle insertion, and bright red arterial blood began streaming up through the hub of the arterial catheter. He slid the wire through the needle, then advanced the catheter over it, rotating it slightly as he went, to avoid traumatizing the artery during the insertion.

"OK, can you hand me the line?"

The OR staff had been busy placing a Foley catheter so that the man's urine output could be observed with some accuracy over the next 24 hours or so. The anaphylactic shock had been controlled readily, but Kurt figured the next few hours might yet be very stormy. Massive amounts of inflammatory mediators would be liberated by such an exuberant immune response—bradykinin, histamine, glucocorticoids, and many others. The effect was to dilate the vessels' smooth muscle and render capillaries all over the body porous so that they simply leaked fluid into all tissue beds.

"I need a transport monitor," the anesthetist announced.

Velma, as if on cue, lumbered into the room, carrying the prescribed apparatus.

There was a tangle of wires and tubes, as they're so often was, especially when lines were placed hastily for resuscitation. It was challenging to keep everything organized when the entire focus was on rescuing the patient from some cataclysmic outcome.

"Give me a minute," she said, as she and the anesthetist furiously whipped through the lines, disconnecting some to untwist them, capping off others.

"OK, we're good. Lines are sorted out, monitor hooked up, pump running fine, art line zeroed, oxygen on and the tank full, foley is up . . . let's move him over on my count, and we'll get going."

Natalie was again at his side.

"What else do you have going? I can cover your rooms till you get back."

Indefatigable, she swung into action, scribbling some notes for herself and adopting his cases while overseeing her own. He was very fond of her, found her terrifically dedicated to the practice, energetic, and driven. She had three small children at home, somehow was able to juggle getting them to their school and a bevy of athletic and musical activities, running the house, and seeing to the needs of her husband, a general surgeon—with an even more demanding schedule than her own. Kurt had no idea how Natalie made it all work, wondered how much sleep she'd sacrificed in the name of getting things done over the past decade. After she'd started in the residency, Kurt had mentored her through a research project, one that had resulted in a prize for "best abstract" at a meeting. Later, they'd written it up for a publication in the anesthesiology literature, to her delight. Then, when it had come time for hiring, Kurt had approached the chief and energetically supported that he keep Natalie on, despite a hiring freeze. Somehow, the old man had made it work.

"We're here," the anesthetist called out as the elevator doors opened in the ICU.

"Here's the EKG. I'll hook up the pulse ox. Can you get a temp for us?"

There was a whirlwind of attaching monitors and breathing circuits as the respiratory therapist arrived to hook up and program the ventilator. The sedatives that they'd administered were begging to ebb away, and the patient had begun to move.

"Pressure looks better, and he's starting to make some urine—good."

The anesthesiologist nodded to the group as he left.

"Hey Kurt, they've got an airway issue down the hall there—can you help us out?"

The head nurse for the ICU, Peggy, caught him just as he was headed back to the elevator. He turned and scurried back into the unit, past some frightened and skittish relatives whom he figured had been chased from the bedside.

He found himself in a small room with a crowd of medical personnel that was swelling by the second.

The intensivist, Khalil, was already at the head. He had gowned and was assuming control of the airway from a therapist who'd been providing mask ventilation. The bodies parted as Kurt came to the bedside. A large man with very dark pigmentation lay on the bed in severe distress; it was clear he was heaving mightily for air and would likely go into respiratory failure in short order. As all air-hungry patients did, the patient fought the mask; he would do so until he became delirious or until his carbon dioxide levels became so high that he was comatose.

"Bruce, I need you to breathe with me, don't fight me!" commanded the intensivist, who was struggling to keep the mask in place as the man thrashed his head from side to side. Maggie, one of the respiratory therapists, was assisting him.

Even in his decompensated state, the patient was clearly very powerful. Controlling him with verbal cues was a losing proposition. In addition, the monitors reflected a dangerously low oxygen saturation in the low 70s. The man also had a rapid heart rate, along with very high blood pressure, a consequence of his struggle to breathe and his own intrinsic adrenaline levels.

"Kurt, I intubated him a couple of days ago; it wasn't easy, but I had a half-decent view. Unfortunately, he ripped his ET tube out a few minutes ago while his family was in here with him—he was getting really agitated, but he was not able to communicate."

"Why's he in the ICU?"

"Intracranial hemorrhage, from uncontrolled hypertension . . . we were just weaning him from a nitroprusside infusion."

The man struggled beneath the mask, his vast frame shuddering with each breath he attempted. His abdomen and chest had begun to rock back and forth in a see-saw pattern, one Kurt had seen many times, as patients began to fail in their attempts to breathe. This patient was but a few minutes away from respiratory collapse. The intensivist, for his part, was struggling to deliver breaths in appropriate synchrony. Occasionally, he appeared to be administering a breath while the man was struggling to exhale, a contradictory application that was probably making things worse. It was challenging to synchronize breathing in patients with severe dyspnea.

In those few seconds of observation, Kurt felt a profound pity for the man, who was neurologically compromised with little hope of regaining the usual quality of life. The patient was unable to perceive the context of the situation while struggling against the very ventilation that was applied to help him.

He suddenly realized he was distracted at a time when he needed all of his focus.

"Let me help with the masking," Kurt offered, and moved in beside the intensive care physician, who was clearly becoming fatigued as he tried to ventilate the large man.

The anesthesiologist applied both hands to the mask, pulling sharply up on the chin and tilting the head back. Unfortunately, the patient was obese, with a thick roll of fat behind his neck, so that tilting the head back was almost impossible.

"Great, I've got a solid mask fit. Let's see if we can get these saturations up."

The patient's oxygen levels had rapidly deteriorated after he pulled his tube; they now hovered in the low 70 percent range, while the two physicians worked strenuously to deliver oxygen. Finally, relieved of the need to make a mask seal on the large, edematous face, the intensivist was far better able to provide breaths in concert with the man's efforts. For his part, Kurt struggled to make a mask seal and keep the airway open at the same time. He grimaced as the seconds ticked by and felt himself begin to sweat, but the saturations slowly began to respond.

"Do you all have drugs drawn up?" he called to the room full of nurses.

"I think we're getting somewhere," the intensivist noted, looking up at the monitor.

The oxygen saturation had now risen into the mid-90 percent range, the heart rate had declined, and the man's struggles appeared to have diminished somewhat.

"I don't think we're going to get these saturations any higher. So let's go ahead and intubate. Maggie, keep your cricoid pressure on. Linda, please give 100 milligrams of lidocaine, then give the propofol and rocuronium. I have a laryngoscope here; let's put in an 8.0 tube. But make sure I have a 6.5 tube, just in case he's swollen—put a stylet in both of them."

He felt nervous and a bit queasy. This might be easy, a straight shot intubation, or something terrible, he considered, during the long pause while they waited for the drugs to go in.

Within seconds after the drugs were injected, the man became flaccid, then the breathing stopped.

"Much easier, he bags much easier," the intensivist murmured.

"OK, let me take a look. Maggie, please hand me the tube when I ask for it."

The glottic opening bore little resemblance to what he was used to seeing. Instead, the tissues were reddened and edematous, swollen to the point of obscuring the entrance to the airway.

"I don't see the cords. Too much swelling. I don't want to poke around with a tube in here. Lousy view. Can I get the Glidescope?"

The instrument was wheeled over hurriedly, the handle placed in his waiting hand. The saturations held at 92 percent, and he placed the blade along the midline of the tongue, lifting again as he came to the back of the floppy organ. The screen revealed to all in the room exactly what he'd seen a moment earlier; a silence fell over the attendees. There was simply no evidence of an airway, yet Kurt was sure he could tell where it should be.

"Can I have a bougie?" he asked."Bend it in a tight curve. Maybe I can fish this into the trachea."

He sounded a bit dubious, but no one else in the room had a better suggestion.

Maggie passed the coiled airway stylet to him, still pressing firmly on the larynx.

"And Maggie, can you relax a bit with your pressure? There. Maybe that helps a little."

Kurt was becoming more uncertain. He thrust the tightly curved stylet into the back of the pharynx. He watched the tip move clumsily about as he manipulated its proximal end, fishing for an opening, dipping again and again into the erythematous mass of tissue.

"Your saturations are going down—do you want to come out and ventilate?"

The intensivist apprised him of the situation, making him aware of how the situation was deteriorating.

"You are at 75 percent. I think you should come out."

Kurt noticed, in the background, the sound of the pulse oximeter tone becoming lower and lower. It triggered a visceral reaction deep within, reminded him that there was little time.

"Kurt—69 percent. Come out."

"I think I'm there."

The heart rate had begun to drop, an ominous sign of impending cardiac arrest.

"Maggie. Put the 6.5 tube over the bougie. Quick!"

He kept his eyes affixed to the screen as the therapist slid the smaller endotracheal tube over the airway stylet, the end of which had disappeared within the mass of tissue before them. Without looking at the tube, he slid it along the stylet until its blunt, clear end appeared on the video screen. He advanced it further, only to have it recoil backward, refusing to move along the length of the stylet.

"Shit," he mumbled.

"Kurt, he's going to arrest."

The pulse oximeter tones were desperately low, the heart rate sounded as though it was in the 30s. He pulled the tube back a few centimeters, twisted it on the stylet.

"Hold tight, Maggie, don't let go."

Again, he advanced the tube. This time, its beveled edge disappeared into the airway tissues, which had been bloodied by the attempts to intubate. Not a person in the room was breathing now, awaiting the outcome.

"I'll hold the tube—pull the bougie!"

Maggie complied, and the intensivist quickly attached the ventilation bag.

"$CO_2$ detector?"

This small, plastic indicator Maggie quickly produced, attaching it to the tracheal tube. As they ventilated, the man's massive chest and abdomen appeared to rise and fall. The CO2 color change suggested the endotracheal tube was in the right place. The dark discoloration of his mucus membranes began to resolve, and the heart rate and oxygen saturation both quickly rose.

"Shouldn't be this hard," the intensivist pronounced.

"I know what you mean," Kurt breathed, a whirlwind of stress and emotions escaping him.

"Thanks to all of you. Let's make sure that tube is secure!"

The respiratory therapist was already placing a device around the patient's head, with anchoring straps, to help prevent future extubation. The man was now flaccid, relaxed, unconscious. He appeared peaceful, particularly in light of the struggle that had just ensued.

"I am afraid you'll probably be seeing him in the OR for a tracheostomy soon, Kurt."

He nodded as he made his way toward the stairwell.

"No doubt."


"Glad you're back," Natalie greeted him with a furrowed and inquisitive brow.

"Couldn't get right back down—they had a near-code up there with a big guy who extubated himself. Desaturated pretty low, he was a difficult mask ventilation, and his larynx was a swollen mess. Grace of God that I got that bougie into his trachea."

At that, she invoked the age-old maxim of acute care physicians.

"Well, 'It's better to be lucky than good.' "

A simple statement, he thought, but with profound implications. No one ever found it trite. Lately, Kurt had felt more lucky than good on several occasions.

"Anyway, it's all coming down. I'm late; Ernie's on-call. I can get you out of here in a few minutes. Can you just go wake up the patient in six? Should be straightforward."

She ran off to direct other traffic. So much energy and intensity in that little package, Kurt observed.

In twenty minutes, he was changing.

"So, what's on your agenda for the night? Out for fun or home to watch TV?" Farrokh Abdullah, one of his partners, queried as they pulled off their scrubs. His hairy abdomen was so protuberant that his overall body shape was, quite literally, round.

"Long list—supposed to go to my nephew's basketball game, gotta catch up on a paper that I'm working on with the chief, and then put together some kind of supper."

"The chief is very fond of you—like a son. Seems always happy when you step up and do projects with him. Maybe he needs a son."

"He's kinda old for that, Farrokh. And his daughter married a golf pro—makes quite a bit out there on the links, I hear."

"Yes. Playing golf all the time. That's why the chief needs a son. You hold a lot together here, like glue for the division. I'm glad to work with you."

It was unexpected, and for Kurt, an embarrassing expression of regard. The big Iranian was not a touchy-feely kind of man. He felt a little glow inside. Day-to-day, he and the other anesthesiologists managed risk, directed cases, engaged with the surgeons, ushered the patients through by the hundreds. Their charges almost always did well, as they expected them to, and then were moved offstage to recover. At the same time, the anesthesia and OR staff made room for more cases. There weren't many sentimental expressions of appreciation, though a few patients were expressly grateful in the PACU. When a colleague offered praise in a candid moment, well, that was something to be cherished.

His fellow anesthesiologist had his back to Kurt, which was, shockingly, as hairy as his front.

"I really appreciate that, Farrokh. The chief has been really generous to me with the academic projects and clinical trials. I like to contribute. Still, I'd never get them off the ground myself."

"You have a great night," the man called as Kurt left the locker room.

A quick stop in the office to finalize his charts, and he'd head home. As he sat down at this desk, he noticed a letter on his desk, a puffy envelope marked "confidential." Probably teaching evaluations, he thought, then saw the sender. A legal firm, he knew the name, on billboards all over town. Litigators, "med-mal" lawyers. His hands began to shake.

Opening it, he quickly read the first page of the long letter, trying to translate the legal language. He remembered the surname. The lady who'd had the stroke. Off to a nursing home to recover, last he'd heard. But the suit was now brought against him by the family. She'd probably died in the facility. Mortality from dense strokes in old people was high.

He felt nauseated as he read through a laundry list of complaints against him. "Grossly negligent . . . failed to evaluate . . . dereliction of duty . . . engaged in malpractice."

Kurt shook his head, felt the sting of tears in his eyes. They'd decided that he was at fault and were suing the health system as well. No mention of the surgeon. He'd heard many talks, had been prepared to someday have a brush with a lawsuit: one in fourteen anesthesiologists sued every year, he'd been told. Somehow that didn't mitigate the emotional wrenching that tore through him. It suddenly felt as though a great weight had been placed around his neck, one that he knew would be there for years, perhaps permanently. No one wanted to be sullied by a malpractice suit. He'd always regarded himself as a careful and safe provider. Even his peers had not found any significant fault or negligence with his treatment in this case. He carefully placed the envelope in the top drawer of his desk and made a mental note to call the risk management people the next day. They would guide him. He felt a touch of anger—it didn't seem reasonable to hold him responsible for this terrible outcome. It hadn't even happened when he was caring for the patient.

# CHAPTER 23

He made his way home, driving achingly slowly, intent upon what he'd just encountered.

"Did I leave the lights on?" He wondered aloud as he parked on the winding lane in front of his house.

He was careful to steer around the lawn chair that was prominently positioned in the parking lane. This was a sacred placeholder in Pittsburgh, not something to be brushed aside, lest an irate neighbor call him into the street in the dead of night. The city had its odd traditions, which made it that much more charming to him. A lawn chair on the street in New York or LA would simply be run over. He turned the key in the lock and threw the door open.

"Well, good evening! I thought you'd never get home!"

Kurt was taken aback; he had not expected a visitor.

He blinked a few times, sought to confirm the image that presented itself to his startled eyes. She was fashionably clad in tight jeans, a tiny top with spaghetti straps over her shoulders, black boots with spiked heels, and jewelry that complemented the clothes perfectly. Her dark, thick hair was pulled back in a ponytail. The makeup provided the perfect accentuation of her pretty facial features. Every time he saw her, it took his breath away.

He managed an unsure grin. "I gave you my key?"

"Sure you did—Friday night. Don't you remember?"

He didn't and wondered if he'd been so intoxicated that some of his conversations with her had simply vanished from his mind. It was all very unsettling, but his surprise began to ebb as he warmed to the idea of her company. Perhaps, after what he'd just learned, this was precisely what he needed. The research paper could wait, as could the basketball game.

"I've got Chinese food, a lovely Napa Valley Chardonnay, some sparkling water . . ."

"Fantastic—I'm starved."

He grimaced, embarrassed. But he had to ask.

"When, exactly, did I present the key—and what did I say?"

Laughing, she took his coat, draping it over the sofa, then patted the cushion beside her.

"You were exhausted, and we talked until four. Then you told me how excited you'd be to have me come see your place, and you ceremoniously presented me your key. Of course, I was honored."

"Tell me all about your day." The food smelled fantastic, the wine affected him from the first sip, or perhaps it was the heady way she made him feel.

He decided that there was no reason to tell her about the legal issue. It would remain his secret, at least until he learned more and could mount some kind of defense.

"Most people did fine. I had a tough case to intubate in the ICU—huge man who pulled out his tube. But we were able to manage it."

"I have no doubt, with you taking control, that things would go smoothly."

He laughed."No, definitely not smoothly. But it went. And he's alive another day."

She briefly massaged his shoulders; he felt eleven hours of stress begin to escape from his body. He wished she could rub the pain out of his low back as well.

As they talked, he found himself buoyed by her warm personality. She was pleasant, curious, and articulate, interested in his past and profession, wanted details of his daily life, even asked about papers he'd published and their impact. How many girls had he gone out with who couldn't stop talking about themselves, to the exclusion of all else? So often, by the time their date had run its course, his date had not bothered to ask one single question about him or his life.

In short order, the wine bottle was empty, another opened up, and they lay beside one another on the couch. Between kisses, Kurt found himself looking into her eyes, searching, probing the depth of those black eyes that shone with so much verve.

She sat up abruptly, took a drink of wine, opened her purse.

"I have more of these," she offered.

It was the moment to say no, to buttress his principles, to acknowledge that he didn't need any help recognizing the pleasure of this warm encounter. In her palm lay several of the opioid capsules, nestled comfortably in the pink folds of flesh.

He began to shake his head, confident that he could deny the offer.

But she immediately offered a tempting pout. His eyes fixed on her lovely expression, and something gave way within him. Between the trials of his day in the operating room, his backache, and the lawsuit that he'd just learned about, Kurt sadly acknowledged that he would welcome something, anything, to help him feel better.

"Just one," he conceded.

The difficulty of indecision behind him, his mood became joyful, his excitation laden with the promise of fulfillment, his outlook uncharacteristically adventurous. And he knew that he was now balanced on the precipice of a relationship that could completely engulf him.

A few more sips of wine, and the extraordinary uplift overcame every inkling of doubt he had. And they were again intertwined in ways that made him breathless for more, drenched, exhausted . . . every sensory stimulus promised new heights of joy.

# CHAPTER 24

"Well, good morning, Kurt!"

The chief, prowling about the office, found Kurt hunched over his computer.

"You're here awfully early."

"I am, sir. Trying to go through this results section again, make sure we've got the stats right. I'm still fleshing out the discussion as well."

"Fantastic. I appreciate the effort you commit to these papers. As if we don't give you enough to do, clinically and administratively. I think we're doing some very high-quality work in this division. Even the Dean noticed. You know, there's a ton of interest in multi-modal pharmacology and nerve blocks to reduce opioid use. Still, a lot of the presentations I've seen at meetings are weak—low numbers, retrospective, unsound methodologies. We should have something to crow about next year at the ASRA meeting. I believe that publication will not be difficult with this protocol we're working through right now. It's great to have you onboard."

He felt a pang of guilt. His contribution to the paper should have been finished and turned over to the senior author a week prior. He was not usually hesitant to fill his evening and weekend hours poring over the academic work. There was no other time to do it, and there was no way to stay abreast of it without delving into it almost daily. Let it build up, and you were swamped; in short order, you'd be behind on several projects. Then, the offers to participate would stop coming, and you'd be marginalized.

For some of his co-workers who'd fallen away, it was the family obligations that had held them back. Husbands and wives expected them to go home, play with the babies, help with the chores, take trips, work on school issues for the kids, and be available for talking, loving, counseling, and discipline. Kurt didn't have to do any of those things, at least not until now. He had begun to realize how time would slip away on the evenings he spent with Lauren. While they were sharing their thoughts, laughing, cooking dinner, or heading out to a restaurant, all of the time Kurt had jealously set aside for working on his academic aspirations was somehow escaping. It gave him a strange, anxious ache in his stomach. But he kept promising himself that, on the coming weekend, he'd shutter himself up in his house and catch up on the several projects that were weighing on him. A few uninterrupted hours with each, he figured, would get him abreast of where he needed to be.

"Uh, yes, sir. I'm trying to get all this done by next week. I appreciate that you were willing to share the opportunity with me. I should have this on your desk by Monday, at the latest."

There was an edge and an urgency in his manner, he knew, that the chief wasn't used to. The man was nothing if not perceptive, and Kurt was sure that he had divined that something was different. He'd just have to make certain he fulfilled his promise—nothing likely to stand in his way, at least not at the moment. He thought with reticence about a dinner his sister had invited him to, with her family and some friends. But that was easy to postpone; further, he could miss the Sunday morning cycling with his friends and, if necessary, could skip mass for the week. It would all work out.

"I realize, Kurt, that our lives here can get kind of hectic at times—maybe you need to give yourself a bit of personal time?"

There was a searching quality to the chief's voice.

"Uh, I understand, sir. I do try to pay attention to the work-life balance thing; you know, exercise, time with my sister's family, a date here and there, cycling with the other guys."

"OK, good. I just don't want you to lose sight of what's important. A weeklong delay in a manuscript isn't going to kill us. I don't want you to burn out. You're just too valuable to me."

At that, the older man patted his shoulder and ambled out of the office without another word.

He sat in the oppressive silence. He couldn't possibly mention the legal issue, at least not yet; the clinical mishaps were problematic enough. There was a reckoning coming. Perhaps it was here, now.

The phone on his hip rang. It was almost six-thirty, time to get out and see patients. He picked it up, preoccupied.

"Kurt? We're down at the SSOC meeting—where are you? You said you were coming."

How had he forgotten? The chief had pulled away from some of his long-term duties, delegating them to several of his trusted cohorts. The old man hated the surgical oversight committee meetings and was glad to let Kurt represent the service, along with his younger colleague. Natalie had clear leadership potential, but Kurt had never meant for her to carry the weight by herself.

"Be right there," he said, hanging up.

He then realized he had three people to see in barely thirty minutes, and one of them needed a nerve block. So how could he go to a meeting?

"Dammit," he mumbled.

Thoughts flew through his head, too fast to capture or dwell upon. The chief of surgery wanted to talk about the newly enhanced recovery program, which would surely affect how the anesthesiologists conducted their perioperative management. And Kurt would have to defend the anesthesia division in a couple of complications that the safety people would surely try to push their way: A respiratory arrest on the floor, in an elderly obese man with sleep apnea who had somehow fallen through the cracks, who had been treated by the surgery team with bolus opioids for pain, an absolute no-no; this would have been forbidden by the anesthesia team, but communication had broken down. Another patient with profuse bleeding but stable vital signs, who received a transfusion in spite of a reasonable hemoglobin level. The CRNA argued that the surgeon had demanded it, and the anesthesiologist had not been not aware of the situation. A febrile transfusion reaction ensued, and the hematologists were in an uproar.

He flew through the PACU, introducing himself to the patients awaiting him. His heart was pounding as he jotted a few particulars so that he could go back later to write his computer notes.

"Dorothy, I've got to go down to a meeting—set up the fem block, and I'll be back in a few minutes."

He was quiet as he explained this and didn't want the patient to know that he needed to tend to administrative duties. Then, tearing down the hall, he nearly collided with Natalie as she came out of the stairwell. Her look suggested that she was more than a little irritated.

"Nat—sorry. I was caught up in a research project, then I went to see my patients—I was just headed down . . ."

"I get it. You were busy. Look, those vultures almost ate me alive. I'm not sure I did much for the service this morning."

He tried to sympathize.

"I'm sure you did all right. I'll catch up with Adams—I have some sway with him. And I can handle Marilyn, the safety lady. I'll email her the details of the cases and then call her—It'll be fine."

But maybe, he thought, it was OK if he missed this one meeting—only heaven knew who among those administrators down there was aware of the lawsuit that had been filed against him. He did not want to face those inquiring, damning characters at this point.

His partner glared at the floor.

"Kurt, I'm really frustrated with you lately—you show up late, you leave early, you're always distracted. Usually, you're the first one here and one of the last to head home at night. What's going on?"

He felt a dull pain in his gut as the words reached his ears. He'd not been subjected to a peer questioning his performance or his work ethic, outside of the bullshit that flew at M and M, since he was an intern. He remembered when a senior resident had dressed him down for failing to show up at a code that he knew was covered by the on-call team, while he was admitting a patient in the ER. At least then, he'd had an excuse. But, unfortunately, he wasn't so sure he had one right now.

He could not help but recall the first time that he and Natalie had worked together on-call when she had just started the residency. The senior resident had developed severe flu symptoms and was sent home. The night had been frenetic, with little time for teaching, training, or coaching. He'd been moving quickly from OR to OR, inducing anesthesia, checking on patients' status and troubleshooting, when the trauma pager went off. There were too many issues for him to leave the OR and go down to see the patient in the emergency triage area. Natalie would have to serve as his eyes and ears, despite her lack of experience.

"Page me if you need me," he had told her, reassured to some degree by the look of determination on her face.

Moments later, she called, apprising him of the situation."This is a tough airway . . . facial trauma, blood in the mouth and nose . . . uncooperative man with elevated blood alcohol, and blunt head trauma with a GCS score of 8 . . . vitals are stable . . . but they need a head scan, and a tube, now."

"I'll be right down. Keep the patient oxygenated if you can."

And when he'd arrived at the bedside, she'd teed it all up beautifully, as if she was already a senior resident: preoxygenation, drugs drawn and ready, helpers designated for cricoid pressure and in-line immobilization, a Glidescope set up for the laryngoscopy, tube chosen and tested, notification to the trauma surgeon that a surgical airway remained a possibility. While tense, the process of endotracheal tube insertion had proceeded without problems, and Kurt was able to rapidly get back to the mess upstairs. Exactly what he'd hoped for. After that, Natalie had become a favorite of his.

The exasperated physician shook his head as he watched her walk away, fuming.

"I have been slacking a bit," he acknowledged in a low voice."A little attention to detail, and I'll put this all back together."

"OK, let's get this show on the road," a voice roared.

The chairman of the SSOC, Merrett Adams, back from his early morning admin meeting, was now on a rampage. His patient wasn't quite ready to go back.

"Who's the anesthesiologist?" Kurt winced as he approached the bedside.

"I am," he admitted, watching the surgeon, red in the face, pacing back and forth beside the cart.

The man was full of bluster, angry at a trifle, prone to swearing in front of patients. Most of the OR staff dreaded working with him. Still, everyone conceded that he worked very hard, cared a great deal for his patients, and mostly didn't avenge himself on individuals. Instead, he liked to make everyone in the vicinity feel threatened and ill-at-ease, at least until he calmed down.

"Kurt, there's no anesthesia consent. We should have been back there 10 minutes ago."

It struck him that, in his haste to make the meeting, he'd had a discussion with the patient and examined him but never asked for formal consent. Sandy was standing by the bedside, getting ready to take the patient back. She looked a bit embarrassed.

"I tried to call you," she mouthed.

How had he missed that? He glared at his phone, checked the charge, which was nonexistent. Probably hadn't been making contact with the charger during the night. He realized he should have checked the damn thing when he picked it up in the morning. He made a note to grab another battery.

The patient seemed amused at the display. Kurt presented the consent form sheepishly and pointed to the signature line.

"Apologies. I know we talked; I forgot to have you sign."

"Ha, that's OK, doc, just don't forget to wake me up!"

At this, the nurses around the bedside erupted in laughter, along with the patient himself. The anesthesiologist felt a reluctant smile spread across his face. It was the first of a few gaffes that marked that morning: with one patient, he forgot to inject the lidocaine and ketamine before the induction dose of propofol, which resulted in a shriek of pain as a red-hot sensation spread up the lady's arm; in another, he dosed the propofol on total body weight instead of ideal body weight, and they'd had to fight an annoyingly low blood pressure for the next fifteen minutes.

By lunchtime, he was frustrated and dysphoric. With a bit of time between patient assessments, he hurried back to the office, hoping to at least blow through the emails he knew were piling up. It was important to empty the box at least four times a day, or it became overwhelming by afternoon.

"Hey Barb," he called as he passed her desk, without a hint of enthusiasm in his voice.

"Hi, Doctor. You doing all right?" She cocked her head as he hustled by, alert to the change in his usual manner.

"Mm-hmmm. It's all OK. Crazy morning. Tempest in a teapot. Getting better with each passing hour," he assured her.

He went immediately to his email and began discarding the junk. But, no matter how hard he tried, it seemed the spam kept coming through, as did meaningless communications from the hospital, the department, the medical school, and a host of sites. The missives came from all sorts of sites—patient safety, ambulatory anesthesia, acute pain relief, chronic pain relief, ultrasound guidance. But on this morning, few of them offered anything he could directly apply to his life or his practice.

Then, as if to make sure that it had really happened, he gently pulled the top drawer of the desk open. The letter was still there, as officious and foreboding as it had been when he placed it there.

After a minute or so, the phone rang.

"Kurt, can you get in here? I can't get this blood pressure up."

Connie. A strong anesthetist. She didn't call unless she was really having a problem.

"Be right there."

He forgot about the text and the emails, ran back to the OR. In a few seconds, he was tearing into the room. Hip fracture, he reminded himself, an elderly man with hypertension, atrial fibrillation, some renal insufficiency, perhaps a bit of dementia. As he arrived, he noted the blood pressure—65/40.

"That's after ephedrine and four doses of phenylephrine. I can't get it to come up. At first, he was responding, now he's not budging."

"What've we had for fluids?"

"About 1.5 liters of crystalloid. I'm hanging some albumin."

"What's the EBL?" he asked, loud enough to be heard by the orthopedist.

"It's not bad down here, Kurt. And we just placed the components. I'm drying up and closing the capsule. I don't think we've lost more than 200 milliliters of blood."

"Call Velma to set up an art line. I'll get another IV site. Can you also call Ben? He can bring the TEE down, and we can take a look at the heart. If we're not responding to fluids or pressors, maybe there's something cardiac going on. No change in the EKG?"

She turned to the screen.

"Other than tachycardia, I don't see much difference. Maybe some minor ST changes inferior, but probably that's from the rate."

The heart rate had increased to 120s, at times higher, in the irregular rhythm of atrial fibrillation, which made it hard to interpret the tracing. Was this somehow evidence of a primary cardiac problem, or a response to low blood volume, or perhaps some other cause of shock? It was almost impossible to know from the physical examination, but an echocardiogram would help answer the question.

The phone sounded again.

"Hey, we're waking up in OR 7."

The ENT surgeon was finished with his laryngoscopy and vocal cord surgery, in a thin lady, with a small tube that hadn't been so easy to put in. He knew that to ensure safety, he ought to be there for that wake-up, or at least he should find a substitute. Trouble was possible, and a skilled set of hands was necessary to help the anesthetist if things didn't go well.

"Uh . . . I'm stuck here in 12 with some very bad hypotension. I need a few minutes to get an echo. Can you get another anesthesiologist?"

"Right, I'll see who's available."

He turned his attention back to the man in front of him. Just as he hung up the phone, his colleague came in, wheeling the transesophageal echo machine.

"Gimme a second, here, Kurt, and maybe we can get you some answers."

"How're we doing up there? I've got the hip capsule closed. There's really no bleeding at all. At this point—we're very dry," came the voice of the surgeon from below the curtain.

The blood pressure alarm continued to sound. Despite the colloid and repeated doses of vasoconstrictors, the systolic blood pressure continued to hover around 70, with the elevated heart rate bouncing in the 120s and 130s.

"This doesn't look good," Kurt said softly.

Ben began to push the ultrasound transducer tip into the esophagus as Kurt probed for the radial artery. With the thready pulse, placing the arterial line was a challenge. After what seemed an eternity, the red blood began to course back into the long, clear hub, and he slid the catheter in.

"Kurt, look here. The right heart is distended and hypokinetic, the septum is bulging to the left—you've got major right heart overload. Probably acute pulmonary hypertension, from emboli."

"Riley," he said to the orthopedist, "we've got a big-time problem. Gotta get him to ICU, we need to plan on an inotrope infusion for acute right heart failure. I'm not sure if we can rescue this right ventricle. If it gets worse, it could mean ECMO."

The orthopedist nodded gravely.

"OK. I got it. I'll be closed in five minutes. Then he's all yours. I'll talk to the family, let them know. This is pretty dire?"

"It's very dire. Maybe a life-threat."

"OK. I'll call Paul, too. He'll need a cardiologist."

"Yup. I think so. Connie, can you get help from another anesthetist? We need an epi infusion and a milrinone infusion—how quick can we get that done?"

Fat from the bone marrow, or cement that found its way out into the circulation, he reasoned, from orthopedic hardware forced into long bones, then embolizing to the heart and lungs.

"While you get those started, I need to pop my head over into the other room. It's an ENT case with a bad airway, they are just now waking up. I need to be there when the tube comes out, just for security. I'll be back. In the meantime, get those infusions running."

As he opened the door to OR 7, he could see that something dramatic was occurring.

"Kurt—I think we need a surgical airway, and now!"

Phil had come in to supervise the extubation in his absence. Apparently, it hadn't gone well. He'd just taken the laryngoscope blade from the anesthetist, who was busy opening up a new, and smaller, endotracheal tube. Velma was in their midst, taking orders and helping out. In a morbid realization of Kurt's fears, the lady's airway had simply closed upon itself after the tube was pulled, despite a look down the throat with the video-laryngoscope first. Sometimes, that helped, but it could give false reassurance. The tube stented open tissues that could collapse when the plastic was removed.

"I see nothing—it's completely swollen shut. Nothing is recognizable to me," Kurt's partner reported in a strained voice.

Kurt peered over his shoulder at the screen, likewise saw nothing but pink, swollen, irritated mucosal membranes. He could not see the glottic opening beyond them.

"We bagged her up well with 100 percent O2 before we pulled the tube—we're just hanging on with the sats."

The oxygen saturation was still in the low 90s.

"Can you ventilate at all?"

"As soon as we pulled the tube, she started to crow, and I tried to get some gas in with the bag. She was in trouble right then. She couldn't move any air. I put her back down with propofol and succinylcholine—I didn't think I had a choice. We still couldn't ventilate. Amy tried to get a tube in with a Mac blade, then we got the Glidescope . . . she's really anterior—neither of us can get a really good look at the glottis."

Phil wasn't one to panic, but he looked very concerned now, shaking his head. His eyes desperately searched the image on the video screen for some evidence of an inlet to the airway.

"Shimura—are you ready to do a cricothyrotomy?"

"They are opening the instruments," the ENT surgeon assured him."But I am not certain where the obstruction is. We would be better off with tracheostomy. There may be hematoma or swelling in the larynx itself, then cricothyrotomy is not of use." This he pronounced in his Indian accent, with just a hint of the London inflection he'd picked up when he trained in the UK.

The scrub nurse was busy prepping the neck with antiseptic while the otolaryngologist began to choose the necessary instruments.

"It would be very beneficial if you all could obtain for me two to three extra minutes."

Kurt looked at Phil, who'd just pulled the video-laryngoscope blade out of the mouth.

"Let's go to two-man mask, and Velma, get us a size 4 LMA."

"You think that'll work? It looks like the obstruction is above the larynx, to me."

Phil had immediately identified the potential flaw in the plan. A supraglottic airway in the face of supraglottic swelling. It might not be possible to get the airway past the obstruction, and it might be no more effective than the attempts at face mask ventilation.

"I had it work once before in a shoulder case-irrigation fluid from the subacromial space moved out into the planes of the neck . . . we got in trouble in just a few minutes. The guy looked like the Michelin man inside and out. The orthopod looked like he would faint when I asked for a surgical airway, and the man was simply going to die. We popped in an LMA, and the damn thing worked—just enough ventilation to get the saturation up. When I looked through the LMA with a bronchoscope, the positive pressure gave me just a hint of an opening. I was able to go down through that with a small ET tube. It saved a life that day."

"Lead on," his colleague said, stepping aside.

The saturations were now in the mid 80s. The team had completely failed to deliver any oxygen despite three hands on the mask, an oral airway in the mouth, and high pressures on the bag.

Kurt fumbled a bit, trying to stuff the small mask of the LMA device into a very small pharynx. Finally, he slid it in, though the quarters were very tight. The cuff was already taut, the pilot balloon distended. He motioned at Phil to hook up the circuit while the CRNA quickly ventilated with the bag.

"I don't see anything."

"The chest is moving! The chest is moving!" The ENT surgeon was elated.

This, after all, would allow him time to do his preferred technique. The last thing he would want was to perform a "slash cricothyrotomy" in a swollen airway, under the duress of worsening oxygen levels and impending cardiac arrest.

Kurt nodded towards his partner, a sigh of relief escaping him. With incredibly skilled hands, a wealth of experience, and a steely demeanor, the surgeon cut down on the trachea, repeatedly spreading the tissues and controlling the bleeding at each successive level. As he approached the trachea, he announced his position.

"OK. We've got the oxygen off," the anesthetist announced.

It was essential to avoid exposure of the electrocautery to the oxygen-enriched gas filling the airway. One spark and the airway could burst into flame. What the anesthesia team appreciated most about Shimra was his willingness to communicate. Not all surgeons were so willing to narrate their progress as they worked in the OR.

"I am entering the trachea now."

There was a rush of escaping air as the airway was incised, accompanied by a spurt of blood, then a gurgle. Deftly, the surgeon dilated the entry point and then slipped the tracheostomy tube inside.

"We are now having a tube in the trachea," he proclaimed triumphantly.

Kurt closed his eyes for a moment, trying to dissipate the stress, much of which had centered itself in his low back. He pressed deeply into his lumbar region with his fist.

"Phil, can you handle the disposition here? She'll need an ICU bed, ventilator and all that? I've got another crisis next door."

"Course. You're having a real shit-storm of a day, aren't you?"

"It sure seems that way," he responded impassively as he worked his way back into the other OR.

"Do we have the epinephrine running?"

He needn't have asked; the team he'd left in his place was nothing if not efficient. The blood pressure now stood at 145/90, a testament to the adrenaline's effect on the function of the right heart and the vascular tone that responded readily to the drug.

"How's the echo?"

"Better. At least we've got some RV contraction happening, and the ventricle is smaller, with better forward flow. I think it's a viable situation, for the moment."

"Let's start the milrinone as soon as it's ready. I'll bet a little pulmonary vasodilation will be just the ticket."

The ortho team had rapidly closed the wound and applied the dressings. Within minutes, they were escorting the patient up to the ICU. Despite the severity of the underlying cardiac dysfunction, they encountered no problems with the transport. Soon the patient was tucked into an ICU bed.

Racing back to the OR, Kurt almost ran into the tech.

"It's been a bear already—and it's only noon!"

Velma fully understood the kind of day he'd had, nodded in sympathy as she recognized her own stress level.

He rounded the corner into the PACU, took stock of his patients, and then strode into the preop area. There would be a string of patients to see, and there was no time for lunch—maybe he could sneak back to the office for a quick bite in an hour or so. But he found himself daydreaming about Lauren as he went back to meet the new patients. Somehow, he pushed himself through the afternoon, but his efforts became almost automatic, his mind filled with images of the two of them, walking, talking, and laughing away the hours in cafes or movies or at her apartment.

# CHAPTER 25

As the week progressed, Kurt's desire to see her became almost unendurable. The weekend could not come soon enough. On Thursday, however, he found himself in a cramped conference room, a woman in front of him transcribing his every word. His hospital-appointed lawyer was seated to his right, gauging his performance, while a brusque, sharp-tongued attorney from the firm of Holder, Kowzwicki, and Reynolds prepared to interrogate him.

"Just like we practiced. Be calm. You're a believable, caring physician and a good provider. Think before you answer. If I don't like the way things are going, I'll object. OK?"

He nodded to the man defending him, who seemed sober and competent.

The plaintiff's attorney began with a series of queries about his background: his address, his hobbies, his position, his honors, every educational institution he'd attended, every degree he'd obtained, and every place he'd trained.

Then, the man began to set the scene: "Where do you work? What do you do? What are your responsibilities on a day-to-day basis? Were you in the OR on the day in question? What was your assignment? Was it your duty to care for Mrs. Adams? When did you meet her? Did you review the record? What did you learn? Did she come through the surgery without incident? Did you see her in the recovery room? Did she show any neurologic deficits?"

So far, so good. Softballs. Kurt felt surprisingly at ease addressing the series of questions.

"Doctor McCain, were you aware that the patient had had a transient ischemic attack four years prior to this event?"

Kurt was startled.

"I asked her if she had any neurologic problems or disease."

"Do you remember asking that question? "

"Well, it was four months ago. I don't remember the moment."

"How do you know you asked that question?"

"I always do. It's part of the preoperative interview."

"And you ask, that, every time, in exactly that way?"

Kurt shifted in his seat. His palms had become very moist.

"Yes, I believe that I do."

"You believe that you do? Or, you do?"

He felt his jaw muscles tighten.

"I do. All the time. It's a standard question."

"What did she say when you asked her that 'standard question?' "

"Again, it's hard to remember exactly. But I'm certain that she said 'no.' "

"If you can't remember, how do you know?"

"Well, I reviewed the record . . ."

"And what did your preoperative note reflect?"

"It said she had no neurologic disease."

"Doctor, would you agree that a TIA would be pertinent history for this patient?"

Kurt was beginning to feel manipulated. He cast a sidelong glance at his lawyer, who was scribbling furiously on a yellow legal pad. The reporter was tapping methodically at her keyboard; the noise annoyed him.

"Yes, a TIA would be pertinent."

"Can you tell us why?" The man had a supercilious note in his high-pitched voice; he was quite aware of the outcome of this line of questioning.

"It would be an indication of cerebrovascular disease. A risk for stroke."

"And she did, indeed, have a stroke, did she not?"

"Yes, a devastating stroke. Hemiparesis and aphasia."

"With severe loss of function?"

"Yes, severe." Kurt bowed his head as he recounted this tragic outcome.

"What happened to the patient after her recovery from the surgery? Do you know, doctor?"

"Well, I believe she went to a skilled nursing facility to help with rehabilitation."

"And how did she progress?"

He felt a sudden emptiness as he admitted his ignorance. In the hospital, Kurt had gone to visit several times, but the picture was bleak. Once she had left the facility, he was uncomfortable with the idea of calling the family. He knew well that the surgical service had given the impression that the anesthesia course had put her at risk for the stroke. The family's warm relationship with the attending surgeon assured that Kurt and his anesthetist were held in contempt. No good news was likely, so he had simply waited for updates from the surgeon himself. In the harsh light of legal questioning, this would give the impression of utter apathy in front of a jury.

"Do you know anything about her progress, Doctor McCain?"

He shook his head.

"I only knew that she survived and recovered from her surgery, then went to the rehab facility."

"Well, as you may have surmised by now, she didn't survive for much longer. After she suffered an apparent cardiac arrest, she was found in her bed two weeks after her transfer. The underlying cause of death was listed as 'perioperative cerebrovascular accident.' "

"I see."

"Objection!"

His lawyer had swung into action and briefly had a conference with the other lawyer. Something procedural. The two returned to their former positions. Nothing had apparently changed.

"Doctor, as an anesthesiologist, do you have an obligation to maintain patients' safety in the operating room?"

"Of course."

What else, he thought, could he say? But he could not shake the terrifying feeling that he was being led down a line of questioning that would make him appear culpable. There was a "gotcha" moment coming. He sipped water from the glass in front of him.

"And, does that obligation extend to the recovery room?"

"Yes, it does. And I believe that I guided her safely through the operation and her recovery room . . ."

"Just yes or no, please."

He turned to his lawyer, frustrated.

"Can I not elaborate? There's way more here than 'yes' or 'no.' "

The man leaned in close. He'd obviously had something with onions and garlic for lunch, and Kurt winced. But the counselor represented security, and Kurt was grateful for his presence.

"You have to answer his questions. If you provide more than he asks, he can cut you off. In court, he will do this forcefully, in a way that makes you look less than credible. Try to answer his questions, and only the question. What needs to be elaborated, I will ask you in open-ended ways, so that you can speak more freely when it is my time to question you. Remember, we're educating the jury."

"Yes, my obligation extends to the recovery room."

"What about afterwards? Once you sign that postoperative note, would you say that your duty to the patient is completed?"

He had a sense that he should be careful with this response. The answer was obviously 'no,' but was the man laying a trap? The anesthesiologist decided to take the high road.

"In anesthesiology, we care for patients in the operating room and in the perioperative period. It's not simply an OR and recovery obligation. We screen patients days or sometimes weeks before they come for surgery, and make recommendations for optimizing their status. We treat perioperative complications in the OR and in the recovery room. We consult on pain management after patients get admitted, and we follow up to make sure there are no complications related to our care. So, no, the obligation is not completed when I sign the postoperative note in the recovery room."

"Can your management in the operating room affect postoperative recovery? In other words, could your actions and decisions in that hour or two under anesthesia affect the condition or course of the patien later?"

"Yes, undoubtedly."

"Take a look at the paper in front of you, marked "Exhibit A." Do you recognize it? "

Kurt shuffled a small pile of papers on the desk and found the one he'd indicated.

"Yes, this is the anesthesia record for Mrs. Adams' surgery."

"Are you listed as the anesthesiologist of record?"

"Yes, I am."

"For the entire procedure? You weren't relieved? There were no other physicians involved at any point?"

"That's correct."

"Take a look at the grid that displays the blood pressure."

He eyeballed the paper, knew what his next question would be. He'd gone over the document with his attorney in detail. Both of them knew what was coming.

"Are there any instances of low blood pressure—where the mean arterial pressure dropped below 55?"

"There are several."

"Yes, there are several." Triumphant tones sounded in the man's voice; he was leading up to something important.

"Doctor, is a reduction in mean arterial pressure below 55 of relevance? Could it lead to a vascular complication, such as stroke or myocardial ischemia?"

The game, it appeared, was to ask innocently if an occurrence could be harmful. Kurt had no doubt that the attorney was well-schooled on the pathophysiology and the recommendations in the literature. It was an effective ploy to have the anesthesiologist state the obvious as he squirmed.

"It could lead to such complications if not treated."

"I see. Treated how?"

"With fluids or a medication to bring the blood pressure up."

"And was that done in this case?"

"Yes. In each episode, we treated with a vasoconstrictor. It's listed right here on the record."

"So I see. Thank you for pointing that out. Please let the record reflect that the doctor is indicating the anesthesia record at time 0835, 0842, and 0851. This was the time of administration of the medications."

The typist looked up, peered over her cats-eye glasses, and made note of what the attorney indicated.

"Doctor, it appears that in each case, it took over five minutes, maybe more, to get the pressure up to an acceptable level. Do you see that?"

"Well, yes, but it can take a bit of time for the drugs to work. It's not instantaneous."

"Could you have followed her pressures and her response to the drugs more closely? Say with an intra-arterial line?"

"Yes, we considered that, but after these few short instances, she became more stable. We had no further problems with the blood pressure."

"Well, it certainly wasn't stable for this . . . almost twenty-minute period."

Kurt said nothing. He could not disagree. He felt he'd responded appropriately, the way he and his colleagues had in thousands of other, similar cases. Anesthesia almost always made the blood pressure go down. You treated it. It got better. The vast majority of people tolerated this without issue.

"Would the blood pressure have remained more stable during this period if you had initiated an ongoing infusion of the phenylephrine that you used to bring the blood pressure up? Could you have smoothed out this blood pressure lability?"

"After the third dose, we conferred and decided that if she dropped her pressure again, we would start a phenylephrine infusion. But she didn't. We were satisfied with that."

This seemed a reasonable explanation, but Kurt couldn't fight the sense that this line of questioning would be very damning in front of a jury.

"Can intra-operative drops in blood pressure lead to stroke in the perioperative period?"

Kurt grimaced. Again, he would have to agree with a statement that made him look bad.

"Well, yes. If prolonged and inadequately treated."

"I see. Would twenty minutes qualify as 'prolonged?' "

The physician took a deep breath.

"I suppose, but we were continuously trying to treat when the pressure fell . . ."

"Is it possible, even probable, that this period of low blood pressure contributed to Mrs. Adams stroke later that night, given that she was found to have very significant intracranial vascular disease?"

He thought about what the chief had said at the M and M conference. "Not probable, no."

"But possible, yes?"

"I think it would be possible, but . . ."

"Thank you, doctor. Counselor, we appreciate your time and your client's. I have a few more depositions, and we can look at a court date in probably nine months, maybe a year."

The two then began to make small talk about the state of the legal profession and a recent public implication about the misbehavior of a local judge. Kurt felt completely enervated, as though he'd been physically wrung out.

Exiting the room, which had become very warm, he tried to get his palms to dry off. Foolishly, he had not asked for the day off, wishing to avoid calling attention to the legal matter. He knew that the higher-ups in the department were aware of the deposition, but people tended to be discrete about such things. He took a deep breath and changed into his scrubs. A busy call shift kept him up most of the night, between emergency operations and epidural placements for women in labor.

# CHAPTER 26

By Friday, he'd left all thoughts of the malpractice case behind him. Somehow, when the time came for the trial, he would cope. He remained confident that he'd acted reasonably, had not violated any standard of care, and sought to shake any lingering sense of responsibility.

Once he'd napped for a few hours, he spent the rest of the day in joyful anticipation of the evening with Lauren. Of course, she did not disappoint him.

"You look fantastic!"

She demurred, tossing her hair.

"Seriously, that outfit really complements you. I especially like those lively colors in the print. Makes you seem even prettier."

She'd obviously spent some time getting the outfit together, accessorizing, making up, and getting her hair perfect. The skirt and top she'd chosen accented her curvaceous body.

"The firm gave me two tickets for the Penguins tonight—in their corporate box. Interested?"

He was taken aback. All of her virtues, and she liked hockey, too?

She flashed the tickets, he shook his head.

"I really like hockey. But I've never had the chance to go to one of those luxury boxes. That sounds so cool!"

She took his hand.

"You're gonna LOVE this. The view is perfect. Good food, nice wines. It makes you feel like royalty."

He caught his breath. Medicine didn't offer perks like that—too conspicuous, too tainted with affluence. This would be an evening to remember, he told himself. Yet, deep inside, he felt a little pang of jealousy. Who had she taken to the games in the past? Surely, she didn't go alone. Everyone had a past. It was ridiculous to think otherwise. Perhaps if she'd known he'd had a couple of very close girlfriends, one that he almost married, she would have been envious, too. Some night, during pillow talk, he figured, they'd probably both come clean about prior relationships. For now, it mattered little.

The arena was throbbing, packed to capacity, a writhing black and gold mass of fans moving in time to chants, clapping, howling along with the rousing soundtracks and organ music.

"Let's go, Pens!" he called, overtaken by the fever as they made their way into the corporate box.

She clearly enjoyed his energy, smiling at him almost continuously. Kurt sipped craft beers and sampled the cuisine, chatting happily with her partners. He was startled at how engaging and approachable they were and began to feel as if he'd been admitted to some secret society.

One of her partners, Almondo, a tall, dark, furtive man with deep set eyes, fairly drooled over Lauren. He was half drunk, and not in the least embarrassed at confessing his interest. He swirled a large, solitary ice cube around in a tumbler of single malt scotch, raising his ample eyebrows suggestively.

"Hey, Kurt. Nice to meet you. Lovely girl. Every guy in the office—hell, every guy in the building, wanst to date her."

"Right, Almondo. Every guy in the building. They can't keep their eyes off me," she scoffed in a way that suggested to Kurt that she was well aware there was some truth in what the man had said.

She turned to him with an inquisitive expression.

"Ignore him. He's had a few. Tell me more about your sister and her kids. It sounds like you have a lot of fun with them."

He beamed. His nephews were a bright spot in his otherwise mundane social life.

"They're really nice kids. I gotta hand it to my sister. She works her tail off, keeps a great house, cooks fantastic food, and manages to raise two great little boys. They're athletic and energetic, but they're respectful, you know?"

He was conscious that he was slurring his words a bit, couldn't help but layer on the praise for the two boys.

She nodded, somehow paying attention despite the near-continuous eruptions from the crowd inside and outside the box. Two back-to-back goals had erased a deficit and set the arena on fire. Kurt could feel the stamping feet coursing through the concrete and steel beams, which only served to elevate his own level of excitement.

The waiter brought another beer, and a glass of white wine for Lauren. She leaned in close to him, trying to hear all that he said. He was suddenly grateful for the noise, realized that it gave them every reason to incline their heads together to achieve a warm intimacy amid a raucous crowd.

"I love to go to their basketball games—they play so hard. You should see the older one—he's a guard. He passes like he's a high school junior, I swear. 'No look' passes and everything!"

Her face registered mock surprise.

"I'm sure that's astounding—whatever it is!"

At that, she reached inside her shirt and pulled out a locket. She quickly spilled its contents into her hand and pressed something smooth and round into his palm.

He was becoming less successful at denouncing the opioids, was in fact, beginning to simply accept them. For a moment, he looked uncertainly at Lauren, considering how complicit he'd become. But the enticement for the woman and the feeling he would achieve were extraordinary. Shrugging, he took the pill, popped it in his mouth, washed it down discretely with a swig of the savory black lager. And they did help his back pain, which made them all the easier to accept.

Just one of course, he thought.

She held his hand, watching the action on the ice in front of them as a fight broke out.

"Oh, Kurt, this is my boss, Stefan. He's Parisian, only been here a few years."

Kurt stood and acknowledged the handsome Frenchman, who immediately welcomed him.

"It's great to have you here—I hope you are enjoying it!"

A permanent smile seemed to have etched itself onto the anesthesiologist's face.

"Stefan—this is too much fun!"

"You are most welcome. Eat, drink, enjoy!"

He tried to imagine these sorts of perks stemming from medical practice. Somewhere, someone in this firm was awash in money, enough to pay huge salaries and finance this sort of boondoggle. Meanwhile, medicine was slowly being cut to the bone, a victim of its own endless expansion, and perhaps of its failures. He looked around the room at the little cliques of rowdy businessmen and financiers, smiling alongside their wives and girlfriends. He'd never been exposed to such society. It felt fantastic to be here in a raucous luxury box with these witty, fun-loving, well-heeled people.

She had her arm around him now, peppered his cheek with soft kisses and titillated him with some romantic suggestions. It was time to go, the end of regulation with the score tied. The hour was growing late. Holding Lauren's hand proudly, he craned his neck to watch the puck drop in the overtime, but Kurt couldn't get his mind off the sheer pleasure that he felt, He imagined that he'd transcended some unidentifiable barrier that usually cordoned him off from the profound happiness that could be experienced in living.

They were soon together in her bed, her warmth and scent fulfilling him in ways that he'd only dreamed of to that point in his life. Her energies were nearly supernatural; he found himself grateful when she finally sighed and drifted off. In the darkness, lying beside her, Kurt concentrated on her soft, rhythmic breathing. He contemplated the seismic shift that had occurred in his life.

His life had undergone a remarkable change: he found himself attending glittering social gatherings; glad-handing with accomplished, wealthy people; sitting near the front row at sporting events, gliding through his evenings in a state of satisfying contentment. How these joyful moments contrasted with his days! Hours of hectic scrambling from one bedside or operating room to the next, troubleshooting and fixing problems that often could not be predicted, fending off angry surgeons, coping with the oppressive production pressure. Praying for the last case to end so that he could recapture a semblance of peace within himself.

Kurt didn't have a proper grasp of what financial people did each day or how they earned their salaries. But he doubted that their existence was anything like his own. He'd chosen anesthesiology of his own accord, but every year brought new pressures and more innovative ideas from the administration on how to cover more with less, along with new requirements from the government and the insurers designed to reduce or avoid paying for services. As he lay awake beside her, he felt his deltoid begin to tighten and cramp and slowly pulled his arm out from under her sleeping form. Her skin had a sort of silky texture that thrilled him whenever he touched it, and she stirred as he moved.

He was settling down now, the golden glow of intoxication subsiding; his joyous mood began to ebb. He thought about getting up for another drink, perhaps some sort of a liqueur for the late-night, then saw the clock and gasped. It was 3:30. He did the math. He'd only get about three or four hours of sleep—even if he got to sleep in the next few minutes. That wasn't enough. He'd be miserable all day. Kurt began to curse himself for his foolishness. He realized that he could have kissed her goodnight after the game and told her he had to be home on Saturday to work on his various projects. But it was so easy to fall into her arms and her bed; her charms were devastatingly potent. It was clear that she was quite aware of this and could extract from him virtually anything. He turned and looked at the sleeping form, the tiny, upturned nose, the pouting lips, the supple, slender neck. He slipped out of the room, grabbing his clothes, hoping that he could see her again the next night.

For now, he thought, he had at least twenty things to do. Kurt tried to enumerate them. He knew that he was behind in many tasks that used to get done automatically.

"Honey, where are you going?"

He turned and was surprised to see her on her side, propped up on her elbow, the strap of her negligee off her shoulder. Her eyes smoldered; she was interested. Again.

"Uhhh . . . just got a whole slate of things to do today. Paper due on Monday, no flexibility. I need a few hours to myself this morning."

"But I can make us breakfast—eggs, bacon, toast, fruit. I have everything we need. But first . . ."

She patted the bed suggestively. This was a simple gesture that spoke volumes. And a commitment that would take hours. Love, cuddles, confessions, dozing, clean up, cooking, breakfast together, dishes. He'd try to push back, but gently.

"Hon," he explained in a soft voice, for the first time using that favored pet name, "my day is full—research, reviews, reading, shopping, a visit to my sister. Both my nephews have games—I have to show up!"

She smiled knowingly, perhaps patronizingly. Subtly but firmly, she was taking control of him. She cocked her head a bit; her eyes shined with affection and sexuality. A man could not escape that influence, and she knew this. He knew that she knew this.

As he thought it through, breakfast actually sounded fantastic. He wrapped her in his arms, felt the warmth and vigor of her body.

"You're amazing," she sighed.

"We're amazing. This is all amazing. I'm amazed," he agreed, pressing himself against her.

He'd once confided to a friend that "morning after" romance turned him off, that he preferred his mates to be showered, made up, coiffured, ready for the evening. But now, he understood how strong carnal desires rose physiologically in the early morning, and a woman asking for love was an extraordinary opportunity for satisfaction and release.

"Breakfast now?" She asked as they lay, panting, looking at the ceiling, and caressing each other's fingers. It was after 5 o'clock.

"That tickles—no tickling!" he protested.

She giggled.

"I see . . . you have a weakness. Don't expect me to ignore this . . . susceptibility."

She was on top of him, her fingers titillating his belly and chest. He curled up, howling with laugher, writhing with giddiness, attempting to get out from under, trying to grasp her wrists, until the two of them heaved and fell silent, lying side by side.

"OK, I'm off to the kitchen," she announced and sprung out of bed.

He admired her curvaceous body, outlined in the red, simmering silk of the lingerie she wore. It would not have been possible, he admitted to himself, to have framed her beauty more effectively.

Her panties were off, and he admired the dual orbs of her buttocks, visible just under the bottom of the negligee, rising and falling alternately as she paced out of the room. Lauren clearly wanted to treat him to the meal and to stay put in the bed until she called for him. But he wanted desperately to grab his clothes, brush his teeth, and head for his own townhouse. That would be thankless and callous, he decided, and put his hands behind his head, peering up at the ceiling, listening to the clanking of pots and pans and the running of water. Could a woman honor a man more profoundly than by cooking him breakfast after a night of breathless passion? This was a tribute to him, an announcement that he was more than a guy she was acquainted with, and who would be considered a special partner from then on, unless he screwed it up. He wasn't sure he was ready for the responsibility that all this conferred, but Kurt knew there was no recourse. She controlled the chess game now, and he was a willing pawn. Or perhaps a knight. But she was the queen, not readily challenged, imbued with destructive potential should he make the wrong move. He'd been in dangerously affectionate relationships before, but never with a woman who bristled with such power.

"Voila—breakfast in bed!"

She placed a tray on his lap, replete with fruit, an omelet, toast, and orange juice.

He eyed it, astonished.

"You did all this in 10 minutes? And all my favorites? Ripe strawberries? Where'd you get them?"

"I have my contacts. Now eat before it gets cold. I want you to come to the strip district with me. I have a fantastic recipe for this evening. I'm having a dinner party—you've got to be free, right? I'll make sure you are home so you can work all afternoon on your academic stuff. If you can come back at five, we can cook together. I've got Stefan and his latest love interest coming, along with two other couples from my office. They're super-fascinating: well-traveled, well-read, smart as whips. I must introduce you—please say you'll come!"

He was carefully calculating as she spoke—if he went to the strip for groceries with her, he wouldn't get home before noon. He'd have a scant five hours to get everything done. And no time to go to his nephews' games.

Lauren had her hands together, clasped beneath her pretty face, wearing a look of sheer eagerness.

"OK, sure. I'd love to come. But I've got a ton to do this afternoon. I need to protect that time. I can go see my sister tomorrow, I guess."

"And, just to celebrate the weekend, and sleeping, and all the fun we're having, I have a bloody Mary for you."

"Wait, hon. If I start drinking now, I won't get a thing done later today. Let me pass. I'll just have the orange juice."

"Kurt, it's one silly drink. It's very smooth, you won't even notice it, but I'll be it'll make you feel . . . well, smooth."

She was right. There had been times during softball tournaments when he'd started drinking beer before noon and kept going till well after sundown. Those days were a lot of fun.

"Just one, then. Gotta keep my head clear."

It occurred to him that he was saying "just one" more and more often since he'd met Lauren.

"What are you working on? Sounds important."

"Yeah—I work with Jim, my chief, on his clinical research projects. It's really interesting stuff, and it adds a whole new dimension to the practice. Sometimes, we just do the projects in-house, by ourselves, and sometimes we're part of a big collaborative group. Mostly, we test new drugs or compare new ones to old ones. Lately, we've been trialing a slate of drugs given during joint replacement surgery to try to reduce the need for opioids—they cause so many problems for patients. Anesthesia is so much better than it used to be—more effective, more specific, less side effects, less toxicity. We're trying to improve on that, maybe get to surgery without any opioids whatsoever."

He was eating voraciously, grunting with satisfaction as he chewed, brushed the crumbs from his chin.

"This is terrific. You're a really good cook—fluffy omelet! They don't make 'em this well at the diner I go to on the South Side."

"Well, my mom showed me how. She taught me everything I know in the kitchen."

He nodded."Yeah. Mine too. Though I didn't come away with such culinary skills. But I can survive. You know, the old standbys: spaghetti, hamburgers, fried eggs, meatloaf . . ."

"Meatloaf?"

"Old family recipe. It's superb. I'll make it for you some time."

She sipped the red fluid, watched as he downed his own.

"With mashed potatoes?"

"Uhhh . . . could you bring those? All I can do is cook potatoes in the microwave, like a baked potato."

"Oh, no. You have to have mashed potatoes with family heirloom meatloaf. I'll bring the potatoes and mash them at your house."

"Great—it's a date. How about Tuesday?"

"I'm with clients till about 6. Is that too late?"

"That'll do just fine. Me, cooking dinner for you! I'm nervous already."

"You'll do great. I have a Beaujolais from '97 that should go great with meatloaf. Should I bring it?"

"Sounds perfect."

He stood up and stretched, looking around as she went into the bathroom. On the bedside table he saw a pill bottle. It was empty. He felt a bit of a chill when he saw his name emblazoned on the label as the prescribing physician.

# CHAPTER 27

She reappeared, dressed and ready to go.

"You are such a sweetheart! Let's get you dressed and get to the strip. I need to go to Penn Mac and to Wholey's. Then, we can lunch at Enrique's—what do you say?"

It all sounded like so much fun. Kurt felt himself unbundling a decade of uncontested dedication to medicine.

"And, if we have a few minutes, we can go up to my office . . . I've got a super view of the point and the rivers. You'll love it."

"I bet. I always dreamed of a panoramic view to inspire me while I work. Right now, I have a gruesome, dirty little peephole that looks over a cement space between two buildings—and most of the time, I can't get back to my office to even look at that."

He thought for a moment about times spent at his desk, when the office was quiet, when he had no competing demands, and he could sit and think. That window allowed him to see just a tiny slice of the sky, and at a particular time in the afternoon, a bit of sunlight came slanting across his desk. That was precious. Most of the anesthesiologists he knew had a cubicle if that. A desk, a computer, a small office, a window—he actually had it made.

"Well," she admitted, "at least you like your job. How much difference does the window actually make when you're running from OR to OR?"

She'd somehow divined his own thoughts. It was getting a bit scary how often their minds aligned.

From her apartment, they crisscrossed a few streets and within ten minutes had traversed the entire length of the compact downtown. The strip was bustling, as always on Saturday mornings. The neighborhood had once been warehouses and freight terminals, with innumerable train tracks cutting through the streets and between the buildings. Now, the Union Fruit Auction and the other shipping concerns were gone, but the character of the place, as the "open-air market" for the city, hadn't really changed. Crowds bustled in and out of the wholesale shops, filled with imported cheeses, spicy Italian meats, fresh baked goods, and produce. The sidewalks were covered by a variety of purveyors selling all manner of foods, clothes, and memorabilia.

"Here we are," she pulled him into an Italian concern called Pennsylvania Macaroni. Kurt's grandmother had taken him there many times when he was a child; he would stand patiently and ogle the foods behind the counter while she ordered items that couldn't be found in grocery stores.

Startlingly, the place hadn't changed much since he'd visited decades before. But the demand for fresh and unusual foods had clearly increased. They mulled about a bit as Lauren pulled a number, but the wait wasn't long, and she was soon ordering the items she needed for her recipe.

She enumerated the other foodstuffs that she needed as they walked out, then set their course.

"Over to Sunseri's. They have this fantastic mortadella."

They squeezed in through the doorway, bumping up against the plump customers. The line formed a serpentine in front of the counter, then out the door.

"While I'm here, can you go over to Wholey's and get eight pieces of Mahi-Mahi? Maybe four pounds total? I'll meet you at Enrique's."

He was off to the fish store and, as he walked along, mused at how enjoyable it was to do something as simple as shop for groceries to prepare for the evening meal. For over a month, she had shown him how to simplify, to let loose of the anchor that kept him in his home most of the time, to explore exciting and fun aspects of life. There was a strange, dynamic interplay within him, one part of his nature pulling for more freedom and indulgence, another for regimentation, order, and professional preparation. His field was demanding, and he needed to remain well-informed. On the other hand, he was aware that well-rounded people stayed happier, longer. He wondered if he could play both ends against each other. But there was a strain in his life. Time was of the essence, and a simple breakfast followed by a shopping trip had consumed half of his day, time that could've been spent on so many other things.

Enrique's was quieter than the Italian grocery stores had been, a welcome respite from the Saturday morning bustle in the strip.

"I think, after that big breakfast—maybe just biscotti and coffee."

He nodded, looking fondly at her as she perused the short menu.

"How about a loaf of the rustic Italian bread. It's incomparable. I'm not Italian, but I think that this must be an authentic version of country bread that peasants make there."

She turned, saw the pile of crusty loaves.

"I'll get two for dinner tonight—favorite of yours?"

"My sister serves it all the time. I love it. She sends some home, and I warm it up in the oven the next day or two."

They tucked their shopping bags under their coats as well as they could, running down the street in a spattering of rain.

"It's the gray season," she laughed, "We should have expected it."

By then, they were at the base of her office building on Stanwix Street. An imposing gray edifice that dominated the entire block, the tower reached skyward into the afternoon cloud cover enveloping the city. Impressed by the clean lines and sleekness of the structure, Kurt followed her onto the elevator after she flashed a badge to a security guard who'd had to pry himself away from whatever distraction his phone offered.

"Here we are—floor 33."

The suite was palatial. Fine, dark brown leather sofas and chairs occupied the waiting area; a foreboding desk with a chair that was apparently occupied by a receptionist on weekdays.

"Anybody up here on weekends?"

"Not much," she confided, raising her eyebrows suggestively. "People mostly take their work home. It's just easier to work on the laptop than to come in here."

Pulling a key out of her purse, she opened a solid oak door with a brass nameplate on it, her nameplate.

His mouth fell open as the door opened.

"Now that is a view."

Hurrying to the window, he pressed his face against it, looking down at the figures scurrying in the rain, the colorful umbrellas bobbing about the street like tiny, drifting spheres. The office faced the Monongahela, its gray and solemn waters coursing briskly to the juncture with the Allegheny. Both up and down the river, he could see a procession of bridges as far as the vista permitted. The high bluffs of Mount Washington faced them, upon which were assembled a long line of houses and restaurants.

"Maybe the view from the Steel Building is better, but only if you're really high up."

"This is awesome. Must be very inspiring."

"Oh, it is," she exclaimed. There was enthusiasm in her voice.

"But like almost everything else in life, when you have it all the time, it can be easy to take it for granted."

She touched his shoulder lightly, turned his head towards her, kissed him gently, and followed this with a firm embrace. There was a plump leather couch in the room, one of many opulent pieces, a testament to the large sums that changed hands therein. In moments they lay upon it, exchanging affectionate murmurs, sighing, caressing, pressing their lips together. He sought her eyes, couldn't wait until she opened them each time they kissed, fixed his own so firmly upon them that he wondered if the hold could actually become physical.

They made love as the low clouds descended upon the building, ensconcing them in a gauzy curtain that lifted now and again to reveal the city and its busy denizens far below, oblivious to their romantic overtures hundreds of feet above them.

"That was electric," Kurt exclaimed, stretching and reaching for his clothes.

"We should have a drink to celebrate," she added.

"You have alcohol—in here?"

"Of course. Clients expect to be offered something, especially when we agree on a deal. I have scotch . . . an 18-year-old Glenmorangie. It's supposed to be quite "peaty" with overtones of oak and cherry. I don't taste all that. But it's delightful."

Kurt couldn't possibly turn that down."My palate is not so sophisticated, either. But I enjoy a fine Scotch."

She poured each of them a half-glass of the smoky liquid, presented his, tapped the glass.

"It was very kind of you to spend the day with me. I don't want to startle you, but we have like, less than an hour to get a meal together for my dinner party."

He looked at his watch, suddenly crestfallen. The afternoon had nearly disappeared.

Laughing, she chided him.

"Don't worry—I'll leave you to your devices all day tomorrow. You can get all your work done, and be ready for Monday. Meantime, we can have an evening of fun cooking together."

She suddenly sat beside him, took his hands in hers.

"I have so much fun with you, Kurt. It's . . . joyful. Like it's never been with anyone else."

The words were magic to him, his mind spun off into the future, and he imagined a thousand dates, a thousand romantic evenings, and moving in together to share their lives. The fine scotch reached into his brain immediately, and he was buoyed by her suggestions.

"I think it can be even better," she confided.

"Oh, tell me more." He sipped the bitter liquid and let it play over his tongue and palate.

Her eyes were somehow keener now, glimmering with a thrill he wanted to take for his own. Lauren was upbeat, unencumbered, adventurous . . . he loved all of those things, sometimes could not believe his good fortune. The woman was an excellent complement to him, to his tight, restricted, circumscribed existence.

"Do you ever have access to fentanyl?"

"Access? I deal with it every day. It's part of pretty much every anesthetic we give."

He was transfixed by her manner.

"Do you think you could get us some? "

At this point, she was astride him and held both of his wrists firmly, peering intently into his eyes.

"I have heard that just a bit of it to go with some wine or scotch—the feeling is supposedly indescribable. I had some just before my surgery, as I'm sure you know . . . it was awe-inspiring."

His head buzzed pleasantly, and this request, which he would formerly have regarded as simply crazy, suddenly seemed so reasonable. He assured her that it would not be challenging to obtain just a few milliliters for their pleasure. But it was essential that he carry this out with utmost secrecy. Detection would be disastrous.

# CHAPTER 28

He cracked the ampule carefully, removing its upper portion, and admired the clarity of the solution it contained. Peering intently at the delicate, tapered top to make certain that not a single drop of the elixir had been trapped within, he tossed it aside. He swirled the tiny glass vessel, watching the clear solution cling briefly to its sides, the meniscus of the liquid lurching to and fro. Satisfied, he held the translucent container up to the light and was startled to find that he was salivating. Within, there were two milliliters of liquid, less than half a teaspoon, scarcely enough to cover the bottom of a drinking glass or fill a thimble. One of these he would generously provide to the patient before him, an elderly man who was undergoing cataract extraction. He would administer this with a milliliter of normal saline with which it had been mixed, while crediting both units of the opioid drug to the case—who would know the difference? The second milliliter he would carry from the room secretively, take it back to his desk, and he would align it with several other ampules that he had requisitioned. They awaited him there, in a row, like a platoon of tiny soldiers arrayed carefully in the top desk drawer for his inspection at the end of the day. Then, with a pipette, he would pool the contents in a single test tube, place a stopper in it, and carry it home for his and Lauren's enjoyment.

Responsiveness to opioids medications varied widely from person to person, as everyone knew. And since the effect that a single dose of fentanyl would have on a patient was pretty unpredictable, Kurt need merely note that there was some justification—any justification—for the patient to receive an extra dose of the pain-killer. This would be a perfect cover for his surreptitious sequestration of the drug. He knew that he could easily find his way to the bedside in multiple operating rooms, providing breaks and lunches each day, improving his opportunities to steal away with more of the fentanyl. Kurt suddenly became the champion for weary bedside providers, offering to provide as many breaks and lunches as he could squeeze in, given his other duties.

All of this, he thought to himself in a moment of heady self-satisfaction, was a delightful scheme, if somewhat nefarious. Patients were not deprived of their analgesic drug—since they'd get all the opioids that they required—even as he exaggerated their need. And he could readily acquire five or ten milliliters of the fentanyl per day, which was certainly enough to fuel the euphoric, rapturous romps that filled his evenings with bliss. Of course, the cost of the anesthetic care that was billed to the insurance company was increased by a tiny margin, but this would not come from the patient's pockets, so he did not trouble himself in the least about the ethics of the arrangement.

A drink or two of wine in the evening, along with some oxycodone tablets, had recently brought him a blissful plane of existence he'd never experienced, perhaps had not even imagined. But Lauren had been right, maybe even understated the case concerning the fentanyl. This was a whole new playing field. In the three decades of his life, there had been no adventure, no victory, no achievement, no adulation, no monetary reward—not even a throbbing explosion of an orgasm—that had ever been able to bring him the instant joy he experienced with an injection of fentanyl. Even the name of the drug seemed magical, as though specifically created to enhance his life.

"Thanks, doc. I'm back."

He hadn't expected the nurse anesthetist to return from his break so soon. He fumbled with the ampule he'd opened, put his hand behind his back. To his surprise and relief, the anesthetist didn't seem to notice.

"He's doing fine, Ron," Kurt reported."He was moving a bit after they made the incision, even though they'd put an extra round of topical drops in his eye. So I gave him a bit more fentanyl—he's had the two of midazolam and four of fentanyl."

"Well . . . he looks pretty tranquil now."

"Yeah, I think he's finally comfortable," the anesthesiologist agreed.

He marched out of the room, having placed the extra fentanyl in his back pocket, hoping the tiny ampule didn't tumble over and spill its precious contents.

"So, what were you saying about the breakdown in defense in the last period of that Bruins game?" he heard Ron say as the door closed, conversing with the surgeon, who simply lived and breathed Penguin hockey.

Kurt's nights had become extraordinarily pleasurable. The woman, the wine, the high . . . he couldn't wait to get free from work to do it all again. But, as he walked down the hall, glancing into the busy ORs, he wondered if he couldn't enhance his dreary, day-to-day life as well. He knew full well that he became more mentally acute, more aware, more . . . decisive when he felt the fentanyl coursing through his brain. That he'd come this far, through medical school, residency, and nearly ten years as an attending physician—without discovering this key to superior existence—puzzled him. It was all so much better; HE was so much better. But no one else really got it, and he could not afford to be revealed. So, he would have to keep his enhanced existence carefully hidden, to be enjoyed strictly on evenings and weekends.

A few months had passed since he had begun dating Lauren, and his life was now inextricably entwined with hers. Almost daily, he sought her out after work, no matter how late, so they could eat and drink, talk and laugh together. Along with her beauty and incomparable eyes, she had a bright, sparkling verve and enthusiasm of which he wanted to be a part. Intelligent and articulate, she seemed to lead the conversation at every dinner party, charming whoever it was that had come over. His friends, her friends, perfect strangers at hockey games—everyone seemed to admire her, to crave her attention. Which made him all the prouder to be dating her. She'd elevated his existence to a lofty height that he had not previously imagined was possible; the alcohol and opioids were but a small part of it, he assured himself.

It thrilled him, just a bit, to be involved in this illicit, secretive endeavor. The label of the pill container he'd seen at Lauren's apartment occasionally flashed before his eyes: the information that was printed on it was also maintained somewhere in a digital databank, accessible to inquiring eyes. Lauren had recently made a show of complaining of ongoing pain when she visited her surgeon, and he'd supplemented Kurt's prescriptions with the ones he was writing. Still, using different drug stores and different providers could only mask the issue for so long—computerized databases would bring the anomaly to someone's attention sooner or later, probably sooner. Fortunately, fentanyl provided an elegant solution to this quandary. Nobody would miss the tiny volumes he was secreting away each day, and there was no need for a prescription, no documentation, no electronic trail to follow.

# CHAPTER 29

She glowed when she saw him, and he was still stunned each day at how radiant her face became.

"And how was your day? Any notable cases?"

He sat down with a sigh and recounted the challenges and stresses of a busy day in the operating room.

"And were you able to get a bit of our favorite, Ummm . . . libation?"

He grinned indulgently, almost leering at her, while holding up the small tube of clear liquid.

"Ahh, perfect. No problems?"

"No problems."

"Well, guess what? I was invited to a very hoity-toity fundraiser tonight at the Phipps Conservatory. Do you want to go? "

"I love the Phipps. Used to go there a lot when I was a kid, with my parents. They were both gardeners. It was smaller then and quainter, if that's a word. But even back then, it was the best glasshouse in America."

"Well, this is for some very wealthy clients who have been important contributors to the symphony for decades. It's got a Hispanic theme. You know, a fiesta—eating, drinking, dancing, live music . . . should be a blast."

"Sounds terrific."

He thought for a moment."I've got some curriculum work to do, and I'm revising a paper that a resident wrote, which I promised to have back tomorrow."

"No problem. We should be done by 9:30 if you want. Then you can go home and work on the papers."

"Sure. I'll pop home and change now, then be back to pick you up."

It was the new modus operandi. He found small intervals in which to do his work outside of work, but now he could barely fit his research projects in. Even so, he felt as though he was managing to keep it together; no deadline had actually been missed, though he was constantly scrambling to meet them. His newfound life was all very adventurous, and almost every week, he stepped out to do something exciting and exotic that he'd never done before.

Kurt was beginning to feel . . . important. Something he'd never really felt in his life. His girlfriend was connected to many movers and shakers in this glittering city, and he now moved among them. To his great satisfaction, the people he met seemed to accept him immediately. Kurt felt as though he were being initiated into some exceptional fraternal group that was ill-defined but which everyone knew was there, a social stratum well above the crowd of ordinary people. The fentanyl didn't just make him high. It made him someone else altogether. And he had to admit that he liked that man.

He arrived at her apartment at the appointed time.

"Just awesome.," He was stunned by her beauty as she opened the door.

Her hair was arranged in an attractive French braid, her smile radiant, her crimson dress dazzling. The gown was form-fitting and flowed flawlessly along the contours of her willowy body.

"We have time for a drink?

"Oh, yes. They don't always offer the finest of wines at these kinds of events. I have a lovely Chianti from '64. Does that sound appetizing?"

"Hon, you know me. I don't have a clue. But yes, it sounds appetizing."

How, he wondered, did she know so much about so many things? Who knew that wine made in some vineyard in the Chianti region in that particular year was so special?

"Well, it is, uh, full-bodied . . . and very aromatic."

He chose the words carefully; she was expecting him to fabricate something in appreciation of the blood-red liquid.

"Well, shall we break out the accompaniment?"

He sat at her table, placing the tube of fentanyl down beside two tiny tuberculin syringes. He felt a certain degree of satisfaction each day at having successfully absconded with it.

"I should have enough for a couple of doses for each of us. I actually have a little more for later, perhaps after the festivities."

"That sounds positively delightful. But I thought you had to get home to work on your paper?"

"I do, but I don't want to ruin our evening—I can stay up late and work on the manuscript. Honestly, it's pretty much brainless, just plugging things in, making sure the math works, citing the limitations. We've done some rough work already—I just have to bring it up to speed."

He took an alcohol pledget and wiped the skin of her underarm as she held up the arm.

"If you don't do this right, you can get a pretty nasty abscess. But we're not going to let that happen."

"I'm in your hands, doctor."

She fixed her eyes on the tiny needle, flinched only slightly as he indented, then entered the soft skin. He could smell the pheromones from a trace of her sweat; mixed with her perfume, it made for an olfactory enticement that stunned him to silence. He wanted to taste that essence, could not wait until they could come together later in the night.

The milk-white skin of her axilla had collected a few tiny puncture marks from their recent rendezvous. However, he noted with satisfaction that they seemed to heal rapidly, leaving only minute evidence of the skin-prick, one that could easily be confused with a hair follicle that had become inflamed after shaving. In his own armpit, he placed the needle just at the edge of the hairline, holding the hair back so he could enter the skin with as little trauma as possible. Somehow, he noted, the prick of the needle had become a pleasure, as his body voraciously anticipated the stimulation that would follow.

"How curious," he murmured.

"What's that?"

"That the pain I would usually have felt on sticking myself has been re-classified, somehow, by my brain. I know that the pain will be followed

by intense pleasure, so my body has somehow changed the whole message. It doesn't seem to hurt at all, but it did the first couple of times."

Almost like magic. The fentanyl transported him to someplace where
pain or sorrow could not seem to reach him.

"Maybe you're thinking too much about it," she laughed.

"Yeah, maybe. But what a mysterious phenomenon."

He felt an extraordinary warmth and the need to talk.

"You know, there are well-demonstrated models of the nervous system twisting on itself, but the adaptation is in a different direction, a
pathological one. Sometimes, when a patient is subjected to a painful
stimulus of some sort, say a fracture or severe sprain or even a skin injury,
their pain processing centers go haywire. The neurons in the spinal cord
set up some sort of 'windup,' so that, when pain occurs, it keeps perpetu-
ating the feeling, even when the stimulus has actually gone away. This
can set up a chronic pain phenomenon . . ."

"Well, I just hope neither of us ever has to suffer through that. We
should get going."

He was amused at her indifferent response and sat, smiling and deep
in thought as she donned her wrap. In a glancing sort of way, like a
disembodied voice within, it occurred to him that the euphoric feelings
he experienced with the drugs would have a downside, a penalty that
must be extracted—nothing in life could be so impossibly good without
a consequence. But the thought was fleeting, and he turned to admire
her fine form at the door, calling to him.

The pair walked out into the night. Kurt happened to glance up at the
summit of Mt. Washington, across the river. The lights seemed brighter
than he'd ever seen them. The church atop the heights appeared to float
in the air on a cloud. The lights of the inclined railways that ascended the
steep bluffs were likewise magical to him, illuminated ladders ascending
to some mythical place. They kissed and embraced after getting into the
car; the feelings of goodwill that the drugs engendered were so radiant,
so extraordinary, that they simply had to share them.

# CHAPTER 30

Lauren drove impatiently past the conservatory, which was brightly illuminated from within on this festive night. Each of the panes of glass that made up its walls and ceilings had been suffused with a warm, inviting amber light that beckoned to them.

"Isn't there a valet?" she wondered aloud.

She pulled over, and a young man assisted her out of the car, a statement of grace and elegance, her diamond earrings and necklace the perfect complement for the dress she'd chosen. In the darkness, Kurt stood, arms crossed, awaiting her elbow, a smile of profound satisfaction etched across his features.

"There she is!"

The entryway was draped with magical, colorful decorations and well-dressed people who were kibitzing, reacting gaily to each new addition to the party.

"Simply striking, my love," a large and effervescent woman commented, throwing her arms around Kurt's date, so fully encompassing her that she briefly disappeared.

"Miriam—you look lovely, yourself. Always a pleasure. Let me introduce you to my date—Kurt. He's an anesthesiologist with the University system. A real doll. Kurt, this is Miriam Forbes. Of the Forbes family."

He bowed and thought, "of course—the Forbes family." Benefactors, philanthropists, owners of limitless real estate, society page icons, and very high up the pyramid of notable people in the city. They were proud descendants of the unfortunate British General who had led his army to the confluence of the rivers, capturing the smoldering ruins of Fort Duquesne from the vanquished French 250 years prior. Unfortunately, he had only days to savor his victory, as he fell victim to some rampaging infectious disease here in the continent's untamed interior shortly after that. His family had eventually emigrated from Britain to the city he had helped to found.

"Ohh . . . handsome and intelligent!" the large lady bubbled, presenting her hand to Kurt.

He kissed it indulgently, assured her it was a pleasure to meet her, looked around at the groups of happy people. He found himself suddenly in possession of a glass of scotch and some sort of hot hors d'oeuvres that was quite savory. He was charmed by the admiring and garrulous crowd and found himself explaining his personal history and his longtime fascination with plants. Then, buoyed about in a stream of happy people, he ascended a grand staircase and entered a room that was steamy, humid, and filled with tall tropical trees. Papier-mache piñatas hung from some of them, along with festive chains of brightly colored decorations stretched amongst the greenery; a mariachi band played happily in the center courtyard. All of this gaiety left him delighted, floating in a nebulous ether of happiness.

"You must be Kurt!" another woman, resplendent in a gown of many colors, announced.

She was tall and voluptuous, given to kissing everyone she met on the cheek, after which she held their face close to hers and peered into their eyes. This, Kurt surmised, was some sort of test of sincerity, and he felt himself squirming a bit as she gazed deeply into his own. A photographer from the Post-Gazette stood nearby, capturing candid shots for the Society column.

Lauren had reappeared at his side.

"Yes, Delilah, this is Kurt. Kurt, Delilah is one of the co-chairs of the event tonight, so make sure you let her know how much you're enjoying yourself."

"It's terrific," he enthused. "I'm already having fun. And I just got here!"

The woman was effusive. "It's simply marvelous to have the both of you here. I hope you have a wonderful time!" Then, she moved on to another arrival, hovering until she could deliver her warm welcome kisses.

"Isn't this wonderful?" Lauren asked, carefully scanning his expression to judge his reaction.

"Oh, yes. Absolutely. Delightful people, amazing decorations, incomparable setting!"

Nothing could displease him at the moment, Kurt decided.

She seemed genuinely appreciative, squeezing his hand affectionately.

Kurt stood, nodding and smiling to each new person who came by him for introductions. He was struck by the contrast between himself now and in years past when he had often felt an odd anxiety at parties. By his own admission, the physician had been a bit of a wallflower, prone to avoiding large gatherings, much more at home with one person or a small group. On this glittering, festive occasion, he marveled at his own self-confidence among these strangers. He had a real desire to speak with all of them, to meet and greet them on their own terms, and to impress them with his verve and wit. What, he wondered, had he been afraid of? Why wouldn't such people find him articulate and interesting, an excellent addition to the guest list, a bonhomie who left only the best impression?

By now, he had lost track of his date but was content to meander through the crowd amid the stone pathways, checking out the many planting beds on his own. He smiled, nodded, engaged with each new, smiling face that came his way. The spring flowers, the daffodils, tulips, and hyacinths filled the bright building with a mixture of delectable scents. These had been arranged in captivating combinations with flowering shrubs—forsythia, dwarf lilacs, azalea, rhododendrons, vernal witch hazels, Virginia Sweetspire. In one room, the plants formed a series of fascinating designs, while in the next, they lined a long, brick trickle fountain, and in yet another composed a scene of a spring forest, replete with a stream, waterfall, and tiny ponds. The setting was idyllic; he found himself intently reading the inscriptions for each of the flowers and plants, nodding his head in fascination, trying to commit all of them to memory. No doubt he could fill his tiny yard on the slopes with similar herbaceous expressions.

At one point, as the evening wore on, he was drinking a glass of champagne that someone had placed in his hand while sitting on a low wall, which surrounded a planting bed.

"Kurt—what are you doing here?

"Elsa? How are you? Having a good time?"

Elsa was one of the nurse anesthetists, an ample, affable lady he knew well and enjoyed working with, especially up in Obstetrics, where she spent most of her time.

"Fantastic. My husband is on the board. It's great that you could come—I didn't know you were interested."

"Honestly, it's more my girlfriend. She's at one of the financial firms downtown—seems to get invited to a lot of charity events. But this is . . . spectacular!"

He was running out of superlatives to describe his experience.

Elsa was clearly in a playful mood, began to do a bit of a Samba as the strains of the band from the other room became louder. He stood up to join her, though he was unfamiliar with the steps. As they swayed and stamped, a small crowd collected, laughing and clapping. And for that moment, being the center of attention among these enthusiastic, inebriated people filled him with a wild, capricious joy.

Tantalizing foods continued to come his way, and he refilled his champagne glass as he eagerly indulged.

"Aha—there you are," he heard and turned to a slight tug on his sleeve.

Lauren had a small group of ladies around her, each of whose eyes were intent upon him. This, he thought, must be a vital introduction—the boyfriend presented to an admiring group of her friends.

"Ladies!" he greeted them with enthusiasm and a sort of radiance that he did not believe he was ordinarily capable of displaying.

"Bev, Sarah, Gina—this is Kurt."

"Bev, Sarah, Gina—it's a pleasure!" He took each delicate, bejeweled hand in turn, with a slight inclination of his head as he pronounced their names.

"Your dresses are fantastic! Each of you is as beautiful as the flowers that adorn this hall!" Kurt was vaguely aware that he was fatuous, but he felt it somehow fit the occasion.

The group twittered and giggled, acknowledging his compliments.

"Stroll with me," he asked, offering his elbow, which Lauren took graciously.

"These people think the world of you," he offered, aware that nearly everyone in the party had come to her to speak and offer respects.

"Well, every woman here seems quite taken with you. I'm a little hesitant to introduce you around. I'm afraid I could lose you!"

She said this in jest, but there was, he thought, an undertone of seriousness. He felt lighthearted and bubbly. But Kurt knew that this was a phrase that a woman dangled in front of a man with a certain expectation.

"That's silly, love. I'm here with you. I'm celebrating with you. I adore you. Introduce me to anyone, but I want to go home with you."

A comfortable silence followed, with a reassuring tightening of the embrace of their entwined arms.

"Let's go dance," he suggested, pulling her toward the brass ensemble.

She followed enthusiastically, laughing and sloshing a glass of Chardonnay. In a moment, they were gyrating in the center court, Kurt following her vibrant hip-swinging, then twirling her and capturing her supple body for a dip. It was a rhythmic, effervescent expression of sheer delight.

"Have we had enough?" she asked.

"I think so. Let's head for home. I still have to get some work done tonight."

He thought of the joy of being with her, the unparalleled fulfillment. Then he imagined the stark emptiness of his townhouse, without ornamentation, without color, without any of the meaningful décor that adorned her life. He could foresee his thin form bent dutifully over the kitchen table, working assiduously at the computer, the intense white fluorescents beaming down upon him. It was a painful image to behold, and he knew that little work would actually be accomplished. The warmth and satisfaction that she brought to his life had simply negated his prior existence. Something important inside of him had been altered irrevocably. He could not go back, could not immerse himself in the austerity and solitude that had marked his dreary lifestyle before her appearance. Lauren had, in a few short weeks, transformed him into another person entirely.

"Kurt, look!" she called out excitedly, turning to look back at the conservatory as they walked out the front door.

They were now proceeding along the sunken walkway in front of the great, translucent structure. The sidewalk was framed by decorative shrubs now bent low, cowering in the cold air, and by foliage that had sprung boldly from robust bulbs in the harsh weather of early March. A snow squall had dropped a delicate white covering over the ground, wet enough to cling to the branches of the still-bare trees, accentuating the intricate tracery of the branches and twigs. A frozen mist hung in the air, surrounding the warm glow of the glasshouse as though it were ensconced in a snow globe.

"Nothing quite compares to the Phipps in the snow, does it?" he acknowledged dreamily.

She pressed his hand, seemed pleased that he was as taken by the image as she was, and they turned for the car.

"Can we go up on Mount Washington?"

"Anywhere you like, dear."

He took the keys and pulled the car onto the Boulevard, pointing again to the strange beauty of the Phipps as they crossed the bridge over Panther Hollow. Kurt drove as quickly as he could through Oakland and across the Liberty Bridge. The same river, which had seemed so desperately lonely and depressing a few weeks prior, now appeared magical and inviting as it reflected the bright cascades of lights from the downtown skyscrapers. Turning onto the McCardle Roadway, Kurt revved the engine of her sleek, silver BMW coupe, tearing up the steep incline; she turned to behold the city as it shrank away from them, a brightly lit jewel of miniaturization. Turning onto Grandview Avenue, he then parked the car on a side street and turned to face her.

"What a wonderful night—could it possibly get better?" He pulled her body against his, they embraced and kissed gently.

"Fun people, Lauren, thanks for taking me."

She kissed him again, more passionately. He fumbled with the syringes and needles, and she offered her arm to him as a lover would offer her body.

In seconds, they'd both been served with the magical compound and kissed a few times more. He opened the door in the cold air, ran around the car, and helped her out. There was an immediacy about their actions;

it seemed somehow essential to get to the rim of the observation deck as quickly as they could. Pitching forward into the stiff breeze and the onslaught of icy crystals, they clattered onto the concrete surface of the overlook, footsteps resounding in the quiet night.

Below them lay the world, or all of it that they wished to see. The tall, slender buildings of the Golden Triangle glittered in the night, and the rivers embraced and reflected them dutifully. The lights of distant automobiles threaded their way through the ribbon-like, meandering streets. Breathless, they clung to each other and leaned out over the railing, trying to discern every detail of the city hundreds of feet below. The pair did not speak, but, excited and shivering, hurried back to the car. Inside, he could not remove her clothes quickly enough. She could not assist him with any more energy. Their impassioned embrace was energetic, celebratory, climactic—a soaring manifestation of the new life that Kurt had discovered.

"Why are you going so fast?"

"It's almost 1:30. I have to get some sleep."

"Why don't you stay at my place? It's not any further away from the hospital than yours."

He was frustrated and angry as the euphoric feelings subsided, replaced by a sudden and almost pessimistic acknowledgment of reality.

"There are only so many hours in the day. I thought I'd be home by ten, so I could get some work done before going to sleep."

She remained quiet in the front seat, carefully addressing the mess that her clothes had become.

"Look, Lauren, I'm burning the candle at both ends, and it's getting pretty hot in the middle."

"Well, you can always say 'no.' I can't predict how much fun we're going to have and how long it's going to take. Things got a little out of hand up there, and neither one of us was worried about the time. You'll be OK. You have tomorrow afternoon to work."

"I'm the late guy. They'll badger me with all sorts of calls. I don't think I'll be able to sit and work—I can't concentrate when I'm being paged all the time."

He felt a pang of guilt and was suddenly angry at himself. Those pages were his job, his dedication to patients and their problems. Kurt needed some protected time for his administrative work and research projects, but that wouldn't happen when he was scheduled for the late shift or on-call. The anesthesiologist was becoming ever more aware of the stark reality that his new, exotic existence was coming at the expense of his old, successful one. Something had to give, or perhaps he could carve out more time for work—but how?

Lauren was silent, sullen. Perhaps she felt that he was blaming her, and he knew he should speak up.

"Look—our time together is wonderful for me. It's . . . sacrosanct. I don't want to lose it. But you have to understand why I'm so frustrated. I'm not meeting my obligations. I have to stay devoted to patient care during clinical hours, and I'd like to have some success in the academic arena. But, right now, the way things are going, that's not possible—it's all going to unravel."

"I see."

She sat in silence as he maneuvered the tortuous roads on the way down the slopes.

"I just need to work this out better. I can't wait to see you every single day! But it's getting so that I can't get my work done. I need to figure this out."

Idling in front of his house, he put his arm around her shoulders, then leaned his forehead down on her arm.

"Surely you see what I'm going through. I just need some time to get it together. We have a date Thursday, right? I don't want to change that. But tomorrow, I have to go home after work and get some serious editing done on this paper. I know you mentioned a hockey game—I love those hockey games. But I can't go tomorrow. And Wednesday, I have a research conference—I'm expected to be there. Lauren, a bunch of things are coming due, and I haven't paid them any attention. So let's just go with Thursday, OK?"

She managed a maudlin smile, took his hand.

"Right. You get work done. I have a meeting late tomorrow evening, anyway. Let's plan for Thursday. Dinner out? And the Pirates are on a home stand—we have a great corporate box. Maybe we can go catch the game?"

A smile spread across his face. Kurt adored baseball. Even more than hockey. He imagined sitting in the box, watching the game up close, eating peanuts and quaffing cold, dark beer. The chilly spring air would mean little while they were warmly nestled in the luxury box.

"That would be awesome! Let's do it."

"OK, we're on. If you get time in the next few days, let me know. We could just have a coffee or something."

He parked in front of his townhouse and held the door for her as she circled around the car to get into the driver's seat. She leaned over for a quick kiss and held her skirt down as the wind lifted it, her hair flying up in the breeze.

If only, he thought, we could simply get coffee. Every encounter was fueled by alcohol and now the delicious sensations of the fentanyl that they injected, with magnificent lovemaking to follow. No, coffee alone wouldn't do. The elevation of his life experience to previously inaccessible heights was not something he intended to forego, time constraints or not.

# CHAPTER 31

"You're late again," Natalie hissed when she saw him skulk out to the preop area.

"The damned alarm clock—it's giving me a fit. Not reliable. I need to replace it. I should still have enough time to see my people."

But actually, he didn't. If things were not plain and simple, Kurt was going to get into a time crunch. He'd make it work, somehow, he decided, and cheerfully approached his first patient.

"Hi, Mr. Bucolia, I'm Dr. McCain. I'll be taking care of you today, along with a nurse anesthetist, Tina. The schedule says that you are going to have a total hip replacement on the right side. Is that correct?"

The man's English was broken, but his wife was eager to converse. She was animated, had an accent that he judged was central European, perhaps Czech or Slovak, with white, tightly curled hair, tiny intense blue eyes, and an air of both kindness and intensity.

"Yes, doctor, hip replacement on right."

"Have you had other surgeries?

"He had left hip one year ago over at Allegheny Memorial."

"Fine—did it all go OK? Any problems with the procedure or anesthesia?"

Her expression took on an air of gravity."My husband almost died."

Kurt looked back and forth between the two, waiting for an explanation. Instead, the pair remained placidly content to stare back at him.

"Died from what?"

"From anesthesia."

"Hmmm . . . did he have a reaction to a drug? Do you know which one?"

"No. The doctors just said that he almost died from the anesthetic."

"Well, that could mean one of many things. People get a lot of medications during an anesthetic. Or it could have been that the doctors had difficulty placing his breathing tube. Or that he wouldn't wake up easily. Any idea at all what part of the anesthetic or what drug caused the problem?"

The two remained blissfully silent, nodding to each other. This made it very difficult to proceed. Anesthetic drugs were reasonably standardized, but if the offending agent wasn't known, how could he avoid it?

He rapidly examined the man, noting that his airway didn't look particularly forbidding.

"Sir, could I get you to sign this? We'll send it off to the other hospital and see if they can get us some records. This surgery wasn't in our system, so I can't call the records up with the computer. It would really help if we could get the anesthesia record from the other hospital. You sign here," he indicated.

"And we need the date. Do you know what day it was, or even what month?"

The man looked blankly at his wife, who appeared to be concentrating very hard.

"It was spring. Sometime in the spring. March? April, maybe."

He nodded slowly, "well, that's somewhat helpful. We'll see what they say."

There was no secretary yet since it was so early. He'd have to wait until seven or try to find the correct fax number himself. He decided to wait and hurried back to the bedside.

"Well, let me have your signature here for permission for general anesthesia. But we won't specify what drugs to use until we get this information if that sounds OK."

The patient smiled and shrugged, signing the consent as Kurt looked at his watch. It was already six fifty-five. He hadn't yet completed one interview. Grinding his teeth together, he moved over to the next bed space.

In front of him lay a young woman, covered with tattoos, even on her face. They were quite vivid and appeared to tell a tale of some sort, with an oriental motif.

"Your tattoos are amazing," he said, introducing himself."I'm your anesthesiologist, Dr. McCain. What are we doing for you today?"

She held up her right arm and supinated it to show the forearm. Kurt could see an ugly and sizable abscess among the bright red and black hues of the tattoo.

"That must be really painful . . . Jaclyn. How did it happen?"

She leaned towards him, her green eyes damp with tears. She was clearly anxious about the surgery and probably about the injury itself.

"I shoot heroin."

"Have you used up all your veins?"

Her lips came together in an embarrassed half-smile.

"Yeah. They always have a tough time."

A resident kneeling at the bedside on the other side of the patient examined her non-operative arm. Kurt felt a surge of frustration. A new resident, a difficult IV stick, and he was already feeling the lateness of the hour.

"Oh, hi, Doctor McCain. I'm Jerry. I'm in my first year. I've only been on the rotation here a couple days."

Jerry was stocky, muscular, enthusiastic. But maybe a bit overconfident, Kurt judged.

"Do you have anything over there?"

"Oh, yeah. She has a good antecubital vein right here."

There was a cord-like structure that Kurt could see, outlined against the skin. That may have been just the luck he needed.

"Great—put in the IV. I'll run through the preop eval."

He began firing questions at her about her health, all of which were negative except for hepatitis C. He'd just turned away from the bedside when he heard her cry out.

"OUCH! You're killin' me," she crowed, her face contorted.

Jerry was struggling with a moving target, blood oozing from the skin penetration he'd made.

"I think I was in . . . until you moved," he said, a bit dejected and obviously embarrassed in front of the attending physician.

"Can I feel?" Kurt asked.

She gave him the arm, glaring at the resident.

"Sorry," Jerry confessed, bowing his head.

Kurt palpated the antecubital area in front of the elbow crease, where veins usually stood out.

"Jerry, I don't think we're getting into this one. Feel how hard it is. This vein is long ago thrombosed."

The resident nodded contritely.

"Alright, grab the ultrasound machine. I'll be over in bed 14. Get me when you're all set up."

He knew he had to move. It was now after seven.

"Mr. Lutadutz," he began, eyeing the chart so he could cite the man's name.

"Hi, Doc! Remember me? I was here a year ago. You took care of me. I had my shoulder done—I told you I'd be back for the other one. Here I am!"

A chipper, portly, loquacious man who was all too ready to put his confidence in Kurt.

"Call me Hiram! By now, we're old friends! I was hoping I'd get to see you again when I came back. What a great coincidence."

"Well, Hiram, it's great to see you again, too. You probably remember, we usually will start out with a nerve block for shoulder surgery and then go to sleep in the operating room."

Hiram was all smiles.

"Course, doc. I remember it all from last year. Well, sort of . . . I had a lot of drugs, you know. Some of the details are sketchy. But I do remember getting a nerve block, and you were showing me that ultrasound screen . . . then we went in the room and 'lights out!'"

"Hiram, has anything changed about your health since we last met?"

"Well, maybe a few things. I don't know if you can remember, but I wasn't really going to the doctor much back then . . . in fact, you inspired me to get more regular checkups!"

"Uh-huh."

"My new doctor sent me for a bunch of tests. You were right, I have sleep apnea now. I have to sleep with one of those CPAP machines, but it really helps me get a good night's rest."

"I see."

"I had to get a glucose test, and it turns out I have diabetes—you know, the adult kind. So I'm on two drugs for that, too. And I have to watch my diet. No more chocolate-covered Krispy-Kremes for me, no sir!"

Kurt realized he would have to commandeer the conversation, or he'd never get the man assessed.

"Very good—let me look you over, here. A couple of deep breaths. Open wide. Any loose teeth? Hold on, I'm listening to your heart. Try not to speak. Just for a few seconds."

This had the desired effect.

"I'll be back shortly. First, let me round up the team."

He moved back to Jaclyn's bedside and was suddenly crestfallen.

"Jerry, have you got a target?" he asked, shaking his head as he looked at the image on the ultrasound screen.

"I had a few, sir. I just couldn't get into them. The catheter wouldn't thread."

Jaclyn offered her own assessment.

"Yeah, it hurt like hell."

"OK, let me give this a try. Can you go over to four and get set up for an interscalene block? Find Dorothy, our pain nurse—not sure where she is. You two can get everything ready to go. I'll be over for a time-out as soon as I get this IV in."

"Kurt—can I help you get started? I've only got two rooms to start. I have some time."

Natalie. Despite her recent frustration with him and how well-placed it was, she was more than willing to help him. He waved it off. Couldn't be seen as weak or incapable.

"Thanks, Nat, it's all good. They're getting me some records for my first guy. I'll pop this IV in, then do the interscalene block over there in four. Got it all in hand."

She squinted at the screen, looked back at him.

"That doesn't look too fruitful. But, hey, take a look at the back of her forearm—isn't there something sticking out back there?"

"Well, most everything she's got is thrombosed. IVDA, you know."

"I know what that means," Jaclyn pronounced."I'm not ashamed. I screwed up my body something bad by shooting those drugs. But I found the Lord, and now I'm on the right path. I haven't shot any heroin for over a week. And I pray Jesus guides you to find my vein, 'cause this just sucks."

At least she could remain on the jocular side, he thought, palpating the region that Natalie had suggested. Sure enough, there was a vein that seemed patent and full of fluid rather than a scar. He nodded to her as she walked away.

"Yup, I think you're right. Hold still, Jaclyn. Just a pinch."

"Uh-huh. Everything is just a pinch."

He popped the catheter in quickly before she could withdraw.

"You see. Prayer helps. Prayer always helps," the patient announced.

"I can't deny that, Jaclyn. Thank you for the prayer. Now, we need to get you back to the OR and get this taken care of."

He sailed to the center desk, sensing that not only the OR teams but the surgical teams were beginning to show up at his bedsides. They sensed delay. Not good.

"Arlene—do we have those records?"

"Doc, they just responded to me. I sent the request to them. Probably be a few minutes. At least we know they're working on it."

"OK, Jerry, ready for time out?" Jerry had set up for the nerve block on Mr. Lutadutz.

"Ready, sir. I introduced myself to Hiram here. We went over risks and benefits, and side effects. He's ready to proceed. Now, do you like to do your interscalene blocks high, up by the roots, or a little lower, where the roots are about to form a trunk? I was talking the other day with doctor . . ."

"Jerry, just scan. Prepare to show me the anatomy when I get back." He was now short on time, short on patience, and very irritable.

"Doc, I've got those records," Arlene called from the desk in the middle of the room.

"Kurt, Amundson is here. How soon are we ready to start this shoulder scope?" Sandy asked, intercepting him as he knifed his way over toward the secretary to collect the records.

"Aggh." He groaned. It was getting very tight.

He turned towards her, his face red with frustration. She appeared briefly startled, realized his predicament, and moved back to the bedside.

"I should have the block in within five minutes."

"Why haven't you guys gone back?" He asked the team clustered around Jaclyn's bedside.

"The IV blew. We have to start another one."

"How can that be," he growled, looking at the swelling in her forearm." I started it myself. It was a good, clean stick. I told you to keep that arm at your side!"

He was nearly shouting at this point, angry at himself, frustrated with the patient, horrified at the circumstances. The preop area, filled with the din of busy practitioners checking patients and escorting them to the operating rooms, now became virtually silent. Jaclyn, for her part, appeared humiliated. A tear appeared in the corner of her eye, and she turned her head away from him.

He looked at her and realized she had numerous small scars on both sides of her neck, from sticks and small abscesses that had occurred during her drug use. No opportunity there. He sighed heavily.

"Kurt—go do your nerve block. I'll get the IV. You have to get these rooms going."

Again, Natalie. She was determined to help him despite his intransigence. This time, he had no choice. It was all falling apart before his eyes.

"You're a gem. Thanks, Nat."

He handed the situation over to her. As he strode through the room, he realized virtually all of the patients had been taken to the OR. Except for his.

A few yards away from him, a curtain parted. The resident stuck his head out.

"Doctor, I'm ready to look at the anatomy here for the interscalene block. We're just waiting for you."

Jerry. So upbeat and utterly oblivious to the situation unfolding around him.

"I'LL BE RIGHT THERE!" he suddenly shouted.

The resident turned white, retreated behind the curtain, and snapped it shut.

The few who remained in the room turned away from the scene, pretending to be busy. Kurt realized how red his face was, how much the resident would sting from that admonition.

"OK, Doc, I got 'em on the phone for you."

Arlene watched him, alarmed as he hurried over to the phone, a snarl on his lips. He caught himself, smoothed his expression, nodded to her in thanks, and took the receiver. The person on the other end barely spoke English, clearly had no idea what he was looking for.

The anesthesiologist now realized that he'd have to take the patient back without the record. It would've been beneficial but perhaps was not essential. After all, the man remembered no specific problems with the anesthetic drugs. The attending surgeon was already at the bedside, having appeared for the second time, glaring at the anesthesia team, especially Kurt.

"Kurt, can we not go back now?"

The man moved menacingly towards him, his muscular arms folded across his chest.

"Yes, Bob, we've just got to go. I can't seem to get the records—really, they're probably not essential. I think we can just do a careful, controlled induction."

He knew he was talking in circles. There was little justification for the delay of the case if it had been for unobtainable records that were unnecessary after all.

"Tina—go ahead back to the OR and get the monitors on. Make sure we have a Glidescope in the room. And ramp him up. I"ll be back as soon as I get this nerve block in."

The anesthetist rapidly unlocked the bed and began to move the patient through the preop area. Even Tina seemed frustrated and angry with the actions and attitude of the anesthesiologist. Kurt resented her steamy silence and thought she could have at least offered a word of encouragement. He satisfied himself with the thought that he'd never really liked her much anyway, wasn't sure her skills were up to his standards.

Behind the curtain, he found the pain nurse and the resident, tight-lipped and cowering.

"Jerry," he said, "please show me the anatomy. Start at the subclavian artery and take me on a tour of the interscalene groove."

Kurt tried to sound professorial, as though nothing had happened. Still, he noticed that the resident was trembling as he guided the transducer into the supraclavicular fossa at the base of the neck.

"When do we do the time out, Sir?"

He felt his jaws tighten.

"After you show me the anatomy. Can you do that? Jerry, they're waiting for me back in OR 11 to start an induction. I have maybe three minutes. Can we get this done?"

"Here," he put his hand on the transducer, encompassing that of the resident, and began to guide his actions.

He grasped the hand beneath his own firmly in his quest to re-direct the probe, and he felt the resident's grip grow slack.

"Keep hold of the transducer, Jerry," he spit out through his clenched teeth.

Now, he could actually feel the young man shaking. A hundred bad feelings welled up inside of him. But there was no time to address any of them.

"Just freeze, OK? Don't move. I'll be right back."

He had to get the hip case started. The delay was already lengthy and likely to be reported. Fortunately, the man tolerated the induction drugs without incident. After the endotracheal tube was placed, he rushed back to the preop area, where the resident stood, in exactly the position he'd left him. Again, he put his hand around the transducer, encompassing Jerry's hand as well.

"Here's the artery. You were too medial. Hiram, here, is not an easy study—you've got to push harder. Can you feel how hard I press?"

"I don't know if he can feel it, doc, but I sure can!" the patient quipped.

Shut UP, Kurt thought. No time for fooling around right now.

"Now, guide it up—follow the superior trunk to the roots."

The image of the nerves was vague at best.

"Can you see the C-5 and C-6 root? They're pretty hard to make out at this level."

"Uhm, I think so."

"Jerry, I need you to see them in order to block them."

The phone began to buzz on his hip.

"Shit," he grumbled. Clearly, they needed him for the induction.

"OK. I'll do this one. You watch me. The next is yours."

He didn't look at the resident, who, having spent 20 minutes with the patient in preparation for his block, was going to be very disappointed. He quickly injected some lidocaine into the skin and subcutaneous tissues, then asked for the block needle.

"And Jerry, I want you to inject for me. You need to learn to feel the injection, as well as guide the needle. Wait—this isn't an echogenic needle. I need an echogenic needle with such a steep approach! For the love of . . ."

Again, he felt the vibration on his hip, heard the annoying tone. He looked at the clock. It was now after 0730. While waiting impatiently for the nurse to bring the desired needle, he snapped his gloves off and answered the phone.

"I know, I know," he growled."I'm almost done with this block—I'll be right there."

His stress was becoming unendurable, and he felt himself losing control of events. He turned to the resident, now pale and wide-eyed, nervously avoiding eye contact with him.

"Tough morning, Jerry. We'll have more time to discuss things and work on technique, don't worry."

He tried to sound reassuring but wondered if it simply came off as patronizing. Pulling a resident off of a case or a procedure was considered very derogatory, something that should be done for cause. This was something that would stick with him for a very long time.

"Great, that's just what I need. Hiram, can I get you to turn your head and look over to the left side," he indicated with his gloved finger.

The phone went off again.

"We're beginning to inject, sir—does that cause any pain in the arm or shoulder?

"Nah. I feel fine. In fact, I feel great—what did you give me?"

"One minute more, and we'll talk. Don't move your head or talk just yet. See, Jerry, how the fluid moves into the groove and the nerves bounce around, floating in it? That's perfect. Just give a few milliliters at a time, then wait a few seconds, then aspirate and do it again. We'll aim for 15 ml, OK?"

"Yes, sir."

The curtains parted abruptly, and Arlene stuck her head inside.

"Dr. McCain! It's OR six. They need you NOW. The patient's blood pressure is really low!"

"Jerry—clean his neck, get him comfortable, watch him closely and check the block in five minutes—if it's OK, tell them to take him into the OR. I'm going back to room six. Call me if you need me . . ."

He flew from the bedside and down the hall as fast as his feet would move him. Barging into the room, he hustled behind the screen and nearly collided with Tina, who appeared anxious but somehow in control. The blood pressure was 136/85, not what he expected.

He faced her, an inquisitive look on his face.

"His pressure just tanked—I thought it might be an air embolus. Out of the blue, he went from 130 to 60. No blood loss; nothing happened in the surgical field. I turned off the anesthesia and gave ephedrine—he popped right back up."

"So I see," he answered curtly."You know, you've called me emergently like this before for things that didn't amount to much. I was in the middle of a nerve block—if I hurry in that kind of situation, I could kill someone. You have to use some DISCRETION."

For her part, the CRNA looked wounded, then indignant.

"Doctor, if I call you, it means, at that moment, that the patient is in danger. And I need you. I treated the problem rather than wait two minutes for your arrival. Should I have left the pressure that low, just so you could witness it?"

He caught her eye, angry and spiteful. He was forging no alliances this morning. Still, he had a case out there that hadn't gone back yet, and it was seven forty-five. Very soon, the next group of patients for his three rooms would arrive. He began to feel nauseated.

He snorted and left the room, confident that the patient was once again stable. On the way down the hallway, he ducked into the bathroom, emphatically locking the door. He turned to the dirty mirror that hung over the sink. The eyes that looked back at him were hollow. He closed his eyes forcefully, then opened them again, as he rubbed his temples. The visage had not changed. The morning had been a series of frustrations, none of which he'd dealt with efficiently. His plans seemed so appropriate and specific in his mind, carefully crafted to overcome the obstacles that lay in his path. And yet, they had been distorted, one by one, by the unpredictable occurrences that he faced. When he considered what was expected of him and the grave responsibilities he had, he grimaced. It was becoming his typical work face; a smile or even a neutral expression seemed an unusual and perfunctory indulgence.

"I have got to get it together," he pronounced quietly.

Taking a deep breath, he turned back towards the door, intent upon getting things under control with all the energies he could bring to bear. As he did so, he brushed his hand against his OR smock. A firm cylinder inside the pocket pressed back at him. Kurt then realized that he'd picked up the fentanyl syringe just as they were completing the last nerve block, and had not said a word to the others. He reached into the jacket pocket, pulled out the drug, and held the syringe up to the bare, dingy light bulb.

Perhaps the time had come, he reasoned, to improve his disposition here at the hospital. The hours, the trainees, the patients, the uncertainty—they all offered their own brand of stress. He'd been internalizing these for years. Why not smooth them over with a bit of a chemical indulgence? Indeed, on a day like this, he could not come up with a reason to withhold this eminent satisfaction from himself. A warm smile spread instantly across his face, and he regarded this change of expression in the mirror with a feeling akin to pride. His morning would soon be glorious.

Slipping off his jacket, he lifted his arm and let the sleeve of his scrub shirt slide up towards his axilla. He inserted the fine needle into the skin and then just a bit deeper, using his index finger to depress the plunger. The pale skin swelled slightly as the tiny volume of fentanyl collected beneath the dermis. If there was pain from the injection, he was blissfully unaware of it, looking fondly at the rivulet of blood that trickled out as the needle was removed. Holding pressure on the spot, he collected his thoughts. This represented an almost inconceivable breach of his duties and responsibilities. But, somehow, he didn't care. It was something that he NEEDED to do. Now, with satisfaction spreading rapidly through him, he figured it was time to put the day into reverse.

The phone rang again.

"Doctor McCain, it's me, Tina, in Six again."

There was a pause as if she expected him to admonish her.

"Well, these episodes of hypotension keep recurring," she continued."There's no blood loss, no changes in the EKG, no change in the heart rate or saturation. I think the guy is just unstable under anesthesia. Maybe this is what happened last year at Allegheny. Should I hang a phenylephrine infusion . . ."

Her voice was high-pitched and wavering. She was clearly afraid of making him angry again.

Within seconds, he was in the room, addressing her, scanning the monitors and the patient.

"I see nothing really sinister here. I think that a neo infusion makes perfect sense. I'm glad you thought of it. Can I help you set it up?

She was immediately taken aback at his willingness to assist but took him up on his offer.

"Need me to program the pump?" he called enthusiastically over his shoulder as he hung the infusion on the IV pole.

"I'll be back in a few to check in on you. Meanwhile, let me get back out there and see the next patient. And I think you're doing a fine job providing anesthesia for this man, given the unpredictable responses!"

He simply couldn't hide the enthusiasm in his voice. Noting that the blood pressure had quickly rebounded with the injection of the vasoconstrictor, Kurt then turned and headed for the preop area.

He entered to find his resident cleaning the ultrasound machine, making ready for the next block.

"Jerry!" he called.

The resident appeared to jump several inches off the ground, then turned to face him.

"I just went by OR 9. They're just getting started. The block is set up perfectly. Great job—we'll get you more involved with the next one."

He patted the puzzled young physician on the shoulder.

Effusively, he offered his sunny observations to almost everyone in the preoperative area. The shift in his persona was so significant that Arlene pulled him aside.

"Doc, are you . . . OK?"

"Of course I am, Arlene. I'm absolutely fine. Just got off on the wrong foot this morning—dominoes toppled in the wrong direction. Once we got things off the ground, it all fell into place. I have to thank you for getting that anesthesia record for me—it really helped!"

"Well, it was a little late, I'm afraid."

He took this cheerfully in stride, "But you got it, and that's exactly what I needed."

He marched over to his next patient and loudly introduced himself. Kurt was suddenly unquenchably chipper, ebullient almost to a fault. His eyes twinkled, and his face shone with irrepressible joy.

The man would undergo a shoulder arthroscopy to repair a torn rotator cuff. He noted that he was constantly in pain, had been miserable since the tear occurred while lifting bags of mulch out of his car two weeks earlier.

"No rest, doc, no sleep. I'm in pain all the time. I can't find a comfortable position, I swear. I sleep in a damned recliner."

"Sir, you've come to the right place. Dr. Amundson is a superb orthopedist. And we're going to take great care of you."

"Jerry, let's do it!" He called ceremoniously, filling the room with his booming voice.

Jerry quickly appeared, pushing a small table covered with the necessary equipment, trailing the ultrasound machine. Dorothy, indefatigable as she glided from one bed space to the next, joined them.

"And now, Dr. Jerry, here, will demonstrate the superior trunk and the C-5 and C-6 nerve roots for us."

Taking his cue, Jerry used the ultrasound transducer to trace the nerves up to the level of the appropriate nerve roots in the middle portion of the man's neck.

"Superb, Jerry. Absolutely perfect. That's exactly where I would have chosen to perform the block. By the way, sir. Great anatomy! We appreciate that!"

While Kurt directed the placement of the local anesthetic, he became keenly aware of his stature. He was shining so brightly, his delight was so infectious that no one in the room could avoid paying attention to him.

As he looked back at the last two hours, he wondered how he could have been so morose, so downcast, when life held so many fine things for him.

He sat at the desk to type his notes, and Arlene leaned over to him, speaking in a subdued tone.

"And, what's this I hear you have a girlfriend? What's she like?"

He propped his elbows on the desktop and turned his gaze towards her, supporting his chin gently in his hands.

"She's absolutely wonderful. I can't tell you how's she's changed my life. Every night, I can't wait to go and see her. We do so many fun things—she actually likes sports, and she cooks, and she has terrific friends"

"Sounds like you may have finally found the right girl," the other offered.

"I think I have. I really think I have."

The phone on his hip buzzed for what seemed the twentieth time that morning.

"Hmm . . . Ready to wake up OK, I'll be right there!"

He'd secured another ration of the fentanyl during the sedation process for the last block. Soon, he administered it to himself in the bathroom, on the way to the OR. He could almost count the individual molecules as they entered his bloodstream and proceeded to his brain.

"Kurt!"

He turned to find the general surgeon who'd lanced Jaclyn's abscess proceeding menacingly in his direction. There was nothing to do but weather the storm. He leaned into it, pulled off his mask, greeted the angry man with a smile.

"Why did that case get off the ground so late? I work till noon, then I have office hours. I need to have my cases in the room on time—is that understood? If you can't do that, I'll talk to your chief, and maybe he can find someone who can."

"Ken, there's no excuse, really. I didn't get the IV in as quickly as I should've. In fact, I should have pulled out the ultrasound earlier. I'll surely do that if I encounter another challenging patient like her."

The man's eyes narrowed as though he were momentarily confused by what appeared to be a sincere apology and admission of responsibility. Grumbling an acceptance of what the anesthesiologist said, he pushed past him.

The anesthesiologist made his way back to the room where the hip replacement was ongoing, only to find that the surgeon had just finished the case. Tina had made ready to awaken the patient. The suction made a loud slurping noise as she shoved it deep into the pharynx, and the man turned his head violently from side to side.

"OK, let's pull it. We have to get this room turned over," Kurt said, with a note of urgency, grasping the endotracheal tube and removing it.

He turned to the machine, began pulling apart the circuit and suction.

The startled anesthetist wheeled the patient out the door while he furiously began to set up items for the next case. At the very least, he would make sure that the anesthesia was set up and ready to go. If there was to be a delay, it wasn't going to be on his watch.

He chatted merrily with the OR team while making preparations. He felt he could work steadily, energetically, without interruption, all day, perhaps all night. An extraordinary sense of accomplishment coursed through his entire being, and his surroundings simply glowed. His co-workers were more affable, their conversation more interesting, the lighting in the room more pleasing than he'd ever noticed before.

"Kurt, we have to talk."

Natalie had stuck her head in the door as he finished his preparations. She looked frantic.

"You have two patients out there that you haven't even seen yet! Why are you doing the techs' job? I can only help you out, so much—I've gotta get up to OB."

She focused her fine, dark eyes on his, looked puzzled, then concerned.

"Are you all right? Are you sick?"

"Nat, I'm fine. Better than fine. I've got this under control. I had to get the room ready—the orthopedist was ready to tear my head off. Mind you, he had his reasons. Can I help you? Can I cover your rooms while you're up there?"

She looked defeated.

"I just need you to see your own patients. Farrokh has my rooms till I get back. Now get down there before they start calling you."

"Nat. I can do the morning breaks for your rooms. I'll let the charge CRNA know."

She turned, shook her head.

"Kurt, you're not going to have time for that. I think we have enough people to do breaks."

"Well, I can help. I'll just offer. I can do the breaks in my rooms, too."

The day somehow contracted as he meandered happily through it, and he found himself bidding his colleagues and the surgeons a good evening. His soul brimming with felicity, he sat at his desk and cast a glance outside, peering at the tiny slice of sky that was permitted him. Gray clouds hung low over the city, a curtain of rain sweeping down upon the downtown and fast approaching the East End.

# CHAPTER 32

"Another beautiful day of liquid Pittsburgh sunshine, hey, Kurt?"

"Hello, Sir!" he said, looking over his shoulder at the chief, who was, as usual, working until late in the evening.

"I'm glad I caught you. I have to talk to you about something."

"You bet, sir,"

He turned to face his superior, looking him squarely in the face. He wondered if the chief was going to bring up the legal matter.

"Kurt, a couple of surgeons have complained to me about things not getting started on time in the mornings—today, and a couple of other days. Most of these were about you. And this is extremely uncharacteristic of your performance. I've known you for seven years—is there something going on? Something personal? Something I could help you with? You're a strong point in my division, and I need that to continue. Can you talk about it?"

The chief didn't flinch, sat motionless, concentrating on Kurt's expressions and demeanor.

"I've had a problem with my alarm. Twice, it failed me, and I got here a half-hour late. I really struggled to get the cases started on time, and I had a few of them start late. I thought I made up for it later in the day, but I can't blame the surgeons for being pissed off . . ."

"Is something else going on in your life? You've been a model of dedication. Maybe too dedicated—it had to end at some point. But this is destructive, you know that. We can't have a continuation of this . . . behavior."

There was a somber gravity etched into the chief's face as he pronounced this. Kurt understood that there could be no tolerance of repeated failures to get patients to the OR on time.

"Yes, sir . . . uh, Jim. I've replaced the clock, of course. I expect to be here in plenty of time."

"Anything else amiss in your life? This seems bigger than an alarm clock."

He bowed his head, felt the chief's eyes boring into him.

When he looked up, the eyes had not moved.

"Well, sir, I do have a girlfriend, and I've been spending more time with her. That may have played a role in being late. But I have it under control, really, I do."

The older man nodded, stayed silent, waited for Kurt to continue.

"She's a doll. Really special. Filling my life. It's never been like this," he explained.

"Kurt, that's terrific. I'm happy for you. But don't let passion control you. You control it. Period. You're a doctor. That's a high calling. And a fine anesthesiologist. Don't let the profession slip away from you."

He felt sick inside.

"No, sir."

Left alone in the silent office, he considered where he was—in the last month, he had witnessed a startling transformation in his life. He meant something to somebody, knew that he was essential in her life in a way he'd never been to anyone before. And she'd opened his eyes to stimulation that had brought him to a different place entirely; he felt that he'd become a part of some celestial orbit that others could not perceive. On this day, after a disastrous start, a few doses of fentanyl, spaced out in the morning and the afternoon, had changed everything. This clandestine ritual would now be a pillar of his unflinching dedication to his patients, of his amiable relationships with co-workers, of his unstinting vigilance for those under anesthesia.

He felt his hip pocket, where there was a syringe with ten milliliters of the magic draught, a cap tightly twisted onto its tip so that not a single drop could escape. He thought with a deep desire of the pleasure that he would have with Lauren this night. At the same time, he admonished himself for getting to bed so late. Guilt briefly surfaced within him, a bit of lingering doubt that he somehow kept managing to suppress. The demands of the woman and those of the profession were so often in direct conflict! But the fentanyl would surely make up for his shortcomings. They would all soon see: Kurt McCain had become a new man.

# CHAPTER 33

When Thursday arrived, Kurt was pleased to find that the afternoon grand rounds conference was canceled. His OR day ended relatively early, and he drove to Lauren's apartment to discuss dinner plans.

"Italian tonight? Maybe La Scala? Pasta and Zinfandel, perhaps tiramisu for dessert?" she suggested, playing gently with his hair as they lay together on the bed in her room.

"That sounds wonderful. Meatballs, or sausage—or maybe both. The bread, the red sauce, the wine."

He sighed lustily, imagining the gustatory indulgence, then pulled the covers up over both of them.

"What's the matter?"

"I do have to pay more attention to my hours and my sleep. I've shown up twice this week on the late side, and people are beginning to notice."

"Really? Who? What people? Have you actually been late? Or just later than usual? You strike me as an incredibly punctual person."

"Yeah, I am. Well, I used to be. All three of my cases started late a couple days ago. A series of minor glitches, but all of them held me up. I was under so much stress I thought my head would blow up. I got it together by mid-morning, but I caught it from one of the surgeons and from the chief."

She reacted, surprised.

"I thought he was such a supporter of yours."

"He usually is. And he went out of his way to compliment me. But he's got to make things happen on time. All of the service chiefs are under a lot of pressure—everybody is watching from on high. These things get reported, and surgeons complain to administrators. He probably could have been a lot harder on me than he was."

"Well, let's go drown your sorrows. Get dressed, and I'll call La Scala," she offered, then looked at him, teasingly."Do we have something for a little extra fun?"

"Absolutely."

He produced the syringe and quickly injected a small volume of the drug into each of them.

"Doesn't take long, does it?"

"No, it's simply superb."

They embraced, kissed quickly, and proceeded to dress.

The Italian food was better than either remembered, the Zinfandel the perfect complement, the service starched-white and supremely attentive.

"I have these seats in the Box for the Pirates," she said, holding up the magic pair."And the Yanks are here. Are you sure you can still go?"

He grimaced.

"I'd love to go. But I can't afford another short night." He contemplated for a moment.

"Let's see . . . 7:30 start, about three hours, that gets me home a little after eleven. I'll have to get right to bed. But I can do it!"

Deep inside, there was a hint of a misgiving—what if the game went long, or there was a rain delay? But he quickly suppressed the notion, thought of the beer, the excitement, the camaraderie. He could not imagine missing this opportunity.

"Let's see. Tomorrow night, I'm late. Then I have to go home and work on this grant for a study—I should've had this back to the chief last week. He hasn't mentioned it, but I know he's looking for it."

Time was becoming very precious; Kurt moved the days and evenings around on his calendar like numbers in a slide puzzle, constantly seeking a few hours of free time for people and activities.

"OK, love. But didn't you tell me that your sister was having us for dinner tomorrow night?"

He froze, startled.

"Ahhh. You're right—that is tomorrow. I figured I could get there by seven. How could I forget? I'll have to call her and postpone it."

"You did that last week. You were going to introduce us tomorrow."

He closed his eyes, thought through the possibilities.

"Maybe I can get some quality work time in on Saturday morning. I'll have to beg out of the basketball game. My nephews play on Saturdays."

"I'm sure they'll understand. Your family all know how hard you work."

"Well, maybe, but they'll be disappointed. Basketball is like the common thread in our lives—it's what bonds me to those boys. I like to see their games and give them some critiques. They love to hear me yelling for them up there in the stands. I canceled two weeks ago, too. I can't make a habit of it, but I think you're right. I need to right the ship and get back into the chief's good graces. He's done a lot for me."

"That's a plan. Let's get an Uber and get to the stadium," she said, pulling out her phone.

In ten minutes, they were walking into the brightly lit baseball arena, the city's lights a panoramic backdrop in the right field. The game was already in the sixth inning.

"Love that view. Best ballpark in the majors," he commented to two men who were in the box as they walked in.

"Oh, yeah! Hey Kurt, great to see you! The Yanks put it hard on our starter, it's three to nothing, and the Bucs are just coming up. Let's hope some of our guys can get the bats on the ball. Those two homers really shut this crowd up."

"Kurt," the other man offered, "have an Extra Stout."

He accepted gracefully, admiring the dark bottle as though it were a work of fine art. Despite the score, there was a buzz in the box.

"Was hoping you two might come tonight. I think we'll pull out of this."

"Even if we don't," Kurt offered with a smile, "this can make all the difference."

He held up his bottle, touched it lightly to the others, and requested a white wine for his date. Every night was a festive, mirthful occasion when he went out with Lauren, and he felt a pang of regret that his profession made it so hard to go out and socialize late into the wee hours. He downed the frosty draught in just a few seconds.

"Another, Kurt?"

He couldn't say no. The dark beer had a wonderful, rich, bitter flavor. No need to drive. He could simply take a river taxi and then a short Uber ride home. Despite the haze of inebriation that came over him, he clung tightly to his goal of getting home and into bed by eleven. The next day's schedule was hectic, with a ton of nerve blocks, as well as many short cases . . . getting there late would not do.

The staff from Lauren's financial firm were as pleasant and chatty as they'd been at the hockey game, and he settled down comfortably among them, babbling about unimportant things, enjoying his evening. She inclined her head towards him, speaking in a low tone.

"I've got to get to the ladies' room. Do you have anything special for me?"

She'd become adept and comfortable at injecting her own fentanyl. Kurt followed her to the exit, putting his arm around her affectionately and pressing the small syringe into her hand.

"Beautifully packaged—thank you. Back in a moment."

He watched her lovely form sway down the hallway, away from him. For just a moment, he allowed himself to wonder what her devotion to him would be should he fail to supply the drugs that gave them both such fulfillment. The thought was cloaked in cynicism, and he immediately rebuked himself, turning instead to his own pleasure. He tripped lightly down the hall to the men's room, which he found empty, and he parked himself in a stall. Working quickly, he raised his sleeve and injected the contents of the tuberculin syringe. It held little more than 1 milliliter, but he'd pulled the stopper back as far as it would go when he filled it, ensuring that a small topper had been added in. An extra ten micrograms would ensure that the evening's heady pleasures would endure. It was all an extraordinary mind-bend, the course to a crystal-clear intellect and to unparalleled euphoria. Alcohol, marijuana, even hashish—which he'd been goaded into trying once in a very fudgy brownie in college—offered nothing compared to the feelings that accompanied injection of fentanyl.

He arrived back in the box at an opportune moment.

"Boom! That's gonna be out of here!"

Cecil, the eldest of the men with whom he'd been drinking and chatting, called it out.

"Gone!"

He needed to reorient. He'd only been gone for a few minutes, but the score, which had been frozen the entire game at 3-0, was suddenly tied at 3-3. The bases had been clear and the situation dire for the home team when he had left for the men's room, but the elation in the box was now wholly unfettered.

"Kurt, can you believe it? Two down in the bottom of the ninth, then a walk and a broken-bat single? A homer, and it's tied!"

A surge of excitement coursed through him, and suddenly, he was also jumping with glee. There were high-fives, fist-bumps, chest bumps, even a hug from one of the young women who worked the reception desk for the firm. He espied Lauren, just returning, trying to process the tumult that was unraveling around her.

He vaulted across the room, swept her into his arms.

"It's tied!"

"Now, can we cash in and steal this game?"

Cecil was pressed against the window, calling over to him.

"Two more Stouts," Kurt yelled to the wait staff, most of whom appeared as joyous as the patrons.

The toasts became more frequent and boisterous as the next two Pirates found their way onto the base paths.

"C'mon baby—just a base hit!"

Kurt steadied himself against a chair, realizing he was a bit off-balance, but guzzled the cold beer as quickly as he could. The game, he sensed, would soon be over, and he might need a bit of fortification for the boat ride home. He pulled out his phone and was stunned to find that it was 11:02. He began to laugh. So much for being home by eleven. He felt innervated, alive, energetic, so much so that he took it upon himself as a challenge to endure a short night and perform his job as effectively as he always did the following day.

The celebration seemed without end. Long into the night, the Pirates valiantly battled the vaunted Bronx Bombers. Every inning, the crowd watched in high expectation as the Yankee reliever yielded a Pirate runner or perhaps two, only to see them stranded on the bases.

Kurt and Lauren managed to stay atop the uproarious cascade of good feelings, as they eagerly enjoyed the wine and beer that the company so graciously provided, even adding a few oxycodone tablets to the mix. The spirit of the group in the box could not be broken, and the romantic pair seemed to gather happy people around them, wherever they went, so infectious was their goodwill and affability. Even so, many of the sleepy patrons in the other seats drifted out of the stadium. It was, after all, a weeknight in Pittsburgh.

"Last little dose?" she whispered, her lips just brushing his ear.

"I'll meet you outside," he confided, finishing his beer.

Holding her hand and gazing into her eyes as he passed off the fentanyl, he acknowledged the sense of supremacy that the two of them experienced in tandem. He could barely inject himself fast enough, and moments later, stepped once again into the box.

"You're back," called Cecil, laughing and pointing to the field.

"You don't know what you missed—I hope you looked at a monitor out there! We got men on first and second with two outs!"

Kurt trained his eye on the field and saw the two runners leading off as the pitcher delivered a fastball, low and outside.

The crack of the bat was of the sort that electrified a crowd, that communicated to them immediately that something very good had happened, if the ball would simply land in fair territory.

Cecil was bouncing on his feet, screaming, "No, man, stay fair. Stay fair!"

Kurt appreciated the full-on movement of the baserunners out of the corner of his eye as he strained to see the play unfold. The Yankee outfielder was in full gallop, the fly ball angling for the right-field bleachers, dropping in a trajectory that would clearly be just out of his reach. The ball plummeted back to earth just inside the foul line, then ricocheted toward the foul pole. The man rounding third, the Pirate catcher, was big, muscular, and slow. He would likely have been gunned down at the plate had the ball not mysteriously bounced away from the fielder, who was just able to bare-hand it on the second bounce. The runner became airborne perhaps ten feet from home plate, diving over the back legs of the catcher, who could not will the ball into his well-oiled glove any faster than its velocity allowed. At that moment, ten thousand souls exploded in ecstasy as the entire Pirate team ran onto the field.

"Awesome, totally awesome!" screamed Cecil, making body contact of some sort with everyone he could reach."Way to go, Bucs!"

"Stunning. Just stunning." Kurt could not stop grinning, he was so heady with the thrill of the victory. "Does anything beat a walk-off in extra innings?"

Lauren was suddenly close beside him, gleefully holding his hand. Her eyes sparkled as she sought his gaze.

"OK, we're outta here!" he called, trading high-fives with the entire staff as they exited.

"Kurt, a moment of composure—you've got to be at work at 6 A.M. Maybe we should get you home.."

"Nah, I have an overnight bag at your place. We'll go home together and celebrate with style, I'll get three hours, and I'll be fine. I've done it plenty of times."

"But you said today that . . ."

"I know. But hon, this is exceptional. The Bucs beat the Yankees in extra innings! Too good a time to cash it out. This is a great omen for our whole season! Let me come to your place, you can hold me close, and we'll make the night even better, then snooze together on your fine linens. I'll make a few sacrifices tomorrow, I know. But I can get through the day, and I have the weekend to catch up with my work."

She quickly took his arm. The two promenaded briskly across the Clemente Bridge, in the swirling, chilly wind, then along Sixth Avenue, angling for her apartment. The city was filled with fans, streaming back to their cars, chatty and ebullient as they recounted the plays of the evening. The multitude of bridges, arcing across the Allegheny, glowed exceptionally bright in the fine spring air. He could barely keep his hands off her lovely, lithe body in the elevator, and when the doors opened, they raced to her apartment.

# CHAPTER 34

He awakened with a start, the room still dark. His head felt as though it were filled with fuzz, the thoughts coming dense and slow. The alarm had been going off, but for how long? The pair had been up till all hours, laughing, talking, making love in every way that they could arrange their taught bodies until his back was throbbing with pain and he'd had to beg off, embarrassed that he could not continue. She would literally have had sex all night, he figured, if he could have sustained it, and he wondered if, in her adventurous past, she had.

Now, on so many mornings, he could barely arise. He was beginning to feel betrayed by the woman, by the libations, by the never-ending felicity. His head often hurt, his stomach was sour from the wine or beer that simply kept flowing, along with the injections of fentanyl, all evening long. He curled up, trying to ease the aching in his low back, using the blanket to wipe the thick, dry paste that had congealed in his mouth and on his lips. The taste was intolerable, his tongue caked and cracked. It was hard to move, and he wondered if they'd engaged in some new, violent tumbling act during the night that he simply couldn't remember. He rose and yawned, then dressed, trying to stretch his lumbar muscles.

He hurried out the door, down the darkened stairwell, and out into the cool morning. If he was lucky, he could get to the hospital by 7:20, with barely enough time to see the first two patients and get them into the OR. God help him if either of them was complicated. It struck him as odd that the things that bothered the hell out of him in the morning meant nothing during the frenetic, joyful evenings that they shared—the highs they rode simply dwarfed small concerns, like promptness and job performance. Recently, during his on-call nights, when he was stuck in the hospital until very late, his need to be with Lauren had become almost intolerable, as he fantasized about what he was missing in her arms, and in her company.

He stormed into the locker room, his clothes flying off as he approached his locker in full stride.

"You're in a very big hurry."

Farrokh was sitting on the bench in front of the row of lockers that both of them called home, appeared to have been dozing with his head forward upon his chest, until Kurt slammed his locker door in his haste to get out onto the floor.

"Shit, Farrokh, I'm late. I have two rooms of ortho cases and most of the patients need nerve blocks, along with a Gyn room."

"Yes. They have been paging you with great frequency," the big Iranian man pronounced in his curious, deliberate accent.

"Oh, God—when did that start? I was at the Pirate game—it went late, really late. Extra innings, then they won. I didn't get to bed till after three. But the stupid alarm didn't go off at six like it was supposed to."

"You went to game? It was on in a patient room. She was in late-stage labor, but the husband kept watching the game. I was ducking in and out to see what happened to Pirates, told them I had to check the epidural. Fourteen innings—great game!"

Kurt pulled his scrubs on in a frenzy.

"Yeah—REALLY great game. Too great. Too long—I gotta get out there. You have time to see a patient for me? I'll help you out on another day."

There was a pitiable, pleading note in his voice.

The man looked at Kurt, his eyes bloodshot and the lower eyelids drooping in the curious fashion of a Basset Hound.

"Kurt, I am up hustling for the last 16 hours. Three C-sections, two of them scary as hell. Five epidurals, one lady with a drop in blood pressure scare me almost to the death. I thought 'amniotic fluid embolism, she gonna arrest, Farrokh there goes your career!' Wondered if she would die. The lady responded to fluids and a little epinephrine, turns out to have placenta previa with bleeding that we did not see at first. We caught up finally—after two hours pouring in blood and products! Baby OK even with all that! I can hardly even move this morning, Kurt."

"I see, I understand—I'm outta here. Get some sleep, Farrokh!"

He skidded around the corner, nearly bowled over the startled resident.

"Jerry, did you see the first block patient?"

"Uh, yes, Doctor McCain. Pretty healthy, a 45-year-old smoker for a wrist arthroscopy. The surgeon requested a block. I have everything ready."

"Great. Pull the curtain, start scanning. I'll be there in two minutes for a time out, be ready to go. Where's Dorothy?"

"Looking for you, I think."

"Well, find her and get over there so we can do the block."

Jerry hurried off to find the wayward nurse, while Kurt went the other direction, to speak with a patient about his knee surgery.

"Mr. Jones—I'm Dr. McCain, your anesthesiologist. I'm looking over your history and physical, here. Looks like you have a stent for your heart, high blood pressure, and a thyroid condition. Anything else?"

The man nodded at each suggestion, then tilted his head, thinking.

"Not really, doc. I'm pretty active. Golf in the nice weather and ski in the winter. Tore up this ACL on some moguls down at Wisp. Scary trail, probably the double-black diamond isn't my thing."

At this, he put his stethoscope on the man's chest and thrust the consent form in front of him, indicating the line upon which to sign. Nearly overwhelmed by the efficiency of the interview and examination, the man opened his mouth, tilted his head back, inspired as deeply as he could, and struggled to get a signature on the chart, which was difficult for him to focus on, given the position of his head.

"Excellent. In a few minutes, we'll get your nerve block placed, then we'll go back to the OR, put some monitors on for your heart, lungs, and blood pressure, and get you off to sleep."

The bewildered man thanked him, and Kurt moved briskly to the next patient, a large, round woman who was scheduled for a hysterectomy related to persistent, dysfunctional uterine bleeding. He had a sense of foreboding as he saw the patients around him moving, one by one, back to the ORs, while his group remained in place. It was only a matter of time until someone began to protest, that was clear.

"Morning, ma'am. I'm Dr. McCain, your anesthesiologist. I work with a nurse anesthetist, Robert, who will be with you in the room."

She was a pleasant woman, bright and intelligent.

"Yes, I've just met him—he was here and gone. Asked me all sorts of questions, then went back to the room to get things ready, he said."

He turned his back to the woman, and threw a fusillade of questions at her, while furiously typing his note into the computer. He cast a wary eye on her airway while listening to her lungs, and pronounced her ready to go.

"Doc, we still need that consent," noted Karen, the circulating nurse for the hysterectomy case, as he began to move back toward the other bedside where Jerry waited for him to do the nerve block.

"Ahh, yes—so you do." He tried to be pleasant, but there was a note of irritation in his voice, as he flipped the chart open to the consent page.

"Let's go, ladies, let's go!" he heard as he headed off for the nerve block.

The surgeon, an elderly and polite gynecologist, had arrived to shepherd the process along. Kurt knew him well, understood that he'd keep his peace about a late start, but might well mention it in passing to his chief. He saw with satisfaction that the team had now begun to take the surgeon's first patient back, but, almost simultaneously, a new patient was brought into the same slot for him to see. It was only 7:30 and he was already significantly behind. It was becoming a trend.

"OK, Jerry, let's time out. Did you find Dorothy?"

The resident looked panicked.

"She had to go to the bathroom. We were here and ready, then she said she couldn't wait."

He shook his head, growling.

"You gotta be kidding me. Well—get someone else back here to help us. GET SOMEONE ELSE BACK HERE!"

His voice boomed through the preop area and out into the hallways, startling staff and patients alike. He realized he was about to completely lose his composure, poked his head out of the curtain, looking from side to side.

"Uh, sorry folks. Just trying to get things started on time."

He closed the curtain, bowed his head."Apologies to you both. Sometimes it's very stressful in the morning."

The patient appeared wary and apprehensive, and Kurt put a hand on his shoulder.

"Things will be fine. I just need to make sure my assets are in the right place at the right time."

This appeared to appease the gentleman, who managed a wan smile.

"It is awfully busy. Is it always like this down here?"

"Well, in the early mornings it is. Everything has to get started at once. For the rest of the day, all the rooms are staggered, so it's not so bad."

He had an idea, excused himself to the bathroom. He'd managed to remove the fentanyl syringe from the IV set, which Jerry had placed there in anticipation of the nerve block. He could get back in an instant, he knew. He'd taken the midazolam as well, knew that he could use a bit of that to help settle his nerves. The combination was tantalizing. Inside the darkened restroom, he flipped on the light, quickly applied a needle to both syringes, and injected about three-fourths of their contents into the skin under his armpit, which of late had become reddened and irritated. In seconds he felt a warm sense of pacification sweep over him. He refilled both syringes with water, re-capped them, and marched out to the bedside.

"Dorothy! Finally, we all connect!" he announced with sincere triumph, gliding back to the bedside.

"Yes, doc, I'm sorry. I thought I had a spare minute to go to the bathroom."

He was at this point glowing.

"Not a problem—not a problem. Let's time out!"

He approached the IV tubing and furtively replaced the syringes, while the nurse checked the consent forms and Jeremy studiously evaluated the man's wristband.

"Very good—it all checks out. Jerry, let's get a mark on that left shoulder, and I'll start the sedation."

"One milliliter of each, doc?" the nurse asked, beginning to document the procedure on the block form.

"Actually, two mils of each. I figured with all my ranting, he could use some real settling down."

He beamed at the man, who brightened.

"OK, let's see the anatomy."

The resident applied the transducer and began to delineate the anatomic structures beneath the skin. He was growing in confidence as his experience grew.

"Excellent. That's right where we want to inject. Sir, how do you feel—are you more relaxed from our sedatives?"

The patient shrugged.

"I don't think I feel too much different, doc."

"Hmmm. Dorothy, perhaps he's a bit on the resistant side. More nervous than I appreciated. Can you open up another amp of midazolam and fentanyl?"

She appeared surprised but followed his directive. They rarely used more than one ampule of either drug for the nerve blocks.

"I gotta tell ya, doc. It takes a ton of drugs to bring me down. You're not the first doctor I've surprised."

The patient was obviously pleased with himself, and so was Kurt. The situation, as it unfolded, covered his actions nicely, and even opened up another opportunity.

"Well, let's give another one-and-one. I want him comfortable for the block. Jerry, trace the roots up to the spine, show me where they enter, while we wait."

A scant minute later, the man allowed a grin to spread across his face.

"OK, now I feel it."

"Great. Now, some local for the skin, and let's get the block in."

He watched intensely as the young man attempted to image the needle, just beneath the skin.

"Here. Swing the transducer gently over the spot where you know the needle resides, like a pendulum with a very limited arc. You'll find it."

His advice had little effect, and the struggle to find the needle continued.

"I see your pathway—can you see the needle pushing through the fascia, here? You just have to improve your alignment."

The resident gritted his teeth tightly, intent on getting it right.

"You guys doin' all right?" the man asked, lightheartedly.

"We're fine—just don't move, or talk sir, for a couple of minutes. We're just getting a better needle image. Are you having any pain?"

"Only the pain that comes from having a big needle stuck in your neck," he quipped.

"We'll be done soon."

Or so I hope, thought Kurt. His patience was beginning to wear thin. Jerry's enthusiasm did not quite make up for his psychomotor challenges. The phone on his belt rang, predictably.

"Hi, Kurt here."

It was Robert. Had he forgotten the induction for the hysterectomy patient? Caught up in the frustration of the nerve block procedure, he certainly had. It would be foolish to abandon the procedure now, and he couldn't leave the nurse and resident to carry out the block without him. They could certainly wait another 90 seconds until he got the block in.

"Here," he said, hanging up the phone and taking hold of the needle hub, the other hand grabbing the young doctor's hand as it embraced the transducer.

"Let's find this thing."

In a few seconds, he had the needle perfectly imaged, much to the embarrassment of the younger man.

"It's not rocket science, Jerry. You have to align the needle with the center of the transducer right down the middle, like a kicker splitting the uprights in the NFL. You know, like whatshisname, for the Steelers—right down the middle, every time. Now, keep this aligned so we can capture an image, and I'll turn on the stimulator."

While the nurse printed an image, he gradually turned up the electrical current, until the man's biceps began to jerk rhythmically.

"That's a hoot," the patient called out, enjoying the phenomenon.

"Hold still, please," Kurt exhorted the man.

"It's at 0.5. Now I'm injecting—any discomfort, sir?

"Naww. It's fine. I can see the fluid there on the screen."

"Very good—great spread, Jerry, just what we want. That's it. I want you to check his block in five minutes, make sure he's ready to go back. I have to go do an induction."

He found himself grabbing the fentanyl and midazolam syringes. While the pain nurse filled out the block note, and the resident cleaned the man's neck of ultrasound gel, he pretended to squirt both syringes out in the trash.

"Ok, that's 50 micrograms of fentanyl and a milligram of midazolam wasted—make sure you chart that, Jeremy. Dorothy, can you witness?"

She was distracted, looked up, nodded vigorously, and went back to her documentation.

Smooth, he thought to himself and dashed off to the operating room. Perhaps, he thought, I can bring this whole thing to bear. I'll have all three rooms started in a moment, and so far, there doesn't seem to be anybody who's too upset.

"Thanks, doc, for coming back," the surgeon announced, rather loudly, with just a trace of sarcasm as Kurt entered the room.

"Right, absolutely, should've been back a few minutes ago—the residents are new and the blocks take a little longer," he explained, avoiding eye contact and knowing that a justification based on training would be more acceptable than a simple admission that he was late. After all, he thought, we wait forever for some of your surgical trainees to prep, to learn arthroscopic and laparoscopic techniques, to close wounds that an attending surgeon could close in a few minutes.

"Ready, then?" he asked the anesthetist, who was placing the laryngoscope blade and handle by the patient's head while holding the mask on her face.

"Ma'am, take a few deep breaths, we'll go off to sleep, now."

The patient was composed, quiet, already significantly subdued by the pre-induction sedation drugs. She opened her eyes briefly as he spoke, tried to focus on his face as the words came out, could not, and closed them again, accepting the effect of the drug as it broke over her, like a wave carrying her under the surf.

"Easy to ventilate," Robert announced, a signal to the anesthesiologist to give the muscle relaxant.

"Good view?" he inquired, as the seconds ticked by, and the nurse anesthetist placed the laryngoscope blade, ever so gently, in the back of the throat.

"I see the epiglottis," he confirmed, sounding a bit dubious.

"Good—the airway?"

"I can't see it. I know where it is, but I can't see it."

"You want a bougie? Can I help your view?"

Robert moved his right hand away from the mouth, and placed it upon the larynx, moving it back and forth, attempting to press it back so the glottis opening would come into view.

"No. Still can't see it."

Kurt felt a pang of anxiety deep inside. It was always difficult to cope with an airway that you couldn't visualize well, placing the tube up under the epiglottis in the hopes that it went into the right space, like a pilot performing an instrument landing in a dense fog. But when you were watching someone else deal with that situation, the uncertainty doubled—you didn't know where the tip of their blade was, you didn't know what they were seeing, didn't know what the effect of laryngeal manipulation was. This was more like landing in impenetrable mist with the instruments on the fritz.

"Can I look?"

He assumed control of the laryngoscope, which the anesthetist yielded only reluctantly. Robert was experienced and proud of his abilities—it would certainly be an insult to him to fail to place the airway. The tone of the pulse oximeter had not changed, though several minutes had passed without ventilation. He pulled the tip of the blade back, then gently reinserted it. Lifting, he was discouraged to find that his placement of the blade revealed nothing that resembled the entry to the airway, just a pink chasm deep in the hypopharynx.

"Dammit," he growled, and began aggressively manipulating the larynx with his right hand on the front of the neck.

To no avail. The view did not improve. If he kept pressing and lifting this hard, if he kept re-situating the tip of the steel blade, he knew that bleeding, swelling or both would occur, making things worse.

But they could ventilate with a mask. Thank God for that, he thought.

"Let's ventilate. Can we call for the Glidescope?"

This was a fly in his ointment. It would be five or so minutes before they could get they get the patient intubated so the case could begin. Then, he'd have to skate back to preop as fast as he could to check the nerve block and approve that patient for going back to the OR. And his third patient would require his presence for induction any minute. By now, at least two other patients were probably sitting in the preop, awaiting his interview. Jerry might be alert enough to do a preop evaluation on one of them, realizing Kurt's situation, but the resident was a bit on the hesitant side, so maybe not. Worst of all, the gynecologist, who expected to be operating by now, had adopted an arms-folded position while sitting on a stool, glaring at the airway proceedings while awaiting his opportunity to begin the procedure.

Ventilation by mask continued and appeared to be effective. The door burst open, and Velma rolled the Glidescope in, breathless.

"I've got the difficult airway cart outside the room, in case you need it, doctor."

"Great. Are we still able to ventilate with the mask?

Robert nodded vigorously, holding the mask in place firmly.

"Vitals look great—we've got extra induction drugs on board, she should be nice and relaxed."

He couldn't shake the anxiety that was pulsing through him, noted his hand was trembling. Having done this so many times before, he assured himself, he knew just what to do.

The nurse anesthetist pulled the mask off, and Kurt inserted the blade of the video-laryngoscope deeply into the pharynx, lifting gently as he proceeded. The tongue seemed to ball up and precede his tip, and he tried to flatten it out as he proceeded.

"Where is this lady's glottis?" He grimaced, dipping repeatedly with the blade while he lifted.

He could hear the tone of the pulse oximeter change ever so slightly.

"What can I do to get you a view," the anesthetist asked, rocking the head back for him.

"I'm fine. I'm fine. Don't help me!"

He felt a note of panic creeping through him. The visualization was terrible. Nothing looked even remotely familiar. This woman was not big, her external airway features were not abnormal. What the hell is going on, he wondered. Some sort of anomaly of the airway? Finally, he seemed to get past the bulk of the tongue that was holding him back, and proceeded, more firmly than before, lifting repeatedly.

"Watch the teeth," the anesthetist cautioned, knowing that Kurt was concentrating on the screen view, not on the blade itself.

"I am watching the teeth," he replied, tersely, immediately frustrated with his emotional reaction to this case.

He looked down and realized how he was impacting the incisors.

"Thanks, got it. I should be seeing the airway. Where is the airway?"

The room was silent. The pulse oximeter tone was dropping, and the sound chilled him even more. It was as though every individual therein—the surgeon, the OR nurses, the anesthetist, the surgical resident, the anesthesia tech—had a sudden sense of foreboding. The man in charge did not sound like he was in charge.

"Should we call for help?"

It was the voice of the circulating nurse, reluctant and hopeful at the same instant.

"Call for HELP? I AM help! You've got an entire anesthesia team right here in front of you. How much more help do you need?"

In his attempt to sound disdainful, he sounded pitiful, riddled with self-doubt, even to his own ears.

"Call for help, Velma," he stated, flatly.

He didn't hear the call go out, was too busy searching for an airway that he could not visualize. He recounted it in his head: The response to failed visualization should be to pull out and consider other options while providing mask ventilation. And, if ventilation became difficult, insert an LMA. But he knew, absolutely knew, that he would find the airway within seconds. These anxious seconds turned to a minute. The saturation began to sound quite low.

"We should come out," the anesthetist recommended.

"One sec, I'm right there."

But he wasn't right there. There was no opening to the airway where he was certain the airway should be. None of this made sense. His panic began to give way to anger. He was doing everything correctly. How could the glottis opening not be there—not even a hint of it?

By now, the saturation was becoming desperately low. Robert had grabbed the mask, was gently pushing against him to remind him to disengage. He would not give way, he determined would resolve this problem, without a nurse anesthetist taking charge, without anybody else taking charge. He was in command, would issue the orders.

"Doctor Martinez," he called to the surgeon, "I may need a surgical airway—can you prep the neck and check the landmarks?"

He did not look up from the video screen but heard a commotion from the bottom of the table.

"Christ, Kurt, are you sure? Okay, I'm at the neck. Melinda, prep the front of the neck, I think I've got the cricoid cartilage right beneath my finger. And for God's sake, put out a stat page for an ENT surgeon . . . this is a very fat neck. Get me a number 11 blade, a curved hemostat, and a small ET tube. Kurt, have you got a 5.5 tube? Can we just temporize and get some ventilation for a minute or two until we can get an airway surgeon in here?"

At that moment, another voice was audible, and Kurt welcomed the confidence that was manifest within it. It was Natalie.

"Kurt—just pull back! I think you're in too far!"

This bold proclamation nearly bowled him over, a simple thought that he had not considered. Could she be correct? He prayed that she was, and dreaded that she was at the same moment. Even in his panic-stricken, ego-driven state, he hoped that she was on the mark, no matter how foolish he would appear with the revelation of such a simple solution. He gently pulled the tip of the laryngoscope blade back, then eased up with the extraordinary force he'd brought to bear on the base of the woman's tongue. The tissues unfolded, the laryngeal cartilages suddenly popped into his sight, along with a superb view of the glottis inlet, now ringed by blood from his aggressive laryngoscopy. He'd almost had his knees buckle in his fear that the patient would succumb or require an emergent surgical airway. Now, the path was quite clear, the simple answer in sight. The size four Glidescope handle, applied in anticipation of a difficult airway in an obese patient by the anesthesia tech, had simply been too long and had led both Robert and him to place the tip too deep.

"Hand me the tube," he said, allowing a hint of a smile to cross his face.

He'd been in error. He'd failed in important ways, letting fear overtake his capacity to reason. Failed to use his tools to their optimum capacity. Failed to heed the advice of a knowledgeable anesthetist at his side. Failed to adhere to the algorithm he'd memorized and practiced a hundred times. And he knew it. But none of that mattered at this triumphant moment. The patient was out of danger, as he pushed the endotracheal tube home.

"Confirmed," he said, flatly, Robert squeezing the bag as Kurt watched the $CO_2$ traces show up on the screen, listening for breath sounds at the same time.

He looked at the team assembled around him, noticed that no one made eye contact.

"Are we good?" the surgeon said, craning his neck to look over at the video screen.

"We're good."

"Thanks, everyone," Kurt announced, anxious to move on.

"Time for some maintenance anesthesia."

The sevoflurane had already been turned on, and the anesthetist had his back to him, entering data into the computer. No doubt, he was also documenting what had transpired during the induction.

There would be an inquiry into this episode. His protégé would have to bear witness against him. Indeed, she had saved him and the patient from his own, uncharacteristic anxiety and panic. He was still trembling, couldn't stop the involuntary shakes. Adrenaline, he figured, coursing through his bloodstream.

He held the door open for the procession as it emerged with the equipment, rolling the video laryngoscope and the difficult airway cart back to the storage closet until it was next needed. Natalie's head was inclined as she walked past him.

"Nat—thanks. I don't know . . ."

Her face reddened as she turned to him.

"None of us know, Kurt. This isn't you. That should've been an easy intubation for someone with your experience. What is up with you?"

She didn't wait for an answer, walking away as quickly as she could manage. He was conscious of the need to get back to preop. There was a gnawing sensation in his gut, an odd feeling. Anxiety? Fear? Perhaps hunger, he reasoned; he had eaten nothing since the night before.

Never mind, he thought, back to see the patients. Further delays would not be tolerated. He could make things up with Natalie later. It irked him that she'd turned on him; every practitioner had a bad case now and then. Had he not come to her assistance a few times? Perhaps she believed that this was different, given their relative stature in the department and their degrees of experience. Whatever. He had work to do.

# CHAPTER 35

He passed the tiny staff bathroom in the corridor, the door ajar just enough to catch his attention. There was no one inside, and this gave him pause. He still had a milligram of midazolam in his pocket, along with the milliliter of fentanyl, courtesy of the sleight-of-hand he'd employed during the nerve block. These powerful tonics he could make use of in the aftermath of the frustrating episode that had just unfolded. If they'd been coursing through his veins a few minutes prior, would he have immediately understood the mystery of the lady's airway? Did these substances not bring his state of consciousness to an almost miraculous acuity?

Slipping inside, he closed the door forcefully, fumbling for the light. The phone hanging from his waist began to ring, and a light flickered across its front, like lightning tearing the fabric of a black sky. "Not now," he said to himself, clicking it off.

"Whatever mundane shit they're calling me about can wait. One minute and I'll be with you, but I need that minute," he mumbled.

He found the light switch, and the amber bulb reluctantly energized, lighting the tiny space, but only just, as though it was a struggle to achieve the necessary illumination. There was barely enough light to distinguish the two syringes, one with an orange label, promising anxiolysis and a warm sense of security, the other bearing a blue label, providing relief of every discomfort and a re-ordering of disorganized thoughts. When he contemplated the effects that the two drugs would have upon him, he suddenly felt that he controlled his destiny. There would be no further ill-conceived direction stamped upon his life, courtesy of idiots who sat in offices with computers and spreadsheets. He would control his existence, and that would be apparent to everyone who encountered him.

A lustful moan escaped him as he injected the midazolam, and he leaned against the wall, awaiting the drug's reassuring embrace. The warmth began to take hold of him, ever so subtly, and he held up the syringe of fentanyl, removing its cap. The tiny, 25-gauge needle that he'd used for the midazolam slipped out of his fingers, falling to the floor. In the dim light, he struggled to find it, falling to his knees in the cramped space.

"Oh, come on," he growled, shifting back and forth and tilting his head to peer into the shadows made by the toilet bowl, behind which he was certain the implement had fallen.

Groping, he perceived an object, felt it pierce his finger, noted an odd satisfaction. The tiny prick was meaningless, but the needle was now in his grasp. Lasciviously, almost rapturously, he screwed it onto the syringe and looked at the skin of his forearm. Wan and vulnerable, it invited him as he crouched in the half-light. He pierced the integument and the subcutaneous tissue beneath it, driving the diminutive needle tip home. Pressing the plunger of the syringe, he prepared for the incomparable feeling that was sure to follow.

At that moment, the door to the restroom burst open abruptly, accompanied by the sound of a familiar voice.

"I don't know, I just can't wait for the weekend . . ."

The edge of the door impacted Kurt's head with astonishing force, and he stiffened, then slid back against the wall, momentarily insensible.

"Dr. McCain!"

The voice was now shrill, reflecting surprise and horror at the revelation before the onlooker. How, he wondered in some obscure corner of his mind, could Velma be everywhere at the same time? But here she was, a silhouette in the bathroom doorway, and he now felt a blinding pain in his head. He somehow could tell the hallway was bustling, full of staffers moving back to their rooms or taking patients to the PACU, or perhaps simply going on break. He'd forgotten why he was on his all fours in the bathroom, and he slumped to the ground as blood began to pour from his scalp. The fentanyl syringe was cradled in the crook of his elbow, the needle still embedded in his skin.

"Ohmygod!"

Velma was almost overcome at the sight of the anesthesiologist curled up, helpless on the floor, blood pooling about him. As he reached for his bleeding scalp, the needle sprang free from his arm and suddenly the syringe was lying on the floor beside him, in plain sight. He was dimly aware that a small crowd had coalesced in the hallway outside the bathroom.

He felt a kind hand on his shoulder, a strong, gruff hand that somehow managed to touch him with compassion.

"Your head bashed . . . you need to go to emergency."

It was Farrokh, for some reason still in the hospital, and he was pressing a wad of paper towels against Kurt's forehead, attempting to staunch the flow of blood. Why, Kurt thought, had the man not gone home yet? He could not look up, was too stunned by this episode to even begin acknowledging the reality that was unfolding before him. He understood that he was too ill to continue, that he would have to abandon the care of his patients, and even that his life was about to change, irrevocably.

A sharp voice called out.

"Here are some gloves."

The big man was known for his casual approach to his profession, and he scoffed, shaking his head at the very notion.

"But Farrokh—he's shooting drugs."

It was a matter-of-fact statement, among health care providers, from someone in the crowd whom Kurt did not even know. The voice was flat, impassive, but it cut him like a scalpel blade. The words fell like a thud in the crowded hallway, which had become profoundly silent as the implications of this scenario became clear. A palpable sadness seemed to spread through the collected souls, after the shock of seeing the injured man began to wear off.

"Kurt, we've got to get you to the emergency room. That's a nasty gash," Natalie had elbowed her way to the front of the onlookers.

There was nothing accusatory in her voice. Instead, it held a note of sympathy or perhaps pity. The tone of her voice was that of someone who had just solved a complex puzzle, but in finding the solution, received no satisfaction.

"Let's get you up on this cart,"

"We'll steady you. Can you stand?"

He did not expect such compassionate behavior from these people, all of whom he had just betrayed. He would have welcomed a display of anger, a sharp tongue-lashing, a fierce admonition-some means of addressing the guilt that had begun to well up within him like vomitus that needed to be expelled.

When none of that was forthcoming, he cooperated with their assistance as best he could, kept his head down as he seated himself on the cart. Farrokh's meaty hand continued to compress the towels against his head, but he could still feel the blood oozing, and a trickle came down the side of his face, where it paralleled the track of a single tear that had gathered in his lower eyelid, spilling over as he changed position. He sniffed as the salty fluid made its way into his nose.

"I can't believe this," someone whispered in the back of the pack of people who, despite the need to get back to their work, had not dispersed.

He felt a finger, its touch soft and kind, beneath his chin, gently lifting his head. Natalie peered intently into his eyes.

"I'm so sorry, Kurt. You've got to get help. We'll make sure you get help."

Those words rang in his ears as a small contingent of people from the OR, who must have been on their morning breaks, ceremoniously rolled him down the hallway, while heads turned, reflecting genuine astonishment. Chatter began to break out among those in the long passage, who gave way as the cart approached, the vocal reaction to his plight following just behind as he rolled by, like a wave rippling through a body of water.

He remembered little of the next 90 minutes in the emergency department, where blood was taken, his wound was washed out, and a physician's assistant quietly closed the gash on his head. He did not doubt that she knew the full story and assumed she was afraid to speak to him. It occurred to him that he was now a solitary individual, could not count himself part of any association, hospital, or profession. He was not sure how quickly word could travel but now was concerned that he was not even part of a romance. He'd repeatedly called Lauren from the ER, left a detailed message on her cell phone. Had it been yesterday she would have called him back within a few minutes, whatever the circumstances. Today, she did not bother to return any of his five phone calls. His inconveniences continued to multiply, as he realized that he could not go back to work, would have to leave the facility, and probably would not be advised not to drive, given his use of intoxicating substances and his head injury.

"Here are your discharge instructions," the PA said, meekly, brushing a strand of blond hair back from her forehead."You have to get those stitches out in 5 to 7 days. Either at your PCP office or back here in the ER."

He laughed at the suggestion. He didn't even have a PCP, always felt that he was healthy, that he didn't really need a physician. Now, he figured, it was probably time that he got one.

"I better get back up to my office. I think they'll want to talk to me," he muttered aloud, to himself as much as the diminutive figure before him.

She nodded, reluctantly, and pointed to where he was supposed to sign the instructions. Pocketing his copy, he made his way out of the emergency department. Someone had been kind enough to send his street clothes down to the ER, so he stopped to change out of the bloody scrubs.

"Frankenstein," he pronounced, regarding his image in the mirror and the long scar across his forehead, the blue Prolene suture tails protruding at odd angles."But overall, she did a pretty nice job."

# CHAPTER 36

He used the back hallway to get to the anesthesia office. Entering warily, he was surprised to find a collection of his colleagues, clustered around the door to the chief's office. They parted, silently, reluctantly, as he ushered himself inside. No one followed him in. The chief was seated behind his desk. He looked wearily at Kurt, rubbed his hands over his face, then tried to focus on the very uncomfortable matter at hand.

"This is very painful," he pronounced, as though the words were themselves torturing the inside of his mouth as he enunciated them.

"Sir . . ."

"I talk, here, Kurt. You just listen."

The chief's terse manner made it clear that listening was all he should do.

"I am truly stunned, even overwhelmed, by the events of this morning. Your downfall is a very public one, and that might be a favorable point. I have to candidly state to you, that I had no idea that you were stealing and abusing opioids . . ."

"But.."

"There are no 'buts,' Kurt. This cannot be characterized in any other way. You have been stealing drugs that belong to the patients. You charged their insurance companies for drugs you did not administer. You carefully arranged to take those drugs for your own, while inventing the patients' needs for them. I suppose a woman was involved in all this, but I will not press you for details. I told you about my own failings a few decades ago, and I expect this is something similar, though it occurs in an era in which opioid drugs have become cheap amusements, almost a currency."

He sat, silently, riddled with self-doubt, self-spite, and inadequacy. The profundity of his treachery, of his transgression, was increasingly clear to him. Whatever effect the drugs had had on his mood, in the early morning, it was now gone, leaving him in an utterly morbid state of depressed sobriety. Still, as he clasped and unclasped his jaw muscles, intent on the appropriateness of this admonition, he realized that something was rising within him, an essence that challenged his impression of himself, an impression which had descended into a chasm of self-deprecation earlier on this dismal morning.

As these feelings beset him, he allowed himself to become distracted, gazing off into the corner of the room, contemplating his future—if he had one.

"Kurt!"

He snapped his head in the direction of the chief.

"You've just come pretty close to destroying your life. You're probably stressed out, but I think you need to pay attention to what I'm saying!"

Even with a junkie sitting before him, someone who had infiltrated his department, become addicted to opioids, treacherously removed the drugs and used them for his enjoyment, then ignominiously revealed himself in a dim bathroom in front of the entire OR staff—even with this despicable man slumped at his desk, the chief managed to address him with a degree of decorum and fatherly affection.

Kurt widened his eyes, raised his head, looked intensely at his superior.

"I can't sugar-coat this, Kurt. You have betrayed every one of your colleagues. You have compromised the vigilance and care that your patients deserve. You have stuck a knife right into my back—indeed, into the back of every member of this division!"

The words registered in his head like an alarm, seemed to bounce around in his skull as though they were balls in a racquet court. There was no way to dampen their effect, or to deny their import. He understood this and opened himself to the raw harshness that they carried.

"But Kurt, I will tell you this. You are not the first practitioner, anesthetist or anesthesiologist, whom I have seen fall prey to the drugs we use daily to suppress pain. You may remember, three years ago a senior resident was found in a coma in that same bathroom. Or perhaps it is still in your memory that less than a decade ago a first-year resident was found dead behind a curtain in the preop holding area? Five years ago one of our most reliable and trusted anesthetists was caught removing fentanyl from syringes to abet a habit that grew out of treatment for her chronic pain. And one of your mentors, two decades into his tenure as a Professor of Anesthesiology, had to be removed from the department for opioid use. Good people, all. But you are the closest ally that I have seen stumble in this fashion. And, as important as you have been to my division, as supportive as you have been to our practice, I am cut to the quick. I am so aggrieved by your actions that words are beginning to fail me. I suppose I should have seen this coming—you were coming unraveled. You are not the same man, the same doctor that I knew. Opioids have nearly extinguished you."

At this, Kurt shifted uneasily in his seat, wished he could throw up to expel the rot within him.

"You know that I can no longer employ you. This system will no longer employ you."

The effect of this expression was as a spear thrust through his chest, though he knew that their veracity could not be challenged.

"I believe in the power of men, laid low by the consequences of their actions, to right themselves. If anyone can do that, you can. The state runs a program for addicted physicians. It is arduous. If you are willing to enroll in it and fulfill the requirements, you can perhaps be employed as an anesthesiologist again. I would be willing to provide a testimonial to the potential that you have as a physician in our specialty, should you decide to conquer this addiction."

At that, the chief folded his hands and looked down. There was nothing more for him to say.

# CHAPTER 37

"This isn't going to be much fun, for any of you. But it's my job to reconstitute you. You have fallen away from your true paths, and descended into the realm of personal depravity, courtesy of substance abuse. What you thought was pleasure has nearly destroyed you. Look around. About 80 percent of you will go back to using drugs and then further descend into the pit of self-destruction. If I'm lucky, one out of five in this audience will heed what I have to say, and right themselves."

"Jesus," Kurt heard the man next to him whisper, disgusted at the pessimistic presentation.

The weary physician looked over, nodded, understood the sentiment. During a short break thereafter, the man made his way over to him. He was unshaven, unkempt, profusely tattooed, a middle-aged portrait of hopelessness. His silver-gray hair, thin and greasy, was gathered in a short ponytail, which hung limply off the back of his head.

"You been through this 'rehabilitation' before?"

The anesthesiologist shifted uneasily."No. First time. Only time, I hope."

The man laughed a cigarette-tortured laugh, some mix between a guffaw and a series of raspy hiccups, culminating in a cough that rattled with loose phlegm.

"Yeah. We all thought that. But the stuff just keeps coming into your life, and it GETS ya. Right there."

He pointed a meaty, crooked index finger at his temple. Kurt looked at the man's eyes, saw only dull, gray, forsaken orbs, without a glint of promise. His pupils were tiny, barely visible, and the physician wondered if he was using opioids even during this stint of education and rehabilitation.

"Well, maybe this time it can be different. Maybe you can really get your life back together."

"There is no 'together,' brother. There's no way back at all."

"You gotta keep trying," Kurt said, unsure of how to approach this onslaught of misery.

The tattooed man just shrugged."Okay, I'll keep trying."

At that, the stranger left him, and walked to the door, probably, Kurt thought, to smoke a cigarette. Sheets of rain were falling outside, and the man shook his head, crestfallen.

This was the introduction to a post-crisis, drug-free existence. Surrounded by disheveled, impassive, miserable people, Kurt sat for days and listened to lectures on the effects of drugs on the brain, the outcomes of addiction to various substances, the pharmacology of different narcotics. All of this was delivered by an angry, tiresome man who'd been hired by the State, and who probably had a Bachelor of Science degree in biology, at best. Kurt was certain that he could have taught the course himself, unprepared, with considerably more verve.

Still, it was a means to an end. Having hit bottom, Kurt now concentrated on one thing: returning to anesthesiology. His fall had been costly, destructive, shameful. But he hadn't harmed himself, or anybody else; this one small comfort had occupied his brain for days after his ignominious dismissal. Then, on one forlorn night, a week after he'd been ushered out of his office, he descended the long, crumbling staircase down Billy Buck Hill to the flats, and while wandering the dark streets of the Southside, he had discovered something of great importance: he wasn't gone. Inside of his body, the same heart was beating, the same lungs were breathing, the same brain that had been taught how to care for patients in the operating room was still filled with meaningful thoughts.

Flushing the few remaining oxycodone tablets down the toilet had come easily, and the wall he thereafter erected inside of himself against them was solid. There would be no further transgressions. The stakes were too high to trip up again. For the first two days of his abstinence, he had felt miserable, nauseated, had even experienced some coarse rigors, shaking so hard he could barely control his hands. One of those nights, on his hands and knees over the toilet, he wondered how it could possibly have come to this. But, overall, it was a comparatively mild withdrawal, and he thanked God for that.

Having fallen until he felt he could fall no further, and now having a chance to see what was in store for him, he thought about all he'd been through. Anyone who could work his ass off in college, get into medical school, obtain the M.D. degree, get into a good residency, survive the four years of hard work and sacrifice, and then maintain a solid reputation in a university practice—well, he had to have something going for him. As tragic as his decline had been, there may have been a glint of a silver lining. His craving, his dependence, his willingness to forego all else in pursuit of the magical substances had not fully matured; he had not crossed over to the dreadful point of no return. Kurt still yearned for the feelings the drugs had given him. But his addiction had been in its infancy; it was not yet able to completely control his brain. Velma had quite possibly saved his life when she smashed his head with the restroom door. If the cycle had continued for another month or so, his ability to conceive of life without these drugs might have been destroyed entirely, all of his spirit wrung out of him by his chemical-mediated existence.

The confrontation with his sister, just a few days after it had all become public, was perhaps the most painful thing Kurt had ever endured. She'd driven over to his townhouse, unannounced, rapped angrily on the front door. Inside, he sat, gloomily, in the darkness, wondering what direction his life would take. Kurt had hoped, somehow, to break all of this to Katy gently, once he'd begun to rehabilitate himself.

"What the hell happened to you, Kurt? How could you do this? How could you let it all just slip away?"

She was shouting at him, swearing—she never shouted. Or swore. He'd nodded solemnly in the face of this fusillade of angry words from someone he loved deeply and could not venture a word. At least she put the blame where it was due. Too often of late, it had been suggested to him that he was a "victim" of the drugs he'd taken, something he didn't believe. At some point, with the opportunity to refuse the indulgence, he'd accepted the invitation to use them. Then, in pursuit of pleasure, social stature, and passion, he had allowed the Trojan horse into his body. The decision to use had then become easier and easier to make, as he succumbed to the seductive effects of the opioids, but he painfully acknowledged that it was still HE that had made that decision, of his own will. Maybe other people were victims; Kurt was well aware that he had screwed himself.

"Now what? Is there a plan? You ruined your life!"

She was crying; he tried to formulate a reasonable answer.

"You worked so hard to get where you were . . . everyone in this family was so proud of you. All this for some goddam romance? I can't understand how you could let this happen!"

Her rage was unchecked at that point, and she kicked fiercely at one of the legs of his kitchen table.

"You were in the f--king newspaper! What should I tell the boys? You were a hero to them. For the last two months, when you stopped coming around, I was making excuses—because you're a doctor, because you have to work all the time, because you have a girlfriend . . . they didn't understand why you stopped coming to their games. And Scott says he doesn't want you coming to our house anymore. Now look at the position that you put me in—I have one brother, one solitary remaining member of my family, and my husband has no use for him."

"I'll make it up to you. To all of you," he had told her, bleakly, summoning as much conviction as he could muster in the circumstance.

"I'll believe that when I see it."

He knew at that moment that her bitter expression of doubt had left the door ajar, if only a bit. Without promising too much, he wanted to give her some hope.

"You'll see it."

At that, she turned away and marched out of his apartment. He hurried out to his balcony and watched her car speed down the hill, back toward the glittering lights of the city, which were just coming up in the gathering darkness. As he looked across the river, towards downtown, he tried to figure out which of the tall buildings was the one that housed Lauren's apartment and to discern which tiny points of light might represent her windows, behind which he'd had so much breathtaking excitement, even fulfillment. The woman had never bothered to respond to his calls or messages. Doubtless, she knew the score—in the eyes of society, he was now a tainted man.

But somehow, it seemed, she was untouchable: radiant and beautiful, artful and accomplished, impossible to sully. By now, he imagined that she'd located some winsome, well-heeled lover who would hold her and walk arm-in-arm with her at the society functions and the sporting events. That Kurt was a physician, an anesthesiologist no less certainly had facilitated her habit, but he did not doubt that she had other ways of obtaining her favored libations, even outside of the realm of the medical profession. Somehow, she could dance above it all. Untouchable.

When he thought of their love affair, of the promises and caresses, and the joyful sense of being part of a tandem, a warm sentiment washed over him. But when he tried to remember the details, pictured their nights together, he realized that any real emotion that had existed between them at first was quickly transformed into a frantic pandering for pharmacologic satisfaction, devoid of actual devotion or caring, with love and lust somehow derived from the ecstasy that the drugs provided. The two quickly became co-dependent consumers of the tantalizing chemical formulations, exploiting each other for the rapture that their bodies could provide, even as they enjoyed the ecstasy that the opioids instilled into their minds. Kurt missed the early feelings of affection that had charmed him so, but he understood that, eventually, his caring for her meant no more or less than the next episode of euphoric intoxication—there was no way he could go back to her without indulging in drugs, even if she would accept him. As their relationship had matured, he'd been barely able to distinguish between Lauren's essence and that of the fentanyl, as though the woman and the drug had become the same . . . he could not think of her, could not conceive of her being, without simultaneously imagining the rapturous effect of the opioids.

# CHAPTER 38

After Katy's car disappeared from sight on that solemn evening, he stood transfixed on the small balcony that was off his bedroom and craned his neck, taking in the view. Peering southward, down the Monongahela, he'd been able to picture in his mind the sprawling steel mills that once carpeted the flood plains on either side of the wide river, great industrial hulks that turned out enough steel to supply the world, perpetually immersed in clouds of smoke, steam and soot that poured from the towering furnaces. When he was a boy, visiting his grandmother's house high on Mount Washington, he'd often sat outside on her porch on the sultry summer evenings, and looked at the flames licking skyward from the tall stacks, barely visible through the haze, taking in the metallic scents that wafted out of the valley on the humid breezes.

The mills were no more, replaced by venues for shopping and entertainment, and fun. But Kurt knew about the men who had worked those mills, on rotating shifts, every hour of the day, every day of the year, and about the work ethic that they shared with their comrades. His grandfather had been one of them, a strong proud man who sacrificed his body over the decades to the hard life of a steelworker. Aches and pains and industrial injuries were a part of the job for many of them. Still, they always went back—bent and broken, their bodies eroding as surely as did the mud and silt under the ever-flowing rivers; they went back, ceaselessly until the day came when it was well-nigh impossible to work anymore. And then, they simply dissipated, like the smoke that poured from the machines at which they labored, as the years and the toil consumed them.

The anesthesiologist knew also that he had that same work ethic instilled within him, by his forebears, and that he longed to do justice to the working men and women that had once built this city, the foundation of which lay in coal and coke, in glass and steel. So grave had been his misstep that he was no longer welcome to work anywhere in the university health system, but he knew that there was a way to retrace his steps into medicine. He would find it, embrace it, adhere to it, and once again report to work, to his calling. His shame, he knew, was well-deserved, but he would return to accomplishment and self-sufficiency. There was no recourse, but to pour his heart into his redemption, and re-create himself.

While he peered steadily downriver on that terrible evening, lost in thought, his cell phone had suddenly begun to ring, startling him.

"Kurt, the PSA has a program that you should enroll in."

A call from nowhere. The familiar voice of Natalie, someone who cared enough to assist him, despite his betrayal.

"Nat?" He paused, not sure what to say. Her voice was flat, impassive. But the call was of enormous importance to him.

"If you complete the program, and then spend time under supervision, you could actually practice again. But it's a one-time deal. If you relapse, you are finished. I have a friend that you could call . . . if you want to."

"Natalie—I'm dying to find a way to practice again."

Tears began to fill his eyes.

"Look." he assured her, "the drug habit is gone, dead, as far as I'm concerned. I guess I'll always be at risk to start up the habit again, but I'm sure I can keep the drugs out of my life. Maybe it's no use to reassure people about my intentions—I doubt anyone will ever trust me, at least anyone who knows what I've done. But I'm patient, and I'm determined. The only real proof I can offer of my sincerity is my service . . . over time. I'm willing to tolerate the cynicism and skepticism from the people around me. I still believe in myself."

His words, as he pronounced them, had the gravity of his sincere desire embedded within them, and he hoped that this was also apparent to her.

"Kurt, it's wonderful to hear that." A modicum of feeling had crept into her voice."Really. I just want to hear good things about you from now on. I'm sorry you can't be with us—everybody is. To see you fall is to understand that any of us could topple over that precipice. And shatter."

"Nat, I was . . ." he hesitated, then regained his composure. "Well, I fell for a woman; she invited me to places I shouldn't have gone. It was my choice, foolish as it was. If I go back in my mind for a few months—I could not even have imagined at that time doing the things I eventually did, or that they would lead me to where I am right now. Life is unpredictable, Natalie, but you've got to be in control of it, whatever it brings you. I gave up my control, in exchange for certain . . . indulgences. And this is where it brought me. I think I'm stronger now, and my backbone is straighter. But I will have to prove it over and over again, through the years. ."

"I need to tell you about something else, Kurt."

"What's that?"

"Not long after you left, the chief found out about your lawsuit. He's been on a campaign to exonerate you. Got after our counsel to bring in some very big guns for depositions. Neuroradiologist from Emory, a neuroanesthesiologist from Pritzker who is an expert on perioperative stroke. He shared with me that he believes this will really tip things in your favor. Neither of these men believes that you violated a standard of care, or were responsible for that terrible outcome."

He was astonished, incredulous. Why such an effort for him?

There was a brief, quiet interlude.

"Kurt?"

"Yeah."

"It was a real pleasure working with you."

"And you, too, Nat. Your future is very bright—keep up the great work."

At that, she'd wished him a good night, and hung up. He'd looked down at the number of the contact she'd given him, and made faith to call the woman in the morning. This might, he'd considered, just be the leg up he needed.

He remembered looking downriver, just after that call, toward the point. The tiny green and red lights that marked the piers of the bridges were visible, their reflections bobbing playfully upon the fast-moving waters, stirred by spring winds that blew chill across their surface; the lanterns demarcated a course for the river captains moving their barges along the waterways to other cities that lay down the Ohio River and, further along, on the great Mississippi. Up over the hills to the northwest, a roiling cloud bank exerted itself against the orange glow of the Western skyline, promise of storms in the night.

# CHAPTER 39

"Hold the mask like this," he instructed.

The student anesthetist, who had just begun her clinical training, was as raw as could be. But she was personable, eager, and, having just come through the many wickets of her pre-clinical, science-based curriculum, was brimming with knowledge.

"The saturations are low—why do you think that's the case?"

She looked down, made a better seal on the face, and assisted the ventilation of the patient, who was just losing consciousness.

"A few reasons. Lying supine, low tidal volumes after our sedation, her cigarette smoking . . ."

"Sure. And she's obese, with a higher closing capacity; when she lies down, she gets significant atelectasis. We can improve on this with her positioning."

He grabbed the bed control and elevated the head of the bed, as she accommodated the mask to the new position.

"You may feel an improvement in the lung compliance while you bag, as the abdominal contents settle downward, away from the diaphragm. This should allow better diaphragmatic excursions, should minimize the atelectasis, and improve our ability to aerate her basilar segments as we take over."

Seconds later, the oxygen saturation moved steadily and quickly from 92 percent to 99 percent. Terri, the student, looked at him and nodded.

"I love it," he said, smiling beneath his mask, "when things work the way they should."

The induction went smoothly, and the endotracheal tube was placed without a hitch. After taping it in place, he turned to her.

"I'm injecting another milliliter of fentanyl. I showed you the first one. This completes the ampule."

Pausing, he held up the empty syringe. The anesthetist who was working with the student nodded, acknowledging his action. He offered his pen.

"No waste. I have to have you sign for me when I provide opioids to a patient."

The student was curious but did as he said. Doubtless, the scuttlebutt had made its way around the department to her, even though she'd just started the rotation. Each month, he had to dutifully explain to the new trainees that he had become addicted to opioids, had diverted them to himself from patients, was under strict observation, and that he could not afford to miss a step in his documentation.

"We, all of us, are at very high risk. We handle these substances daily. They are in our lap. And for a subset of providers, the temptation is very great. I could give you my whole story, but it doesn't matter. What matters is that I succumbed to these insidious drugs, and the more overtly I reveal this to others in the profession, especially young people, Terri, the more I think I can help to protect them from that first step. Once you make that first compromise, the slope is very steep, and it's almost impossible to stay in control."

Meeting his eyes with her own, she appeared to grasp the import of what he was saying. He would approach her about it several more times when they worked together. No lecture or online presentation was as effective as the bedside confession of someone who had wrecked his own life. Here, in this tiny community hospital, which was barely surviving in a downtrodden neighborhood on the outskirts of the city, he was doing his penance. Already, he had run much of the proscribed gauntlet: given up his license, subjected himself to the mercy of the state board of medicine, accepted their directives, and been admitted to their impaired physician rehabilitation program.

Once he was cleared of the drugs, the real fun had begun. A six-week, intensive outpatient rehabilitation program, daily drug testing, ongoing classes. The wrenching, confession-laden twelve-step meetings, every night for three months. And, for the next three years, he would have to attend them four times a week, religiously. Very few of the people he sat within that circle of restless souls appeared to be intent upon getting their lives back together—most of them seemed to accept their plight. A pall of depression hung over many of the meetings, along with the pervasive odor of cigarette smoke, as they went round and described their lives, newly unembellished by drugs or other stimulants. For some of the men and women, it seemed the years of abuse and dependence had wrung the spirit right out of them.

But, having obeyed the dictums, Kurt had received his license back. Conditionally. And his new practice was a bright spot. Working with two other anesthesiologists, he managed a variety of cases and some very sick people for such a small place. The intensive care unit, the fallback for patients who were too sick to wake up and return to the wards, was a little shaky, compared to the university, but the hospital had recently hired a full-time intensivist to direct the unit, which was clearly a step in the right direction. There were six nurse anesthetists in the department, with two of them hovering at the precipice of 'too-old-to-practice.' Still, even in their late sixties, laden with a variety of ailments, they got themselves together each day and got to work early enough to pull it off. What they lacked in energy they made up for with settled bedside wisdom, and he liked working with them. The surgeons tolerated their slower pace, seemed appreciative that someone was staffing the room at all, as they saw services throughout the hospital being reduced in the name of efficiency. The new department had openly welcomed him, which was a shock. They had set up a rigorous oversight program for his use of opioids, which he eagerly embraced. He refused to draw up fentanyl, accepted it only for the induction process, and was overly demonstrative with his administration of the drug to his patients, quickly handing it back to the anesthetist after announcing the quantity he'd given.

Taking his leave of Terri, Kurt walked over to the other OR that he was supervising, in which a patient was having a hip replacement, for which purpose he'd provided a spinal anesthetic. The patient was slumbering peacefully through the violent hammering, which jolted the man's entire body, as the surgeon forced the long stem of the prosthesis down into the marrow cavity of the femur. Propofol. How wonderful. The anesthetist gave him a brief report on the situation—a modest drop in blood pressure after the spinal, which was readily responsive to the usual pharmacology, only a minimum of blood loss to this point, the patient seemingly comfortable. It all looked to be pretty stable for the moment. He found his way back into the main hallway and went back to the cubby that was the anesthesia office. It was sort of a long, narrow closet that someone had managed to cram three desks into. There was no secretary—the institution was too small, and certainly couldn't afford to pay one.

He picked up the phone and dialed the now familiar number.

"This is Kurt. Do you need to test me today?"

Each day, he would call in to see if he'd been chosen for a random drug test, which required him to provide a urine specimen in a shabby, unadorned downtown office, in the late afternoon. There was no dodging it, and no predicting it. He had to be careful to avoid any sort of stimulant drugs or even foods that might cause a positive test, like poppy seeds.

Also, each day, he would call his case manager and discuss his activities, making arrangements for attendance at the local Impaired Physicians Support Group meetings that he was required to go to each week. He had found some real camaraderie there, among a selection of men and women who understood what he had gone through, and what he had done to himself. Mostly, they were acute care physicians—emergency medicine docs, anesthesiologists, even a surgeon who'd buddied up with an anesthetist to provide the drugs he needed. All of them had been slain by opioids. But to a man and woman, there was a strong devotion to the idea of returning to their practice, of taking off the shackles of dependence and shame, of contributing to something larger than themselves.

This, Kurt was convinced, was the most important element of recovery. You had to believe that the service you were providing to some greater cause was far more important than you were, that the products of your exertions were clearly of benefit to the people around you. Only that abiding influence could allow you to overcome the ceaseless call of the drugs. Nothing else could propel you past the irrefutable attraction of those substances, guarantors of incomparable pleasure, and overseers of wanton self-destruction. People who focused on themselves, their comforts or relationships or finances, were lost, he thought. It wasn't enough. Anesthesiology had facilitated his destruction, and anesthesiology had allowed him a way back to health and self-respect.

"Are you afraid?" the student asked him, in a quiet moment, later that afternoon. She was unusually frank, compared to some of her classmates, who seemed intimidated by him.

"Afraid of relapse?"

She nodded, aware that she might have offended him.

"Yeah. I think everyone who ever crosses that line and uses these drugs for the wrong reasons, who finds himself in their powerful grip, is afraid that he'll fall right into their control again."

She waited. The patient was stable. And he had no need to leave the room. He gazed reflectively at the bucket into which he'd thrown an empty fentanyl syringe a few minutes before.

"When you learn how an opioid drug can control your brain, make you its slave, exert itself in your every action, then you finally understand how . . . molecular we are. Just complex bags of chemicals within a physical shell. You'd think I would have gotten that before I fell into such a black hole. Anesthesia people literally make a living by chemically altering the function of people's brains. No one understands this process as well as we do. And yet, members of no other specialty or profession fall prey to addiction as frequently as us. Keep these thoughts uppermost in your mind, and you will never succumb to the curiosity or the longing."

With that, he patted her shoulder and left the room.

# CHAPTER 40

"Long day. Headed for home?" Marie, the chief anesthetist, looked exhausted herself.

"Almost. I need to see a lady in the E.D.—she had an LP a couple of days ago. I guess she had a fever and a bit of a stiff neck, so they had to rule out meningitis. Probably the flu. That got better, but then she got this positional headache. Probably needs a blood patch."

"Need my help? I can draw the blood for you. Can be tough down there to get anybody in the room with you."

"Nah. I'll get one of the nurses in the ED to draw it. But thanks! Have a great weekend. See you Monday." It felt right. He was now part of the practice.

Trotting down the back stairs, he recounted in his mind the equipment he'd ask for. It might take a while to get it all together. The ED was happy to call, but too often there was nobody to help. The department was busy, with people lying on stretchers in the hallways, all the rooms full, staff moving up and down the corridors in a sort of Brownian motion that appeared random but had an underlying logic that took a while to comprehend.

"And it clearly gets worse when you are upright?" he asked a prostrate figure, the woman lying on her back, quietly, in a darkened room.

"Doctor, I can't even stand up. It hurts too much, and then I get nauseated. But it's OK when I lay back down."

He put a hand on her shoulder.

"Definitely sounds like a spinal headache. We need to do that blood patch the emergency doctor told you about. It's like a biological bandaid that we put into your back; your own blood will congeal and seal that little hole that's leaking inside—that's what creates the pressure gradient that gets so much worse when you stand up. I'll need a signature for permission right here if you can."

Wearily, the patient made an effort to open her bloodshot eyes, and scrawled her name on the paper he held up. He quickly summarized the minor risks associated with the procedure and pushed the bedside button for the nurse, hoping she'd be available.

"It won't be easy, but if you can sit up for a few minutes, it makes the whole process easier."

She looked dejected."I think I can if someone can help me."

With an effort, she sat up, dangling her legs over the side of the table, brushing back a limp strand of hair from her face. The ER nurse, who'd just stepped in, placed her hands on the woman's shoulders, bracing her.

"So, when I get into the space, I need you to draw 60 cc's of blood. She looks like she has pretty good veins. Use a sterile prep, of course." The nurse, blue-clad, plump, and officious, nodded vigorously and glanced at the clock. Every second counted in the ED.

The room became very quiet as the anesthesiologist prepped the skin of the patient's back and placed the sterile drapes. He numbed the skin and began to advance the needle towards the epidural space, just inside the vertebral canal. The woman bore up well, given her misery. Against the silent background, Kurt could hear a conversation, perhaps from the next room, as another patient described her medical complaint.

"So, what did you do to your shoulder, Ma'am?"

"Well, doctor, it's been operated on before—just last year—but I fell and landed on my bad arm. I'm afraid I may have partially dislocated it. The pain is excruciating."

As the sound reached his ears, McCain's blood froze in his veins. He knew that melodious voice, knew the inflection, knew the beseeching tone.

He swallowed hard, fumbled a bit with the task before him, then struggled to regain his concentration. The needle entered the space, but he couldn't stop his hands from shaking.

"Well, your X-rays are fine," the man's voice continued, "but I'm sure that you injured the ligaments, and maybe the rotator cuff. You should call your orthopedist, and I've written for something for pain in the meantime. We'll keep you in the immobilizer until you follow up."

"Thank you so much. Is it something strong? I'm a bit sensitive, but I think I'll need something like oxycodone. I can't imagine I'll be able to sleep like this."

McCain looked at the nurse."OK, go ahead and draw the blood."

She noted his pallor."Are you all right, doctor?"

"Yes. Yes. End of the day. I'm a little tired . . . I'll be fine." He took the syringe and injected the sanguine contents into the woman's spine. She groaned as the last few milliliters were delivered. Together, McCain and the nurse eased her back onto the bed.

It was surely Lauren. A flood of emotions overcame him as he stuttered some instructions to the patient. First terror, then anger, then curiosity, and finally, a bittersweet note. He hung his head.

"Now, you'll likely have some back pain. Imagine it's a deep bruise. But your headache should feel better very quickly. Just stay here on your back, and we'll be in to check on you in 15 or 20 minutes. If you feel better when you stand, we'll get you going."

He had to speak to her. He had believed for a year that he'd never see her again, and was certain that that was for the best. But now, she was ten feet away. Her voice still brought raw emotions to the surface of his soul, those sultry notes seared deep within him.

He exited the cubicle and took a few steps towards the room next door. It was easier to hear the voices now.

"Well, just my luck. But it did bring me here. And I got to meet you . . ." She was purring.

"Maybe fortunate for both of us," the man inside answered, his voice a bit higher."I'll get your discharge instructions—be right back."

The curtain parted, and McCain found himself face to face with the Physician Assistant who worked evenings in the E.D. It was a small hospital; everybody knew everybody. The man was tall, chiseled, handsome. A military guy, still drilling in the Army Reserve. And divorced. Perhaps most importantly, he had the power of the pen. He can certainly make her happy, Kurt thought.

"Hi, Scott—just did the blood patch. She should be ready for discharge in a half hour. Just have her follow up with us if any further problems."

The tall man was glowing."Thanks, Dr. McCain. Really appreciate you coming down here so quick to see her."

He then bounded down the hallway toward the nurse's station. Kurt thought of the day he'd met Lauren, and how profoundly she'd affected him with her attentions. It was now or never. He held his head up as he walked in, a churning in his stomach.

Lauren looked up, almost startled, quickly controlled her response. She smiled. Beautiful as ever, he noted.

"Kurt! It's wonderful to see you. Do you . . . work here?"

He made an effort to smile."Yeah. For a few months, now. I lost my other position . . . and my license. Took me some time to right the ship."

She looked embarrassed. Maybe even reticent.

"I'm sorry for all that. But, well . . . how are you?" To his surprise, she seemed genuinely interested.

"It's OK . . . I'm OK. I think I pulled it all together. I feel like I'm on the good foot again, you know?"

He studied her face, her impossibly lovely face, for some sign of recognition of what he'd been through. Certainly, she knew. She had to know.

"I'm so glad for you!" She was trying a little too hard.

But there was no sense of the friendship, familiarity, intimacy that they'd once shared. Above it all. The thought kept careening about in his mind.

"You hurt that shoulder again? Hope it doesn't need surgery," he commented a bit sardonically, his wry tone a jarring contrast to her velvety voice.

"It's just really painful. No—hopefully no surgery."

The PA loped back in, carrying a shoulder immobilizer and a script. He seemed surprised.

"You two know each other?"

Kurt nodded."Sort of."

It was a helpful transition in an awkward moment. He nodded curtly, turned, and walked out of the exam room. Ambling down the hall, he was surprised at his lightheartedness after this unexpected encounter. He thought about his life, since the tragic occurrences of the year before. He'd climbed out of a pit of self-pity and self-imposed misery, and re-established the most important thing in his life—the profession. Just a few minutes before, he'd been summoned to the ED to help a woman who was truly miserable and unable to function. He had applied his knowledge and skills, resolving her pain with the careful placement of a needle and the injection of her blood into just the right place. This relatively simple act had required years of training, a decade of experience, knowledge, judgment, skills, deliberation, worry. All of this was part of a sacred calling. His ability to help others made his life something special. And the wanton self-indulgence that had marked his life with Lauren stood in clear relief. There was no regret.

# CHAPTER 41

"Please come for dinner."

That was the message, and he heard within that voicemail the warmth that he had once enjoyed in his interactions with his beloved sister. After a year and a half of his dedication to the task at hand, of abstinence, of self-discipline, of a return to self-sufficiency, Katy had finally let her barriers down and reached out to bring him back into her life, though he could sense her caution. She knew what he'd been through, and knew what he was now involved in. His heart sang; a delighted smile spread across his face as he played the message again and again. He'd won, or at least had accomplished a small triumph. It would mean so much to be able to re-establish the old relations. Thinking of his nephews, he raced down Billy Buck Hill on the cascade of staircases in the gathering dusk, to the flats below, tightly clutching his basketball, and jogged to the closest park, where he shot the basketball for over an hour.

That Friday afternoon, he took the bus downtown, got off on Liberty Avenue, and walked eagerly up Polish Hill. His reception was decidedly mixed.

"Hey, guys. It's been a long time!"

What else could he say, he figured, as he greeted the boys, basketball in one hand and a loaf of crusty Italian bread from Enrique's in the other.

The older one held back, reserved, cool, mindful of the things his father and mother had told him about his uncle. But the little one bubbled over with energy and affection, ran to his side, and hugged his leg, all the while emitting mirthful, childlike squeals.

"Uncle Kurt, where were you—why didn't you come see us?"

He composed himself, thought for a moment about how best to answer, choosing his words carefully.

"I got really sick, Doug. I just couldn't come to see you till I got better. It lasted a long time, and then, it took me some time to get myself back together, to get better."

"Drug-addicted is more like it," the elder brother murmured, hanging a few feet away, glowering from under the rim of a Pirates baseball hat, which he'd pulled down low over his eyes, as though he wanted to disclaim that this reunion was occurring.

Kurt could feel Thomas' eyes boring into him. He looked up, tried to meet the eyes of the boy, searched the shadows under the bill of the ball cap.

"I have no problem with you telling the truth about me, Tom. I was ashamed for a long time, but now I'm better, and I know that I'm not going back there."

He saw the boy swallow hard.

Then, the grip around his leg tightened a bit. "Going back where?"

"Where I was, Dougie. It's just an expression. I didn't really go anywhere, but I sort of became a different person."

"Where is he now?"

"He's gone. I left him behind. Forever. But I wasn't sure I left him behind till just recently. I didn't want to come and see you all till I knew I was really myself again."

"I'm glad you're back."

"Me too."

Thomas spoke up again, this time raising his eyes to meet Kurt's gaze.

"My dad says you never really stop being an addict."

Kurt nodded, tried to explain.

"Your dad is right—that possibility haunts you for the rest of your life. But I think, the further away you get from that monster that you were, the less chance you'll become him again."

The younger one looked up, startled.

"Yeah, Doug. I was a kind of a monster. I didn't care about anything but getting the drugs that made me feel good. The drugs controlled me.

I didn't care about you guys or your mom and dad anymore; I didn't care about being a doctor, or taking care of patients, or anything else."

His eyes became very wide."Did you kill anyone?"

Kurt softened.

"No—not that sort of monster. I didn't kill anyone. But I was stealing drugs from my patients, making it look like they needed more than they did, and taking the extra. It was a terrible thing to do. And I was getting high at work, so I couldn't do my job right. I was putting people at risk of bad things."

There was a silence, and the little one spoke up.

"Are you sure you're not him anymore?"

"Yeah. I'm sure. I know what I did, and I know I'll never, ever go back there. Now, I want to visit you guys again, and play basketball with you, and eat dinner with you. It's gonna take a long time, but maybe things could go back to the way they were."

Predictably, the elder boy scoffed, his cynicism boiling over.

But the younger one refused to adopt his brother's stance.

"Well, we're having hamburgers next Saturday. Can you come over?"

"Your dad grills great burgers. Of course, I'll come. And maybe now—can we play 'HORSE' in the driveway?"

The boy raced away, calling over his shoulder "I'll go get the ball!"

Doug had to shoot the ball with the "Pitt" logo on it; no other ball would do.

"You wanna play?" he asked the older brother.

Begrudgingly, the 12-year-old moved toward the driveway, now taller, thinner, and more awkward in his motions than Kurt remembered. This willingness to accompany him, Kurt understood, was a tacit acknowledgment that the relationship could be rekindled, however slowly.

A few minutes later, the little one was having his way in the game.

"Uncle Kurt has 'H-O-R-S' already," he called out, as his brother finally came to join the game."I just have 'H'!"

"Well, I wasn't here," his brother groused, frowning."Can we start over again?"

The little boy adopted the sunny, innocent expression that moves so quickly across the face of a child. He looked at his Uncle, who stood with his hands on his hips, awaiting the ball. Katy was standing across the driveway, at the garage door, watching them play. Kurt caught her eye and nodded.

"Yeah, Tom." The physician swallowed hard."I think we can start over again."

That phrase, 'start over,' fraught with meaning for Kurt, and spoken unwittingly from the mouth of a young boy, resonated deep inside of him. Yes, it seemed that they could all start again. He rolled the ball around on his fingertips and bounced it over to his older nephew, who squared himself for a jump shot.

As they sat to dinner, Kurt felt an emotion that he had not experienced for many months. In his self-imposed exile, he had chosen to dine alone, to think each night about what he'd been through, what the next day would bring, and how he would cope with it. There had been an ache deep within, a need for meaning that he could not experience without these people.

They bent their heads, held hands, and prayed. His eyes welled up.

"I just wanna say," he began, dabbing his eyes with the paper napkin, "that I know it is a privilege to be here with all of you."

He choked on his words, sniffed, looked around the table at four pairs of earnest eyes.

"And it means all the world to be here. I need to say 'thank you' for letting me come to your house."

A tear spilled, and his sister, who had felt the rush of water into her eyes as well, laughed happily.

"We're really glad to have you back with us."

"Meatloaf?"

His sister looked proud.

"Mom's recipe—you love it, right?"

"Yeah. And the way you make it, Katy. With mashed potatoes. It's incomparable."

His brother-in-law nodded in happy agreement.

"Are you still singing at the Church?"

"Every Saturday at five. Maybe you could come tomorrow?"

"I'll be there—any hymns of note?"

" 'When I survey the wondrous cross.' "

"She'll bring the house down," Scott said, enthusiastically, reaching for more meatloaf.

Kurt contemplated that, and remembered with pride her voicing carrying through the towering church.

"I can't wait."

Katy shot her brother a satisfied look.

"So you've rediscovered your Catholicism?"

He nodded, looking around the table.

"I've been through a lot. Without prayer, I doubt I'd be here."

After dinner, he took leave of them, allowing just a hint of enthusiasm for his future to grow within. He would be back at their modest home again soon, and for that he was grateful. The evening sun appeared briefly through a rent in the gray sky and shone warmly over the face of Polish Hill. Walking up the street from his sister's house to Bigelow Boulevard, he turned down the long stretch into the city, a mile or so distant. The views from the Hill, down over the strip, into downtown, and across the river, were particularly striking on this still evening. The Allegheny, a benign and eternal entity, flowed quietly beneath the bridges that helped to lace the city together, a collection of spindly structures that held tightly to the disparate parts of a metropolis sundered by the great rivers. At the baseball stadium, deep within the shadows cast by the North Hills, the lights were already coming up for the Pirate game.

In town, he picked up the 51C and rode it over to the Southside, where he was deposited next to the rusty railroad bridge at the base of the slopes. He stood for a moment, at the bottom of the zig-zag of staircases that had channeled so many people between the homes that studded the hill in multi-colored tiers. He eyed the deep depressions, cracks, and chinks in the stair treads, created by hundreds of thousands of shoes and boots, by the heavy footsteps of the men who'd descended to their toil, and tramped back up again, exhausted, at the end of the day.

It gave him a special feeling of pride, to walk up those steps, to think that he was following the tradition of the men who went before him, who worked until they had spent themselves in contribution to some meaningful cause, invisible but somehow greater than their own existence. In virtually every walk of life, it was essential to people that they made a substantive contribution to something which touched the lives of those around them. This dedication to men or their systems must undergird every life, in one way or another—all else was mere futility. Upon that belief, that foundation, he was certain that he would rise again, without looking back, without self-pity or doubt.

He made his way up to Pius Street and looked forlornly at the decaying Rectory. Just a few years prior, it was common to have elderly priests who lived there show up for surgery at the hospital. He hadn't seen one for quite some time. Now, the dormitory appeared to be shuttered, except perhaps for some offices on the first floor. The nunnery beside it was an absolute shambles. Behind him, the stately, soaring edifice of St. Michael's had been restored to its prior glory, a proud testimony that was the courtesy of rapacious investors and developers. The noble old church was plastered with signs that advertised the new loft apartments within.

Of late, he'd made time to stop into the church beside the monastery at the top of the hill for mass and the occasional prayer; sometimes he was ashamed that it had taken a crisis in his life to lead him to search for spiritual restitution. He climbed the many stairs up the hill painstakingly, in anticipation of a moment's peace in that serene sanctuary.

Inside, a few people knelt in silence. Kurt took his place among them, wondering how the Church had become simply tangential in the lives of so many. A whiff of incense made its way to him and he turned his gaze downward, closed his eyes. There was much in his own life to be thankful for, not least the inspiration and direction he felt with his newly strengthened faith. The failing evening light barely illuminated the tall, stained-glass windows, their soft mosaics of color falling like a blessing upon the penitent in the pews.

Afterward, he paused outside for a moment, admiring the church building and thinking of what it stood for. The diocese was on the verge of collapse, it seemed, with announcements of church and school closings every year. Marx had once observed that religion was "the opium of the masses." Kurt wondered what the renowned philosopher would think of society now that the church was in the throes of an unceasing decline, and the opium of the masses had become, for millions, the opiates. A pathway to dissolution for uncounted souls.

Walking to the edge of the hill, he looked out across the Southside and to the city beyond. He'd risen above the amorphous evil that lay down in those streets. His life had been disrupted, nearly destroyed, but he had somehow extricated himself from a power far greater than he could conceive. There was now reason for cautious optimism. A slanting ray of sunlight again broke through the dense cloudbank that hovered above the city, illuminating thousands of lives and casting thousands of shadows, all at once.

# ABOUT THE AUTHOR

Steven L. Orebaugh is an anesthesiologist at an academic medical center, whose position requires that he handle or prescribe opioid medications every working day. He has witnessed a number of ruined careers related to addiction among his peers, and has worked with trainees whose lives have been irrevocably altered by indulgence in the controlled substances that anesthesiologists administer to their patients. *The Stairs On Billy Buck Hill* illustrates just how compelling the allure of these drugs is, and how, once ingested, they create within the user a voracious appetite for greater indulgence, followed inevitably by ruinous consequences.

Most of his publications are related to his profession, with some 75 works in the medical literature, including peer-reviewed articles, textbook chapters and review articles. In addition, he is the author of two medical textbooks, and has served as an editor or section editor for several more. In 2006, the Johns Hopkins University Press published his non-fiction book entitled *Understanding Anesthesia*. This patient education manual, which explains the subtleties of operative anesthesia and pain management, empowers patients to ask appropriate questions about their perioperative care. Five years ago, his first fiction work, *A Night in the Life*, which describes the plight of a disenchanted emergency physician in a decaying urban hospital, was published by the Pocol Press.

Dr. Orebaugh practices anesthesiology at the University of Pittsburgh Medical Center, and has a special interest in regional anesthesia, an important means of reducing opioid use for pain control. He is especially enthused to teach these methods to doctors in training.

Made in the USA
Middletown, DE
19 September 2022

10135017R00158